THE CASE OF THE UNDISCOVERED CORPSE

D1826046

An Alasdair & Toby
and Cambridge Fellows
Crossover Mystery

 CHARLIE  COCHRANE

WILLIAMS & WHITING

Copyright © Charlie Cochrane

This edition published in 2022 by Williams & Whiting

9781912582839

Williams & Whiting (Publishers)
15 Chestnut Grove, Hurstpierpoint,
West Sussex, BN6 9SS

Also by Charlie Cochrane
From Williams & Whiting

Pack Up Your Troubles

Alasdair & Toby Mysteries:
An Act of Detection
The Case of the Grey Assassin

For information about this and other books
published by Williams & Whiting go to:
www.williamsandwhiting.com

Peter Norris

ABOUT THE AUTHOR

Because Charlie Cochrane couldn't be trusted to do any of her jobs of choice – like managing a rugby team – she writes. Her mystery novels including the Edwardian era Cambridge Fellows series, and the contemporary Lindenshaw Mysteries. Multi-published, she has titles with Carina, Riptide, Lume and Bold Strokes, among others.

A member of the Romantic Novelists' Association, Mystery People and International Thriller Writers Inc, Charlie regularly appears at literary festivals and at reader and author conferences with The Deadly Dames.

(1952)

2022

I'm grateful to the reader who inspired this book by mailing me to say, "In the early 1950's Jonty and Orlando would be in their early to mid-70's and probably still quite active. Seems there's every possibility the 4 amateur sleuths could have met." As indeed they did...

Cambridge September 3rd 1952

"Good morning, Orlando. Lovely to see you."

Those words had been spoken first thing in the morning on numerous occasions and in many different settings over the best part of fifty years. From lips that had once been young and full, but which were now showing fine lines and downed with white, rather like the hair which crowned Jonty Stewart's head. A full set of hair—he'd inherited his paternal grandfather's locks rather than his father's bald pate—yet the tawny gold had now all gone to be replaced with hoary silver.

"Lovely to see you, too." Orlando Coppersmith turned in the bed, easing into a more comfortable position. He was currently beset with an issue concerning his left rotator cuff, or so the doctor had diagnosed, one that should get better with exercise. It had been a result of over-exertion in the garden and not, as Jonty told everyone, due to Orlando having dealt the bridge cards too vigorously.

"What does your diary have in store for you today?" The airy tone in Jonty's voice as he asked the question immediately put his partner on alert.

"The usual. College business and the like, given the arrival of students is hull up on the horizon. Why do you ask?"

"I'd like to suggest a slight change to plans dinner-wise. Are you free tonight?"

"Ye-es. Why?"

"I had a phone call last evening, when you were at your orgy." That was another line which had been used innumerable times over the years, referring to Orlando being

1

out playing cards. He'd learned to ignore it. "It was to invite us to dinner and a discussion."

"A commission, do you think?" It had been a while since they'd had a really good mystery to get their teeth into. Odds and ends of investigations, yes, including ones bound up with the war that they simply couldn't accept, because they'd have had little chance of fulfilling them. Finding where Aunt Elsie had hidden the family silver because she thought that Hitler would invade—said aunt having then been so inconsiderate as to get herself killed in an air raid before she could share the location of the treasure with the rest of the family—had been a typical kind of request. As were the string of entreaties to locate the whereabouts of men who'd been declared missing in action, at least one of whom Jonty had decided had likely taken a convenient opportunity to get away from home.

At least they could now decline the commissions with dignity, pleading old age and the inability to travel as far as they used to, alongside not being up to the physical challenge of digging up bomb sites to find Aunt Elsie's spoons. These excuses might have been seen through had the applicants observed the pair of them working vigorously in the garden at Forsythia Cottage or indeed still almost as vigorously sharing the pleasures of the double bed.

"It's not about a commission as such, although there's a peripheral link to an old, unsolved mystery." Jonty raised an eyebrow. "One we might have got involved with at the time had we not been otherwise occupied. No, this is something quite different and rather exciting."

"Am I allowed a clue to whatever you're on about?"

"Not a single one. I want you to come to this meeting with an open mind and if I drop the merest hint, you'll mull it over all day. Suffice to say the discussion could lead into pastures entirely new for us, which is rather nice at our time of life, wouldn't you say?"

"I'll only say one way or the other when I know what these pastures new are and whether they'll be green or arid." Orlando was rather pleased with his analogy. "You're not even going to make an indication as to whom I'm eating with?"

"No, because it risks giving the game away entirely. A knight of the realm. Title conferred as opposed to inherited. You've met him before, although that doesn't cut down the field. Very nice chap, who has a proposal for us and—" Jonty cuffed Orlando's arm. "That's quite enough. You're wheedling secrets out of me. I'm easing my stiff old bones out of this bed before you spoil all the elements of surprise."

"Just one more question, then. Will this different and exciting whatever-it-is be the sort of thing to make me jump for joy or run away screaming?"

"I can't imagine you running away screaming from anything, at this point in your life. Quite below your dignity. I might have to see if I can engineer it happening, simply for the novelty." Jonty, now on his feet, stretched extravagantly, like a great cat rousing itself.

"You didn't answer my question."

"True, oh light of my life, although that's simply because I can't formulate an answer. I've been weighing it up since last night and I honestly don't know. All I can state with any certainty is that we'd be stupid not to explore the possibilities. Too young still to be stick-in-the-muds." Jonty made an elaborate bow. "And now I exit, if not pursued by a bear, then pursued by your third degree. Patience, old man."

"Patience my arse," Orlando muttered, although he couldn't help smiling. Whatever happened over dinner would turn out to be gratifying. If he liked this mysterious proposal, then it would add a new challenge to their lives

3

and if he hated it then he could go into a pleasing yet dignified huff for at least twenty-four hours. And tease Jonty over his rashness for the next few weeks.

Despite the ache in Orlando's shoulder, life was still good.

London September 3rd 1952

"Mr Bowe on the telephone for you, sir." Morgan knocked gently, then peered round the door of his employer Alasdair's bedroom. "Are you available to speak to him?"

"Once I've put in this cufflink, yes. Could you ask him to hold for a moment?"

"Of course." The invaluable manservant glided away in the direction of the telephone, while Alasdair Hamilton wrestled the onyx link into submission.

"Sorry I was so long, old bean," he said, when he finally took the call. "Why is it that inanimate objects always misbehave when you least need them to?"

"Sheer cussedness." Toby Bowe chuckled. "What you need as compensation is a dinner out with a handsome co-star, by which I mean yours truly. Tomorrow. I know you're free because Sir Ian checked your diary and unless you've got a bit on the side neither of us know about, you're not due to be busy."

"I could have had another appointment. My life doesn't entirely revolve around the studio and you." Although to be honest a good ninety-five percent of it did and nearer a hundred percent of what Alasdair got up to would be on the radar of the Landseer studio head. Sir Ian Sheringham missed very little when it concerned his stars. "You're fortunate that I have tomorrow evening earmarked solely for finishing Mrs Christie's latest. Anyway, how does Sir Ian come into all this?"

"It's his invitation. Seven o'clock at the Savoy. He wants to discuss a new project with us but can't say anything about it until tomorrow because it all hangs on a meeting he's having tonight in Cambridge. He's being rather guarded about it all, although he says that's because he doesn't want to get our hopes up prematurely. All I know is that if it comes off, the film will be neither a Holmes and Watson mystery nor an RAF romp. I don't suppose they have much trouble with pirates on the Cam so that possibility should be out of the window, too. It's a complete departure from the usual."

That sounded interesting. While Alasdair would never decry the formulaic offerings Landseer produced —starring him, Toby and their customary leading lady, Fiona Marsden—it would be nice to get his teeth into something new. "Let's hope it'll be popular with the public. No matter how much I enjoy a change, I'd hate to sacrifice the box office appeal of the familiar."

"I can't imagine Sir Ian wanting to risk losing hordes of bums on seats. All will be revealed tomorrow. On two counts, actually, if you fancied coming round to the aforementioned handsome co-star's residence afterwards for a bit of see-what-transpires."

"I'll be there as well." Especially as Alasdair knew exactly what was likely to transpire. He put the phone down and returned to the business of his cufflink, which still wasn't sitting quite as he wanted it to.

A new project and with a potential Cambridge connection? Alasdair's mind ran through the gamut of possibilities, from the biography of a notable figure— Byron, perhaps, or John Donne, either of whom would suit his looks—through to something modern day with post-war spies and the like. Whatever the screenplay involved it would no doubt be to the very high standards Landseer was renowned for. Formulaic films, admittedly but never stinting on quality or on providing satisfaction. Which was more than could be said for the cufflink.

Chapter One

Jonty's enthusiasm for their potential bold new adventure had grown from the moment Sir Ian Sheringham had rung him. It had reached a peak at lunchtime the following day but was now fading as the hour for their dinner appointment neared.

Everything had been a distinct surprise at first, to the extent that Jonty had feared the telephone call was merely some student rag. He'd explained that to Sir Ian, who'd immediately commended him on his shrewdness, suggesting that Jonty should check his bona fides with George Broad, who'd provided the Forsythia Cottage telephone number and who could supply Jonty with the one for Sir Ian's private line. Only once he was entirely satisfied, should he ring the studio head back.

All of which process Jonty had gone through, pleased as ever to have an excuse to ring his favourite nephew. George always remained about eleven in his uncle's mind, despite the fact of being in his forties and one of the youngest judges on the circuit. As soon as Jonty had received confirmation that all was tickety-boo, he could call Sir Ian in the confidence that he wouldn't actually be speaking to some long-haired lout from the *college next door*, St Bride's arch-enemy and the source of many an irritation to the college and its inhabitants.

The possibility of involvement in a cinematic project was thrilling and keeping it secret from an increasingly inquisitive Orlando had proved most a most rewarding activity. Yet as the day waned, Jonty couldn't help but be plagued with second thoughts. Despite his remark earlier about wanting to see Orlando run off screaming, they were both getting too long in the tooth for creating dramas in public and the dinner could prove very uncomfortable if he took against the proposal from the start and they subsequently had to pass the rest of the meal in an awkward attempt at conversation.

As it turned out, he needn't have worried, because Orlando—his lover, colleague, fellow detective and general light of his life—proved delighted to meet their dinner host. After introductions had been properly made and the important matter of ordering food had been dispensed with, they could get down to the intriguing business in hand.

"Gentlemen, thank you for seeing me," Sir Ian said, as they took their first glass of champagne. "George Broad said you've both got marvellously open minds and have never lost your sense of adventure. With that in mind, I'd like to discuss a film project with you."

Orlando nodded, having clearly realized what the meeting would likely concern as soon as he knew who their host was. "You want to call on our advice, I assume? Some academic point perhaps or inside knowledge of how the university works?"

"Not quite, although both of those will come into play. Landseer studios would like to make a film which touches on events at the Old Manor during the Great War. I believe it was used to house items of national importance."

"It was, although I'd be grateful if the exact nature of said items were to remain a secret." Jonty briefly glanced around, to emphasis his point. "I can't say any more in a place where we might be overheard, because it's not the only time the cellars at the family home have been used in such a capacity and it's possible they may be again. Perhaps sooner than we think given the way matters are developing under Stalin. I hope I'm wrong in that regard."

"How did you know that the Old Manor had been utilized in that way?" Orlando asked, cutting to the most important point.

8

"From your nephew. Not George, but Thomas, if I might use his name without his proper address."

"Thomas?" Jonty glanced at Orlando, horrified at the present bearer of the Stewart title having had such a loose tongue. Thomas's grandfather would have been appalled, especially as he'd been the one to propose the hiding of the crown jewels in those concealed vaults beneath his family home should the need arise. "There will have to be a family pow-wow to prevent such a thing happening in future. I'll get George's sister Alexandra to sort Thomas out: he's always been a touch scared of his cousin, no matter how much he adores her."

As Jonty spoke, Sir Ian turned pale, apart from two livid spots on his cheeks. Perhaps he was afraid he'd immediately scuttled any chance of the studio's plans remaining afloat. "I've clearly touched on a sore point. Is the matter so important?"

Jonty nodded sombrely. "I'm afraid it is. Did Thomas tell you exactly what we had hidden there?"

"No. Simply that they were items of immeasurable worth to the nation that couldn't be put at risk."

"That's a blessed relief, then. If he'd told you all the details, the family Stewart would be in serious trouble." Stern words would need to be spoken at the earliest opportunity.

Sir Ian passed his hand over his brow. "Does that mean it's unlikely we can proceed further? Some matter of national security?"

Jonty took a glance at Orlando, receiving a shrug in return. "We'd need to know how vital the actual items are to your storyline."

"Only in the sense of being a vehicle for the rest of the plot to be carried on. The hiding of these objects in itself is not a key part of the story and what they are matters not a jot. That element could be done away with entirely if there was no other choice and we could no doubt find an alternative thread. It would be to the detriment of the film, however." Both Sir Ian's tone of voice and sad expression conveyed clearly how much he didn't want to have to take that route. The man must know his business as well as Jonty and Orlando knew theirs: he would be making an expert call.

Orlando had evidently had a similar thought. "I have a possible solution. The Old Manor wasn't unique in terms of being employed to safely store items in a time of war. There was far too much to hide, and one wouldn't want all one's eggs in the same basket. Might I suggest that you retain that element but simply change the nature of hidden items to that which they were not? Make them key works from the National Gallery or objects from the British Museum, such as the Rosetta Stone or the Elgin Marbles."

"A splendid idea, Professor Coppersmith. I believe the Stewarts could endorse that, especially if you were to throw in a Shakespeare first folio as one of the treasures." Jonty watched with pleasure as the relief swept over their host's face. "If we take that difficulty as overcome, what's the main thrust of the story?"

"A murder. And two amateur detectives who become embroiled in solving it." Sir Ian paused. "I'm sorry, have I put my foot in it again and accidentally struck on a real case? You both seem rather shocked."

"*I'm* sorry if we appeared surprised. You've caught us on the hop or, rather, a strange coincidence has." Orlando looked at Jonty, clearly thinking it was *his* prerogative to narrate this part of the tale and explain why they'd been a touch startled.

"You're aware, Sir Ian, given what you said over the phone, that we've had many an experience of investigating mysteries of one kind or another. I daresay that young George will have embroidered some of those tales, so take them with a generous pinch of salt. Esteemed judge or not, my nephew will always be an enthusiastic young boy to me."

Sir Ian smiled. "On the contrary, I'm confident he underplayed them. He said you would hide your lights under a bushel and somebody needed to uncover them."

The arrival of the waiter to usher the party from the hotel lounge to their table gave Jonty more time to plan his tale, not having anticipated this coincidental, rather odd episode could be one which interested Landseer. He'd established the previous evening—and with great relief— that the proposed film wouldn't concern their service in either war or the strange events following the Armistice in 1918. Either of those would have brought an immediate refusal. But he'd got it into his head, because Sir Ian had mentioned the drama being set in the past, that the project would concern one of their earliest cases. Perhaps the one in which Orlando had posed as a professional dancing partner, because that would seem eminently suitable for the cinema. Still, so long as no mention was let slip of delicate matters like the crown jewels or what he and Orlando did in Room Forty or people losing their memories and thinking they were someone else, all should be well.

"So, back to the tale," Jonty said, when they were seated again. "At the start of the Great War, we were serving his majesty doing something which we can't possibly discuss. You'd better be suitably vague about that in the film, too. Perhaps put us in an administrative role with one of the ministries."

"Noted." Sir Ian literally did so, on a small leather-bound pad. "It's as well this is all still in the planning stages

11

or we'd be giving ourselves a lot of re-writes. I'm obliged for your help."

"Our pleasure. It was my father," Jonty continued, "who offered the use of the Old Manor vaults to the country. Those cellars hadn't really been used for years, apart from the occasional cursory inspection to ensure that they weren't damp or the like and sporadic, surreptitious visits from small Stewarts to play there. I believe the last time, previous to 1914 that is, that they'd been given a thorough overhaul was when the old queen was on the throne. The date is pertinent to this business, isn't it, Professor Coppersmith?"

"Yes. Around 1851. They'd been hauling stuff out to loan for one of the displays at the Great Exhibition. Examples of our engineering heritage to be used as a comparison with the then wonders of the industrial age and some rather ghastly stuffed animals that people used to find amusing in those days. The items were subsequently returned, although they weren't properly checked. Nobody had bothered to make a proper inventory, because the items were of little value to the Stewarts, having been accumulated by the then lord's father, Dr Stewart's great-grandfather. We suspect there was a hope that some of the things wouldn't find their way home." Orlando raised an eyebrow. "Alas, they came back with additions, although nobody realized the fact at the time."

"Additions?" Sir Ian remarked.

"Yes." Jonty took up the account. "The kind of oversight which wouldn't have happened on my father's watch. When the vaults were being made ready in late 1914, Papa came across things that had never—he was sure—been a Stewart possession. No doubt priceless parts of our heritage in somebody's eyes, but old tat in ours. It must have come wholesale from the Crystal Palace and the original owners had either not registered its loss or were pleased to see the back of it. He decided not to bother sorting out the wheat from the chaff at the time, although Mama says he made a spirited rendition of 'Any Old Iron' about a box of metallic fittings."

Sir Ian scribbled another note. "We must work that in. A moment of humour amongst the serious stuff."

"Like the porter in the Scottish play? Excellent idea. Anyway, given the weight of the task he had to perform, Papa decided it would be useful to hide the valuable among the rubbish. Who'd look for a pearl of great price among lumps of metal?" Jonty paused, milking the moment. "He also found something less amusing. A dead body amongst the dross."

"A dead body? I had no idea anything like that had happened." Sir Ian froze with his fork in its mouth-ward motion, so great was his surprise.

"You wouldn't. I'm not sure the story made more than a few small paragraphs in the newspapers. The police were notified of the find, as was a local doctor who specialized in bodies of people who had clearly been dead a while. Papa had contacts everywhere, of course." Jonty took a fortifying sip of wine, hit by a wave of longing for the father he had loved so much and whom he still wished he could consult when the occasion demanded. "They decided the chap must have died back in the early 1850's, possibly from a heart attack, although the date was as much determined by the return of the items from the exhibition as from any specific medical evidence."

"Did the police take any action?" Sir Ian asked.

"No," Orlando said. "Even if it hadn't been deemed as natural causes, it would have been too long from the date of death to bring anyone to book. There was a perfunctory inquest, at which it was decided that the chap probably collapsed into the chest, perhaps after moving a heavy item, and had not been noticed because the lid shut on him. He was then simply put away with all the rest of the stuff. A tragic accident. We were intrigued at the time but, as so many other folk back then, had more important and pressing business to deal with."

The waiter appeared, to clear their first course. Empty plates all round, although the food—good as it was—couldn't prevail over the intriguing story.

Sir Ian evidently appreciated what he'd been told. "That's much more interesting than the plot we had in mind, which was all about death from eating rhubarb leaves. There were supposed to be cases of it during the Great War, because people were encouraged to eat the things, bizarre as that may seem. We thought that would prove a novel way of poisoning someone and the culprit could pass it off as a terrible case of misadventure on the victims' part. You two would be investigating the case."

"Us? You want to put us in a film?" Orlando didn't appear as surprised as he might have been. His deductive skills were as sharp as ever.

"Yes. You may not remember but we three met a couple of years ago at a St Bride's function and while we hardly spoke more than a few times, it struck me how you'd have been excellent characters for Alasdair Hamilton and Toby Bowe to portray. Especially given the physical similarities."

"Hamilton and Bowe?" Orlando evidently couldn't help but grin. He and Jonty both enjoyed their weekly trip to the cinema, which had become a household tradition since the talkies first appeared. The old silent films had driven Orlando to great amounts of adverse comment, given the over-acting often on display. The modern Landseer offerings usually found favour with both him and Jonty, whether it was rollicking comedies like *Henry Himself* or the dramatic offerings that featured the two premiere studio actors. "Yes. I can see the general likeness. In terms of background, too. Both men distinguished themselves in the RAF, so I'm told by my students."

"They did indeed. We find that adds an authenticity to their action roles."

Jonty raised a warning hand. "Sir Ian, please keep to the RAF and naval dramas and don't mention Sherlock Holmes, because my colleague can't stand the chap. I have to go to those particular films with Dr Panesar, who's our fellow fellow, as it were."

"I'm sure I met him, too." Sir Ian's brow crinkled in thought. "Is he the chap who was a pioneer aviator?"

"The very same. Polymath, man of mystery, liable to blow us all to kingdom come at any point." Jonty chuckled. "If we are to agree to this project, about which I'm hopeful, I suspect we'll have a number of stipulations. On my part, one of them would be that you'd have to work Dr P into the script somehow. Find a handsome actor of Indian sub-continent extraction to play him."

"I'll see what I can do." Sir Ian employed his notepad once more. "I'd expected you'd have some conditions to lay before me, which we can negotiate once we've established whether we have a basis on which to proceed. Dr Stewart sounds optimistic. Professor Coppersmith, I'm assuming you're not discounting the idea entirely?"

"Not yet," Orlando said, scooping up the last piece of his pate . "Although I'd like to be able to sleep on the proposal before coming to a definitive conclusion. One hates committing oneself without due thought. What would you say, Dr Stewart?"

"I'd agree, no matter how appealing the idea of being depicted onscreen by the dashing Mr Bowe. I think another proviso would have to be no mention of discovering the actual dead body. What were you anticipating in terms of this fictional murder, apart from the rhubarb leaves?"

"One of the people involved in overseeing the move of the…let's call it the Rosetta Stone…is found dead in his office. The police think it's an accident, his having read some persuasive material about eating every part of the rhubarb plant. Waste not, want not and all that. You're not convinced and think his death is linked to the valuable items he has care of. Those, naturally, turn out to be simply a red herring and in the course of your enquiries you realise it's the old story of a jealous suitor who wants the murdered man's fiancée for his own. We thought a dramatic climax featuring a car chase and a gun would work rather well." Sir Ian paused once more. "What have I said this time? Stumbled on another coincidence?"

"Pretty well. I find it quite scary how you keep proposing that your art should imitate our lives, even if the coincident chases didn't happen at that time. We could relate just such an instance or three, could we not, Professor?" Jonty waited for Orlando's agreement then added, "I'd be happy to describe then to your scriptwriter, although he or she might find the real events rather far-fetched. At least one involved a chap in a dress doing the driving, so best not to use that. Perhaps a reference to my colleague not being terribly keen on automobiles would add a nice note of veracity."

"I might stipulate that the wretched machine end up being wrecked, which would make a spectacular scene and give me much satisfaction," Orlando said, with a smirk. "Have you been studying our cases, to have picked up so much?"

"Not recently, although when I was a boy, my father would regale me with the stories about you in *The Times*. Suitably abridged for my tender ears. I suspect some of the

16

detail must have lain dormant and is coming out now." Sir Ian made another jotting. "I've noted the dislike of cars and the avoidance of men in dresses."

"All joking aside," Orlando said, suddenly serious, "as my colleague has noticed, you'll have to pick a careful trail concerning which real events can be depicted in your film. For example, in the matter of our activities in 1914, I'd hate people to think we were in any way shirking our duty. We weren't, although we're not able to speak about it."

Sir Ian resembled a child on Christmas morning who'd had their new toy taken from them. "That's a shame. I had hoped we'd be able to imply the administrative role you suggested was in something hush-hush but clearly that would, again, cut too close to the facts."

"It would. And that's not a matter for negotiation as it would come under the Official Secrets Act. There are implications for what we got up to in the recent conflict, as well, although please note that I didn't say that. I'd hate to be as indiscreet as my nephew." Jonty tipped his head in thought. "It wouldn't do any harm to suggest we were involved with developing some of the prototype aircraft that were around at the time. Fledgling Flying Corps and all that. Then you can work in Dr Panesar."

Orlando nodded, that still handsome visage speaking of intelligence and authority. "Yes. It would be safe to depict the degree of secrecy which must have been involved in such a role."

"Splendid. I should employ your services as consultants on all my screenplays if you're so quick to identify potential problems and find solutions to them. Is it your academic training which makes you come up with ideas which we mere mortals don't?"

"Perhaps. I'd say natural inquisitiveness on our parts is the more likely explanation. Aha!" Jonty beamed at the arrival of their main courses, the steaming plates bearing succulent goodies, if the aroma was anything to go by. Either the continuing situation with food supplies wasn't affecting this establishment as much as it should have done or it had some secret source of groceries, one which it might be as well not to ask about.

"It's not simply our experience in solving mysteries which enables us to come up with ideas," Orlando said, as they started to tuck in. "With any academic discipline, you must develop the ability to come up with and rigorously explore different explanations for the facts you have before you. Imagination can play as vital a role as logic."

Jonty smiled. The Orlando he'd first known back in the year five wouldn't have borne such mature views: he'd not been able to see beyond numbers, logic and objectivity. "As a broad brush for your film, you'll need to depict Professor Coppersmith—although he hadn't been given that post then—as being the man for rational thought, while I tended towards ideas. That's simplifying a more complicated situation, naturally. If we could be given sight of the script, we could point out if either of us were acting out of character, although the public wouldn't know if you'd got it wrong."

"We would, though." Orlando pointed out. "As would anybody who knew us then or now. The porters at St Bride's would be horrified at such inaccuracies."

"I hadn't thought of such wider ranging implications, never having tackled a film concerning persons still alive. Much food for thought. As good as this food for the stomach," Sir Ian added, clearly appreciating every forkful. Even the gravy itself was of pre-war quality. "Overall, I must concede it would be safer with a fictional case being portrayed than a real one."

"Indeed. Not simply for us but for those who've entrusted us with their confidences. As I'm sure you appreciate, we are told things with a great deal of candour, things which our clients wouldn't want aired in public." Orlando speared a potato in what would be called, were it onscreen or in a book, a meaningful manner. "If you're thinking of this becoming a series, for example, you would also need to consider the variety of cases we've undertaken and the challenge in ensuring that the fictional never sails too close to the real."

Which would apply to other aspects of the film, as well: had Orlando been dropping a subtle hint on that front? They'd need to ensure the script didn't accidentally imply that their relationship was anything other than that of friends, academic colleagues and partners in detection. They were too old for dealing with scandal.

"This all appears to be eminently sensible and well within my remit to promise you. I have one more request, which I won't outline until we've done this food justice." Sir Ian turned his attention fully to his dinner, the cinematographic conversation not resuming until the plates were as nearly clear as they could be.

The offer of pudding was declined, although a soupcon of cheese with coffee was welcomed. Just the kind of thing to sharpen the wits for whatever Sir Ian wanted to say.

"I'd be very grateful," he resumed, "if you could meet the two actors who would be playing you, so that they can add as much authenticity as possible to the portrayal."

"It would be a pleasure to make their acquaintance." It was never a chore to meet two handsome young men: Jonty had derived as much pleasure from the Hamilton and Bowe films as the women around him in the audience seemed to.

"It may interest you to know that…" The arrival of the cheeseboard annoyingly cut Sir Ian off just at the point

19

things were becoming even more interesting. Maybe waiters did this sort of thing deliberately, to make their jobs fun.

"Yes?" Orlando prompted, once they were alone again.

"Alasdair and Toby do a bit of detecting themselves. Not as much experience of cases as you've accrued and they've not been blessed with such illustrious clients, but they've helped to run three murderers to ground. Including the *Grey Assassin*."

"Really? I take my hat off to them. Holmes and Watson onscreen and off, eh?" Jonty grinned. "We'll be able to swap stories when we meet. What do they think of this proposed film?"

"They don't know about it yet. It would have been remiss of me to discuss this with anyone bar my chief screenplay writer prior to having discussed it with, and obtained permission from, the various parties concerned. It's all my idea and, given my position, I'm never sure if people will be honest and tell me if it's a bad one." Sir Ian smiled ruefully as he loaded a water biscuit with a smidge of cheddar. "Perhaps your students show you the same deference."

"Professor Coppersmith's, possibly." Jonty's knife went in for the blue cheese. "Mine are never quite as polite as one might hope, although it could be said that I encourage them to think in a more expansive way and to share those thoughts."

"I'm always pleased if my students think at all," Orlando said, as he carefully buttered a cracker. "Alas, they too often come from school knowing their stuff by rote and can't always cope with the new and different."

Jonty concentrated on his food, afraid that his face would be reflecting the fact that the description Orlando had just given could have applied to him when they'd first met.

Not in terms of his beloved mathematics but his understanding of life in general.

Once they'd all filled their faces some more, he said, "So Alasdair Hamilton playing Doctor Coppersmith—as he was titled then—and Toby Bowe as me. An actor and actress of maturity and good humour cast to play my parents, no doubt. What about the lovely Miss Marsden? Where does she come into it?"

"Ah." Sir Ian laid down his fork. "That's the other aspect of the plot I need to discuss with you."

Jonty shot Orlando a glance. As George Broad might have said in his younger days, the thick was plottening.

**

"So, what do we think?" Jonty asked, as they entered their cab outside the *Blue Boar*.

"We think many things. All of which can wait to be discussed until we're home. I don't think Sir Ian would want us to talk in a public place about a project under development." If they'd had young Adam to collect them it might have been different. He'd been brought up to understand the particular nature of the Coppersmith/Stewart household, being the great-grandson of their first housekeeper, but he was still a touch young to be driving the latest metal monster, despite having been helping Jonty to tinker with it from the age he could first grasp a spanner. He'd been promised the job of housekeeper cum general factotum once he'd turned eighteen and was presently undergoing a kind of apprenticeship to the role, which would include chauffeuring them when needed.

"Is this secrecy in case a rival studio such as Tudor is spying on Sir Ian's business meetings with a view to leaping in with their own film on the subject?" Jonty didn't sound as though he was simply making a quip. Their war experiences had made the notion of spying an everyday possibility. "In that case, I think you're being very wise. As ever."

Once safe within their own four walls— *Forsythia Cottage* still felt like a bastion against the world—they opened the flask of cocoa which had been left for them, possibly by Adam himself, and settled before the nicely banked fire.

"So, jumping for joy or running away?" Jonty asked.

"The former, I think. While the old Orlando would definitely have dug in his heels and refused to have anything to do with any film, the new Orlando is intrigued. With one or two reservations, naturally."

"Naturally. You'll have to swallow your pride about the romance plot, much as both of us bridled at the idea when it was mentioned over the cheese."

"Quite." They'd tried to persuade Sir Ian otherwise, citing historical accuracy, but he'd been adamant.

Jonty stared into the flames, a wistful resignation written on his face. "It's expected in the films those three actors make together. And you have to admit that Alasdair Hamilton looks like he kisses beautifully."

"One can't deny that. Why *me* having the romance, though? Why can't *you* be the one taken with the beautiful secretary?

"Because that's what the audience expect. Toby never gets Fiona, except in that film where Alasdair's character died. Or else they'd have had her playing one of the women that Watson falls for and marries, rather than twisting the plot and making Holmes have the romantic entanglement."

"Holmes gets the girl?" Orlando supposed that made things easier to swallow. If the so-called great detective had his stories twisted, forcing him into relationships he never had, then the precedent had been established and the audience—the St Bride's porters, for example—would take it in the spirit intended. "Perhaps I should be brave and go with you and Dr Panesar to watch the next one in the series. I'd like to see Holmes suffer indignities. Not that a romance with Miss Marsden could be called such, it's just so out of keeping with Holmes's character."

"I'm constantly surprised by how you know so much about him, given your dislike of the man."

"I've read some of the books—otherwise how could I have built up an objective opinion of him and his alleged skills? I don't believe in judging merely on what one has been told." Orlando chuckled. "Anyway, I quite like working out where he goes wrong. One of my students wanted to write a thesis about the mistaken assumptions and how Holmes draws conclusions he can't possibly draw from a few observations. He wanted to call it 'The adventure of the lucky guesses.' I'm sad he never got round to writing it."

"Feared the backlash from the Conan Doyle fans? They're supposed to be rather keen about preserving his reputation. They invent far-fetched ways in which the inconsistencies in the books aren't actually inconsistencies."

"No. My student would have stood his ground on that. A brave lad. Served with 617 squadron and never made it through."

"I'm sorry to hear that. The trenches were bad enough but being up in a Lancaster seems immeasurably worse. Brave lad indeed." Jonty sipped his drink, then flashed Orlando a smile. "On a happier note, I think there's another positive to be taken out of Miss Marsden's appearance in the storyline. It acts as a smokescreen for us. People, for better or worse, will believe what they see on the screen. If you get Miss Marsden, you can't possibly be getting me."

"True." Orlando recalled the Hamilton/Bowe films he'd seen and how one or two times he'd thought he'd detected a certain chemistry between the actors. One that could bear a particular implication for those with an eye for such things. "We need to ensure there are no lingering glances between those two male leads."

"You've noticed those too? There's not anything overt in the script or storyline, yet when I go to see the Conan Doyle adaptations, I can't help but observe some of the looks and subtle body language between Holmes and Watson. I'll eat my hat if they're not trying to imply something, probably without the director realising. Certainly without the censor cottoning on."

"Really? Then I definitely should gird my loins and see one of these films. Perhaps Sir Ian will organise a special showing." That would be an aspect to analyse rigorously and hence keep his mind from the foibles of the so-called great detective. "There is another concern which I didn't like to mention to Sir Ian and which isn't so easily overcome.

"Which is?"

"College related. While we'd need to check with the Master that he's happy for us to be portrayed, it's less his reaction that than of the students that worries me. I can imagine some dunderheads ribbing us mercilessly for being depicted onscreen. Not so much our chaps—there's always the threat of a gating or other sanction to hang over *their* heads—but those pests from the college next door."

"I wouldn't worry about them. They're never short of finding ways to insult or annoy St Bride's and if there isn't a good cause they'd make one up." Jonty waved the pests away. "If there's an immovable objection from the Master, then I'm happy to let the project go by the board but I'm not going to give up my chance of working alongside Bowe and

Hamilton simply because of a bunch of unwashed undergraduates. We've faced much worse problems and overcome them."

"My fears are allayed." Not quite the truth but it would do. "I'm keen to meet them, as well. If they're also involved in amateur detection, that could lead to some interesting conversations."

"A comparison of cases? I'd certainly love to know how they helped run the *Grey Assassin* to ground. Nasty business that."

Nasty was an understatement. A series of murders of grey-haired men, which had taken place earlier that year. Despite the culprit having been caught—and said currently to be in Broadmoor, unfit to face trial—men of a certain age were still reluctant to tread the streets on the night of the new moon. "I was less thinking of that than of picking their brains."

"About what?"

"About the dead body in the vaults. Your father believed the man had been murdered and if he thought that, it was probably true. He wouldn't have been fobbed off with that rather too convenient inquest verdict."

"Convenient for who?" Jonty raised a hand. "I'm not quibbling, simply asking the next logical question. I thought at the time it had all been dealt with rather swiftly. I'd merely concluded people didn't want the extra bother of investigating it when we'd just gone to war. Unlikely anyone could be charged and convicted at sixty years remove."

"Agreed. The logical answer to your question of who, would be somebody who could influence the coroner and who had an incentive. A reputation to preserve."

"Their own or that of someone they knew?" Jonty laid down his cup. "I wish I'd had the opportunity to discuss the matter properly with Papa. He'd have been a child at the time of the Great Exhibition, although old enough to know what was going on. Eleven or twelve, I think. I suspect he'd have been rather like George at a similar age, although without a pair of uncles to aspire to emulating detection-wise."

"Do you think he noticed anything when the items were returned from Hyde Park? Assuming he was there at the time they came, of course, and not at school."

"I'd have said not. If he had picked up on anything remotely suspicious, then in the first place it would have passed into family legend, to be discussed every time you visited. In the second, he'd have made reference to it when the body showed up in 1914. *I knew back in the year 51 there was something odd about the situation.*" Jonty's voice was higher and lighter than his father's, but he'd caught the old man's intonation perfectly. "That must have been a hundred years ago, give or take a smidgeon, because I'm not entirely sure when the Great Exhibition was dismantled and despatched. Now would be a perfect time to re-open the investigation. The slender chances of us finding any relevant clues or eye-witness accounts notwithstanding."

"I doubt anything will turn up from a hundred years ago but there should be folk from forty years back who can give us first or second-hand accounts of what went on when the vault's contents were properly investigated." Preferably the former—they'd had at least one case where information had become changed as it passed from mouth to ear. "We've tackled mysteries which are much older. The Woodville Ward for one."

"Ah, but in that instance we had papers, *yellowed with their age* one might say, to help us." Jonty grinned in evident delight at having worked a quote from the sonnets into the discussion.

"Would we be as fortunate this time and turn up something similar? What happened to anything your father kept? Diaries or the like?"

"As far as I know, everything of his was simply put into store, for the benefit of future generations. Lavinia insisted, apparently. I always meant to go through the things but I didn't have the heart after he died and since then there's never seemed to be the right moment."

"Perhaps that moment is now." How splendid to have a case, albeit one that might prove insoluble, alongside a number of fresh challenges that Orlando could never have anticipated twenty-four hours previously. "All in all, I'm more than happy to proceed."

"You've made an old man very happy." Jonty rose, stretching. "Alas, I can't offer to reciprocate in the trouser department as I feel the need of sleep. Hold that on your account as a credit to be called in when I'm not so drowsy."

"I'll jot it in the book right away." There was life in the old dogs yet.

Chapter Two

The *Savoy* was looking splendid, a bastion of style and glamour in a London which still bore the scars of the war years and probably would for a while to come. Toby and Alasdair had taken a holiday to Normandy during the summer and been struck at how close the conflict felt there. It wasn't simply the presence of the German fortifications which still peppered the coast. Poor old Caen had taken a real battering, although she wore her wounds nobly.

Stepping through the *Savoy* doors always felt like stepping back in time, although on this occasion the actors didn't use the main entrance, having been pre-warned by a contact that the hotel was expecting the arrival of an American film star and his latest wife. The press photographers would apparently be out in droves. Given that neither Alasdair nor Toby had the obligatory fake girlfriend on his arm, it might be as well to avoid the lenses on this occasion.

When Sir Ian arrived, he'd not had the benefit of that inside knowledge. He looked buffeted about, having had to force his way through the throng. Not being as well-known as his employees, he'd not been targeted for a snap but he confessed to being in need of a sit down and a drink, in that order.

"I didn't have this trouble in Cambridge," he said, as they were ushered into a private room where they could drink and dine without interruption. "It was worth the journey, too. Gentlemen, as I told Toby, I was there to establish the viability of a new project and earlier today I was given the key permissions I needed to proceed."

"Groves of academe?" Toby asked. "That really will be a departure from the norm."

"Not quite, although you will be portraying two college fellows." Sir Ian sipped his drink, recovering by the minute from his jostling. "The broad storyline is a murder mystery which you'll be investigating, set in late 1914 just after war broke out and against the backdrop of sending items of national importance into safe storage. In this instance at the Old Manor, a real property which is the Stewart family's country seat down in Sussex and which we'll be allowed to access for location shots. There are vaults there which I'm told were devised for some strange purpose back in the days when the roundheads were beating the living daylights out of the cavaliers and vice-versa. Not quite priest holes but a similar principle of an area where people or things could be kept safe and unlikely to be found. The Kaiser would have had to tear the place apart to locate anything."

"This sounds like a great romp. Not for Holmes and Watson, though, I assume," Alasdair said. "They'd be a touch old, although I suppose artistic licence would apply."

Sir Ian shook his head. "Not the old stalwarts, no. Another pair of sleuths and in this instance real life ones. I met them yesterday."

"Stewart and Coppersmith!" Toby drummed gleefully on the table. "I should have guessed."

"Never heard of them." Alasdair's heavily insured eyebrow reflected his frustration at Toby knowing something he didn't.

"My father used to read about their adventures in *The Times*. Those reports would have been primarily before the Great War, although I think one or two of their cases were reported afterwards. They solved one very famous college mystery that was hundreds of years old." Toby paused. "I assume I'm right, Sir Ian. Very embarrassing if I've conflated two different sets of people."

"You've identified them correctly. I met them briefly a couple of years ago and I have to say, once encountered, they're never to be forgotten. Frighteningly clever but good company with it. They could have drunk me under the table yesterday, which is no mean feat in itself. Over coffee, I got a potted history of their detecting career, which started when the century was still in short trousers and they were asked by the police to provide inside information on a series of murders which hit their college, St Bride's. Nasty business but they helped to resolve it. The experience gave them the taste for such things. Not unlike you two."

Toby suspected they wouldn't be *exactly* like him and Alasdair, given the nature of the actors' relationship. No doubt his lover would be thinking the same, although *he* simply asked, "We've not portrayed living people before. Will that add complications in terms of the production?"

"We'll have to involve them at various stages, naturally, not least in oversight of the script. We don't want to risk a suit for defamation of character. They've outlined a few stipulations, all of which I've agreed to. It's a case of art coincidentally imitating life, so we need to exercise care about what we show being stored in the vaults and how we portray their employment during the early part of the war. There's something else, as well, which I'll touch on later."

"I suppose we also need to make sure we don't present them as a pair of unworldly academics."

"Once you've met them—as you will more than once as we develop this project—you'll know that would be the least appropriate depiction. They're great fans of your films, for one thing, and admire your war service, for another, being veterans of both conflicts themselves." Sir Ian paused. "I won't pretend that the reception for the idea was completely favourable. The other condition includes them not being portrayed as a sort of pseudo-Holmes and Watson.

Professor Coppersmith apparently can't stand the great detective. Dr Stewart has to go and see those films in the company of a certain Dr Panesar, whom they'd like to be included in the film as a minor character. He'd make an excellent source of intelligent humour and would feed into the intrigue, although I fear we'll have to tone down the reality or he'd be implausible. IS Johar would be a splendid casting choice if we can get him."

"None of that sounds difficult," Alasdair averred. "We don't portray all our characters in the same way and I for one enjoy the challenge of producing something unique." He didn't refer to the fact that while the characters did change—subtly—the basic formula remained the same.

Toby decided to tackle that matter straight away. "Given that both men are still alive, Alasdair will no doubt be winning Fiona, because we can't manoeuvre her into having me as a consolation prize. Are either men married or have they been in the past?"

"No and no. I knew that from Dr Stewart's nephew, who helped me get into contact with them. Two crusty old bachelors who share a house." Sir Ian lowered his voice. "Whether the same situation applies as with you, I couldn't say. There were no obvious clues but then there are no obvious clues around this table."

Alasdair's eyebrow might as well have borne a sign saying, "Well, well." That would be another factor to enliven the making of this film.

"How will I be suffering nobly this time?" Toby asked. He might equally have enquired about the use of Alasdair's eyebrow in the close-ups or how Fiona might best display the steely qualities that lay beneath her lovely exterior. The paying public hadn't tired of any of these aspects, as yet.

"I'm not sure at present. I had thought of having you at risk of being blown up, because the aforementioned Dr

Panesar is a man of many talents, one of which includes experimenting with explosives. If we could work that into the plot, the whole of the university community would be beating a path to the cinema doors in order to appreciate the in-joke."

The waiter arrived bearing plates of ham terrine, allowing the noise from outside to penetrate.

"That sounds quite a fracas," Alasdair said. "Do you have a rugby dinner on or has the American actor arrived?"

"He has indeed." The waiter's eyebrow lifted in almost as eloquent a manner as the actor could produce. "They are taking a series of publicity photographs although the crowds resemble an enormous scrum. If I may be so bold, you're all better off in here." He took a deep breath then backed into the fray once more.

"I was once asked to include a certain actor from across the pond in one of our films. I declined." Sir Ian set to on his food, while Toby and Alasdair shared a grin. The studio head's view on such matters was legendary.

"To return to the film, what will these hidden treasures be?" Alasdair asked. "The crown jewels?"

Sir Ian looked up sharply. "No. I had in mind a whole collection of items, including the Rosetta Stone and a first folio Shakespeare."

Alasdair elegantly smoothed some butter on his toast, a pleasure to behold. He'd employed the gesture in one of their films, gaining praise and favourable comparison with Du Maurier lighting a cigarette. "Is that to hide the fact it was the crown jewels which were hidden there?"

"I wouldn't be surprised. Messrs Coppersmith and Stewart were rather cagey about it, so don't mention it, especially as the present lord was rather indiscreet when I approached him initially for permission. He's besotted with Fiona so immediately consented to us using the Old Manor, on the understanding he'll get to meet her." Sir Ian lowered his voice again. "Whatever they really hid there in the Great War, I rather suspect they did the same again during the last conflict, only nobody is supposed to know."

Toby chuckled. "I've been told by three different people about three different locations which were used to keep the crown jewels out of Hitler's hands. On each occasion the person swears they had it on good authority that *their* information was correct. None of them mentioned the Stewarts' place, on which grounds I suspect it's probably the front runner. And that's the last we'll say on the matter. Anything else we need to avoid discussing?"

"Ah, yes. Two old bachelors, remember? I was worried I was going to have to ask you two to employ both your charm and diplomacy skills to ensure that a certain part of the plot went ahead." Sir Ian waited, having provided the cue.

Alasdair took it up. "Fiona's role?"

"Exactly. When we finished dinner last evening, I was mightily afeared her part would be the stumbling block upon which the whole would come crashing down and that if we wanted to proceed, we'd have had to feature her as simply a friend. Or Stewart's married sister."

"The public would never put up with that." One day the formula would have to change—unless geriatric romances came into vogue—but the moment wasn't now. "Has it been resolved?"

"Yes. They're happy for the romantic element to remain. As you've pointed out, the public would expect it, not least Lord Thomas himself. He of the crush on her." Sir Ian finished off the last of his toast, giving the opportunity for Toby to speculate about the apparent change of heart on behalf of the Cambridge fellows. Evidence of their being

33

akin to him and Alasdair and using the onscreen romance as a smokescreen?

"Now, for the murder," Alasdair said, once the waiter had been to clear their plates. "Based on one of their real cases?"

"No. I'd never intended that, given the risk that relatives of either the victim or the murderer would still be alive and liable to kick up a fuss. This entirely fictional case will involve a government chap, one involved in getting the valuable items into store. He'll die of oxalic acid poisoning, ostensibly by accident."

Alasdair tapped the table. "Eating rhubarb leaves?"

"Yes. Only he's been given the stuff intentionally and it's been made to look like a sad chance of fate by a rival for his girlfriend—Fiona's—hand. The interesting thing is the 'something else' I referred to earlier." The story was cut short as the waiter returned to serve the main course, with the sommelier in tow to ensure their glasses were topped up. "That hubbub appears to have settled."

"Yes, sir. They're settling into their suite. I believe we will be saved any further disturbance until tomorrow." Once the proper disdain had been registered and the waiting duties were done, the pair departed again, carefully closing the door.

"This is resembling a scene in a farce. People in and out and noises off. Nothing farcical about this beef, though." Toby carefully cut himself a piece. "Sir Ian, the mysterious 'something else'?"

"A dead body. A real one, discovered when the vaults were reopened in 1914." Sir Ian beamed in evident pleasure at having surprised his two actors. "I'm not too sure why it hadn't shown up previously, as it's said to date back to the time of the Great Exhibition. The Stewarts lent some items to exhibit and more returned than was bargained for. Took

34

them sixty odd years to discover the fact, though. The inquest ruled the man had met his death by natural causes, nobody having the time or inclination to go much further with a proper investigation. Suspicions raised among the Stewarts at the time, though."

"How very gratifying." Alasdair immediately raised a hand in apology for his words. "Not for the dead man and his family, clearly. I was being purely selfish and thinking it would be an intellectual challenge to discuss the matter with our fellow amateur detectives."

"Maybe it *was* gratifying for his family," Toby pointed out. "It doesn't sound like they made much effort to report him missing. Or to find him, if he lay undisturbed for so long. Is there any doubt that it was an old corpse rather than a more recent one deposited in a convenient place and made to look like it had been there all that time?"

"You'll have to ask your colleagues in detection that. You won't be short of things to discuss, one way or another." Sir Ian jiggled his fork enthusiastically. "This could be one of your most authentic performances. They even bear a passing resemblance to you, in terms of one being tall and dark—dark in his pomp—and the other being fair. A better resemblance than even we achieved with Holmes and Watson. My assistant has managed to find some photographs from their younger days which we can consider this evening. Once they're no longer at risk from gravy stains."

When the table had been cleared again, Sir Ian laid out the items out perusal. The general physical resemblance was there just as he'd said, particularly in body shape. Professor Coppersmith would probably have been taller and leaner than Alasdair at the same age, Toby guessed, although he and Dr Stewart were much of a height and build. Facially, the type was there if not the detail. The eyebrows would no doubt not be so highly expressive on the mathematician's face than on Alasdair's but there was the same hint in the eyes of vast emotional depths kept well-hidden and well controlled. Whereas the man's Shakespeare-loving colleague wore a beaming grin which would be easy to replicate onscreen. Handsome men, both, and quite the sort to melt many a heart.

"Yes. A satisfactory piece of casting." Alasdair held the photos up to the light. "Do they still possess what you might call the echo of these looks?"

"More than an echo. Neither of them lacks being photogenic, even now. If they weren't so wedded to their studies, they'd make a wonderful pair of character actors."

"Then what about them having a walk-on role in this film?" Toby suggested. "They could be in the background for a scene set in college. Perhaps debating some abstruse academic point in the Senior Common Room or walking past in one of the outdoor shots. What say, Alasdair? Alasdair?"

"Sorry. I was starting to imagine myself into the role and my thoughts strayed back to the dead man. It *is* rather intriguing why he laid there so long."

Toby recognised the subtle metamorphosis from actor to detective. "Would you like to share those thoughts?"

"He may have been an orphan, so wouldn't have had a family to report him gone. Or he may have had good reason to make himself scarce back in the 1850's, so people assumed that's what he'd done. How frustrating that we're unlikely to ever find a solution to *this* mystery. Unlike the rhubarb leaves business, which will no doubt see us triumphant."

"Too defeatist. That's no way for a war hero to talk," Toby said, grinning. "It could be the great case of our detecting career were we to clear the matter up."

"Imagine it. The combined expertise of Bowe, Coppersmith, Hamilton and Stewart." Sir Ian's eyes shone, possibly in anticipation of the publicity value of such a feat. "Could any murderer defy their efforts to pin them down?"

***

The meal done, the bill paid and the hotel manager having remarked—with uncharacteristic indiscretion—that it was a pleasure to do business with *British* actors, Toby and Alasdair caught a cab back to a place where they could discuss the evening in more detail.

Once ensconced in Toby's sitting room with a glass of port as a nightcap, ties loosened and tongues ready to be, he said, "Well well, a pair of lifelong bachelors living together. Doesn't prove anything, of course, because I can think of some crabbity old codgers whom no woman would have anything to do with. But from what Sir Ian said, they don't appear to be in that category. He clearly suspects that the arrangements in Cambridge are the same as here."

Alasdair patted his lover's knee, which was within convenient reach. "Not quite the same if they've set up house together. I wonder when that was. If they've known each other since the start of the century that's rather encouraging, don't you think?"

"Living like an old married couple even if they haven't taken the vows? Yes, I think it's lovely." Toby snuggled closer. "Not least because of the fact it seems they haven't been caught, either officially by the police or unofficially by the university or society in general."

"They've probably more sense than to take the extra risk of being found out." Unlike some actors whom Alasdair could name, at least one of whom had fallen prey to a combination of a toilet that was being observed and a handsome, undercover policeman. "Discretion being their watchword, as ours is. There are ways to reduce the danger, as we know. Happily married men don't necessarily feel the need of acquainting themselves with ladies of the night, so why should two chaps who have all their needs satisfied at their own fireside want to seek their pleasure elsewhere? A pair of Cambridge dons would have the advantage over us of not being in the public eye, therefore not needing faux girlfriends on their arms."

"A traditionally all-male environment, too, so they can hide in plain sight in their college. Not something we can do." Toby drained his glass, sighed and rested his head on Alasdair's shoulder. "Assuming we're not barking up the wrong tree, I'd love to know how they've managed to evade discovery. We might get some tips."

Alasdair kissed the top of his lover's head. Oh, that they could be so fortunate. "Let alone the tips we can get on investigation. They've forty odd years more experience of that than we have. Knocks our handful of cases into a cocked hat. Academic rigour to back it up, as well." Although, while neither actor could boast the brains their detecting counterparts possessed, they weren't stupid.

"We can both act highly intelligent, as we've proven with our Holmes and Watson. Nobody doubts the validity of your onscreen portrayal of the great detective. Our offscreen activities—not those of the bedroom, naturally—add to the authenticity of our depictions and stick a feather in Landseer's cap. Who else has a pair of amateur sleuths to portray a pair of amateur sleuths? Twice over in this instance. We really will have to ensure we make the characters sufficiently different to our Conan Doyle interpretations, especially if what we surmise is correct."

"An excellent point." It should prove easy for them to portray Stewart and Coppersmith as unique, particularly as they would have the originals to study. Yet they'd have to avoid any of the little sly glances that passed between their characters, principally in the Sherlock Holmes films. Glances which not only evaded the director's gaze but flew straight past the censor, only to lodge in the minds of those who had an eye for such things. Alasdair had no doubt, from reading the books, that Holmes bore a romantic, unrequited love for Watson. "It'll be manly interactions at every turn. Ow! What did I say to deserve that?" Alasdair rubbed his arm, which had received a severe pinch.

"It's a reminder that *all* our interactions are already manly, onscreen or off."

"I stand corrected and contrite."

"Good. Now, the aforementioned fireside. We have one of those here in this very room and North has it banked to perfection for such a chilly evening." Toby leaned up to give Alasdair a kiss. "I have all that I want here beside me and a large, warm bed which we could employ to prove that neither of us need to stray to get our pleasure. Are you interested?"

"Am I ever not?"

Chapter Three

Saturday mornings out of term were normally not dented with the hubbub of activity of their term-time equivalents, allowing a leisurely start to the day. Not so this September one, where all decks had to be cleared before noon. A meeting with two distinguished actors beckoned, either side of and through luncheon. A meeting about which word had spread like wildfire and which was rousing a surprising amount of envy from the porters, who seemed convinced Miss Marsden would be there, no matter the reassurances to the contrary.

Jonty had even been given a photograph of the lovely actress by the newest porter, Archer, who said he'd got it from his brother who worked on a newspaper.

"Please could you get her to sign it, Dr Stewart?" he pleaded, when Jonty and Orlando arrived in college to check their post before heading to their appointment.

"I think I should be going around wearing a sandwich board, with the message 'I am *not* having lunch with Fiona Marsden' written in capital letters and underlined three times." Relenting at the sight of Archer's crestfallen face, Jonty felt he had to make recompense. "The best I can do is take this and ask either Mr Hamilton or Mr Bowe to work their magic on the lady herself. You risk not getting it back."

"That's a risk worth taking. Thank you, sir." The porter went off beaming.

"Are they all in love with her?" Orlando asked, unopened mail in his hand.

"Most of the male population—and no doubt some of the females—would come into that category to some extent." Jonty grinned. "I think she combines remarkable beauty with intelligence and the impression that no nonsense will be stood for. She probably reminds people of their nannies or their infant class teacher. Deep psychological depths to be plumbed there." He took his father's walking stick—used more for effect than efficacy, he swore—and pointed towards the gate. "Off on another adventure."

Once out of St Bride's, Orlando said, "I've been having a look through the package of information Sir Ian sent us. Alasdair Hamilton *does* bear a resemblance to me in my younger days."

"He's certainly the same dark and handsome type. I always thought *you* might have made a wonderful matinee idol. I can imagine you in the old films, seducing the ladies with a glance, some mouthed dialogue and a caption."

Orlando snorted. "I shall treat that remark with the contempt it deserves. I know better than to encourage you by rising to the bait. Toby Bowe has a touch of you about him, although not quite your equal in looks. Nobody could be," he added in a murmur.

"Thank you. He's just your type, then."

"I don't have a type."

Jonty knew that to be true, him alone being Orlando's fancy. The mathematician had only ever found one other man in any way alluring and he'd often confessed it had made him very uncomfortable. The late Dr Beattie had been nothing like Jonty physically: and that period of attraction had occurred at a time of great loneliness and emotional turmoil when Orlando had been at his lowest ebb and not thinking straight. Best not to dwell on that. "I've had an idea, one I'd like your opinion on. I've spoken to Thomas and have suggested that when these two actors visit the Old Manor, we could come with them. Take the pressure off him having to do the entertaining."

"And allow us to broach the matter of the body in the body in the vault? If that's what you want an opinion on, it has my complete approval."

Jonty had guessed that would be so, the allure of a case—even one that on the face of it could prove impossible to solve—working its inevitable magic. "They'd be able to justify to the studio any time spent on it. Observation in the field, as it were. Seeing us in detecting action. Ah! I believe that's them."

A cluster of girls and women had formed on the pavement ahead, spilling into the road and so causing swerving of vehicles and beeping of horns. Two handsome male heads could just about be glimpsed in the middle of the throng.

"Autograph hunters and the like, I suppose," Orlando observed.

"I hope that's all those ladies are hunting. I can imagine that pair having the jackets ripped off their backs for souvenirs. Let's effect a rescue." Jonty picked up the pace and, as they neared the group, he both shouted a greeting and began to wave his walking stick in a manner he hoped would look like an accident waiting to happen. The women dispersed, perhaps thinking they were in the presence of an aged madman. Without waiting to make introductions, he said, "Quite a useful prop, this, I find. Let's get you into the hotel before the hordes can descend again."

"It's a hazard of the occupation," the one who must have been Toby said. "I sometimes think I'd rather be facing Messerschmitts."

Only once ensconced safely in a private room in their chosen hostelry, with a promise exacted from the management that nobody would be allowed to enter apart from the waiting staff, proper introductions could be made. Introductions that were conducted in an atmosphere that felt distinctly strange at first. For Jonty, it was almost like peering into a magic mirror and seeing one's younger self staring back. There was also, clearly, some undefined sensation which the actors were experiencing.

"All a bit peculiar, this." Toby glanced from Jonty to Orlando and back again. "We've never previously met the people we're going to play onscreen."

"I feel I need to apologise in advance," Alasdair added. "Because I'll find myself studying you so closely. Would it be embarrassing if we made notes?"

"I'd rather you did than risk inaccuracy," Orlando said. "One has to take one's job seriously."

Alasdair's famous eyebrow—how wonderful to be able to observe the thing in close-up—registered delight. "Thank you, Professor Coppersmith."

"Please call me Orlando."

Just as well that the drinks hadn't yet arrived because Jonty would have been at risk of spilling his. Orlando rarely allowed the use of his Christian name in public and never with people he hadn't previously met. A red letter day, indeed.

"If we are to be involved in this project," Orlando continued, perhaps having registered Jonty's surprise, "then we should do it wholeheartedly, as we might an academic venture. If Mr Hamilton—Alasdair, if I may—is to portray me then he can't be addressing me by my title all the time. It would put up an unwarranted barrier."

"It would indeed." Alasdair nodded approval.

"For the purposes of the script," Toby said, "would I be correct in guessing that you would normally use your title in everyday conversation?" Perhaps he'd also noted Jonty's shock.

"Yes. Dr Stewart and I…Jonty, I mean—old habits die hard, you see—only refer to each other by our Christian names in private, amongst family or on holiday. Please make a note of that for your film."

"I will." Alasdair produced a leather-bound notebook and elegant silver pen, not dissimilar to the one Sir Ian had used the day before. Standard Landseer issue or imitation of the boss? "Are there other things of which we need to be aware?"

The ensuing discussion firstly covered the physical, how Jonty's facial scar post-dated 1914 and how Orlando's dodgy Achilles' tendon occasionally affected him back then, reducing his natural turn of pace.

"Oh, and I do this when I'm thinking." Jonty tipped his head to one side. "My nephew, George Broad, is said to do the same when he's on the bench. Orlando favours a roll of the eyes."

They turned to likes and dislikes—useful background information, the actors assured them—which then naturally led to the surprising things they'd been involved in, such as Orlando having to pose as a dancing partner during one of their commissions.

"It's a shame we can't use one of your real investigations," Alasdair said, clearly impressed at the range of cases being detailed. "Though I can understand that would be fraught with problems. And the real murder in the vaults was never solved, so that wouldn't work."

"I suspected Sir Ian would mention that to you." Orlando delicately speared a new potato, this bit of the conversation having lasted into the main part of the meal. "We'd be very interested to have your views on it. Especially if we can turn up any new evidence when we visit the Old Manor. Jonty has already arranged spending a weekend there if we can find mutually acceptable dates."

"We tried to pretend it was merely about the film but my nephew Thomas, the present title-holder, saw through us." Jonty chuckled. "He knows he needs to get himself back in my good books as he's been a bit too free and easy discussing Stewart business, so is more than happy to accommodate us and let us poke around in the vaults. Likely we can have the place to ourselves as he's in London at present and I'll try via Sir Ian to fix him up a dinner with Fiona at the same time as we're down in Sussex. Would she fancy a handsome widower with a ready-made family but room for more?"

"She's due to be married, imminently, although I daresay your nephew might turn her head as she enters the final furlong. The race isn't won until you pass the post." Toby laid down his fork. "This dead man. What can you tell us?"

"Very little. His name, Peter Drayton, which was confirmed by clothes marks and the contents of his pockets. An approximate age, being somewhere in his twenties given the status of his wisdom teeth. The fact he'd likely been there since the 1850's. Our family lent items for the Great Exhibition, some of which were sent in the crates they'd always been stored in. The then lord, my grandfather, took this as an opportunity to give the vaults a jolly good clean out and disposed of much old rubbish. This is important, because it tells us that the body couldn't have been there earlier. And the crate it was found in was one of those sent to Hyde Park, given the labelling on it." Jonty nodded to Orlando for him to take up the tale.

"At the end of the exhibition, the items were returned, ostensibly as they had been sent, and put back into store. Nobody thought to make a detailed check of them against the inventory of what was sent, partly because the items were of no great interest to the Stewarts—they'd have been in use or on display, otherwise—and partly because Jonty's grandmother was seriously ill after a difficult confinement. That mattered more." Orlando paused a moment, gathering thoughts and words. Jonty couldn't miss Alasdair making a

45

mental note of the exact action. "The fabric of the vaults was regularly checked as part of ensuring the Old Manor was kept ship-shape but nobody bothered about the contents. Until Mr Stewart had a proper look in 1914. He decided a full stock take, as it were, should be done. He'd not expected that the stock would include Peter Drayton"

"*Mr* Stewart?" Alasdair asked.

"Yes. Papa never used his title, although he kept it for my brother Sheridan and subsequently his son Thomas to assume. Papa said he could never stoop so low as to be called a lord." Jonty smiled ruefully. "Had he not fallen victim to the Spanish flu, we'd not be having quite this conversation. We three would have worked together to solve the murder, because he was quite convinced it wasn't an accident or natural causes. If we'd failed we might have come to the conclusion it wasn't solvable."

"He sounds a remarkable man." Toby—who was even more handsome in the flesh than he appeared on the screen, partly because one could see the true colour of his extraordinarily blue eyes—inclined his head in tribute. "Was he the one who found the body?"

"He was in the stock-taking party, yes. Drayton wasn't the only unexpected item, because Papa also found various artefacts that definitely didn't belong to us. That sorely tried his conscience as he wanted to return them to their owners but had no indication of from whence they'd come. Being a pragmatic sort, he decided that the…let's simply say the Rosetta Stone…and other things could be best hidden among the old tat." Jonty fingered his scar in thought, then hurriedly stopped. He hadn't possessed that scar in 1914, so it would be no use Toby mimicking the gesture.

"It sounds absolute madness." Alasdair pushed away his emptied plate. "I have three questions. Firstly, can you be sure that Drayton went into the chest while it was in London?"

"Not geographically," Orlando said, "but there is evidence relevant to the timing. Drayton had a letter in his pocket dated a few days before the crates and other objects were returned. That date is also consistent with the medical evidence given at the inquest. Second question?"

"What happened to the original contents of the chest?"

"That's exactly what I asked at the time." Orlando was obviously delighted at the direction in which Alasdair's thoughts were running. "Nobody knows. They weren't of great value—some zoological and native objects collected in Africa, Mr Stewart believed—and they weren't misplaced among the other things which had been returned."

"My guess is that they ended up elsewhere. Perhaps accidentally, with another family thinking what we did, that they'd been sent someone's old tat by mistake. Or they were deliberately disposed of to make room in the crate." Jonty shrugged. "As with so much concerning this case, finding the likeliest rather than the definitive explanation may be our best outcome."

Toby drummed gently on the table. "There was no clue from the extraneous objects returned to you? That a swop might have occurred, I mean."

"Papa didn't mention that as an idea, but then we all had our minds on other matters in 1914. It's probable those items are still stored in the vault, unless Sheridan cleared them in an excess of zeal. You had a third question, Alasdair," Jonty added.

"Toby has already asked it. Almost. I did wonder what these other objects were and if they could be relevant."

"Various metallic items, nature unknown, although possibly the remains of ancient iron smelting—pre-Roman,

47

supposedly, according to the chap who looked at them for the coroner's court."

"Also, what might be a small mammoth tusk and a collection of flint tools," Orlando added.

At the mention of the mammoth, Jonty had a sudden vivid recollection of Thomas being convinced it was a unicorn's horn, or a narwhal's. "Not a particularly unusual collection for those times and none of the things were labelled. I feel some explanation of the timings is important here. We visited the Old Manor two days after the body was found, so we only saw the chest and the extraneous material, as the grisly contents had been taken away. Anything we have to report is predominantly at second hand, although it should be easy to find a report of the inquest."

"There *may* be some first-hand evidence." Jonty, aware of the slightly disappointed expressions on the actors' faces, wanted to encourage them in case they thought the task too daunting. "After he inherited the estate, Sheridan had the good sense to ensure all Papa's papers were kept. The next step after seeing the vaults would be for us to go through them. I'd lay a tenner that he left some record of what he thought."

"Splendid. I was beginning to give up hope." Toby eyed the door, from whence the waiter would no doubt soon emerge. "Shall we order a sweet or savoury to finish?"

"I rather fancy a soupcon of cheese," Alasdair said. "Then getting some fresh air along the Backs, if that would suit the company?"

"A walk would be very welcome after such a filling lunch." Orlando patted the front of his jacket, where the smallest paunch was developing. "I'd like to hear about your adventures in the RAF, if I may."

Alasdair nodded. "Of course. Two old fliers sharing tales with two old soldiers. We've heard about your distinguished records."

"I doubt you've heard the entire tale." Few people had, Jonty still guarding it fiercely. Perhaps when they were at the Old Manor, settled in the drawing room with a glass of port, he could tell them what the end of the war had brought. Having now spent time with this pair, he could hazard a guess that they had more in common with him and Orlando than simply a passing resemblance and a passion for detection. They'd appreciate the tale.

"Sir Ian told us that you signed up halfway through the Great War but were doing something before then, at the time the film spans. Are we allowed to know what that was?" Toby asked.

"In a word, no." Jonty produced his most charming smile. "That's one of the secrets we'll never reveal. Don't ask us about the last war, either."

***

Initially Alasdair fell into step with Jonty, having told Toby he wanted the opportunity of observing Orlando walking and thereby study his character's gait.

"It does still bear witness to the dodgy tendon, doesn't it?" Jonty said. "You should see him sometimes if he has to break into a run. If it's playing up, he's all dot and carry one."

"Who's dot and carry one?" Orlando asked, slowing his pace so they could catch up. "Alasdair, walk with me so I can explain to you the exact circumstances in which the thing plays up."

Toby let them get ahead before remarking, "What a pair."

"Did you see Alasdair's face when rhubarb compote appeared on the cheeseboard?" Jonty's face creased into a grin, the lines adding to its mischievous character. "I thought he was going to choke."

"Another strange coincidence." One that had momentarily turned the conversation over the cheese from flying Spitfires to the murder which would feature in the film. The two fellows had longed to hear about that part of the storyline but the writers' department would have to flesh it out and mere actors wouldn't be privy to it until the script began to emerge. "Your colleague doesn't appear to want Fiona's character involved in the murder investigation."

"In the interests of accuracy, naturally." Jonty flashed a smile. Toby hoped he could do justice to the younger version of a man who appeared so handsome well into his seventies.

"Naturally."

"He was distinctly *Orlando Furioso* at first about her being featured at all but he's got over his upset. You see, we've never had much call for the female of the species investigation-wise, apart from my sister and mother who were rather good at helping us. Miss Marsden would be far too young to play Mama, of course, although she's blessed with the same rare beauty. And a hint of the same formidable nature." Jonty shot him a sidelong glance. "Can I rely on your discretion? It's relevant to the film, I promise."

"Of course. Even if it wasn't relevant, I could assure you my lips would be sealed." Especially as Toby could guess what revelation might be coming.

"Well, Orlando and I have had plenty of female friends but none of them romantically, if you get my drift."

Toby patted Jonty's shoulder. "I do indeed understand. Such a partnership is not unknown in our business, if you get *my* drift."

"So I've been told." Jonty glanced across again. "We both know that much detection is based on careful observation. Not in the Sherlock Holmes way of stains on thumbs or scratches on watches but of people themselves. Forgive me if I intrude but it would be deliciously ironic if Orlando and I were being depicted by a couple whose relationship is exactly the same as ours. It isn't obvious, I hasten to add, unless one has...specialist knowledge."

"I'm pleased to hear that. You read the situation correctly, despite what the Landseer publicity department would have you believe." Toby looked ahead, wondering if Orlando and Alasdair might be having a similar conversation. "I'm hoping that everyone else will assume that the only connections we have are a passing physical resemblance and the joint interest in poking our noses into other people's mysteries. Fascinating that love should form the third, unspoken, connection. You look rather well on nearly fifty years of something that's almost a marriage."

"Well, I've not murdered him yet, although he alleges he has planned various undetectable methods to get rid of me." Jonty swished at a long piece of grass with his cane. "I'd hate to teach you your business but please don't employ any of those glances you interchange when you're Holmes and Watson. For all our sakes."

"Ah. You noticed those?" No doubt due to that specialist knowledge. "We've already decided that no such things will appear this time."

"Much obliged."

"I think you're remarkable. If Alasdair and I are still together and as content as you are in our seventies, we'll count ourselves as blessed." Toby, lowering his voice, took

51

Jonty's arm. "Please God we don't see another world war as you've done. Quite a varied career in the service of your country, one way and another, I've heard. Not many men would have swopped the safety of Room Forty for the perils of the trenches."

Jonty stiffened. "How on earth did you know about that?"

"My maternal uncle, Jeffery Fitzpaine, worked with you. He's in a nursing home now, frail in body and mind. I visited him a couple of days ago, thinking I'd better take my chance to see him while he was still with us and happened to mention we were coming to see you. I was staggered when he said he'd known you back then. I hadn't even heard of the place before."

"I remember Jeffery. He must be losing all his senses if he's telling everyone what we did." Jonty swished his cane again.

"I think you can rest assured. He rambles quite a lot and if anyone hears him, they'll think he's talking nonsense. Once you've claimed one day that you're the queen's long-lost brother and the next that you're Churchill's father, people take everything with a pinch of salt. I guess, from what you said earlier, that in this rare instance he was telling the truth. Alasdair knows none of this, by the way, and I won't be telling him."

"Thank you. I'm sure he's trustworthy but old activities have long repercussions. More recent activities, too. I'd be obliged if you'd forcibly remind the Landseer publicity department not to touch on what we were doing while you were up in your spitfires. Make it serving with the Local Volunteer Reserve or fire watching or something similar." Jonty pointed at the pair ahead. "Talking of coincidences, we recognized the name of one of the *Grey Assassin's* victims. Was there any connection to the others in terms of what they did during the war?"

"Yes. It was pivotal to solving the case. Again, we were careful not to tell anyone else what we discovered, apart from my godfather."

"Your godfather?"

"Matthew Firestone. Serial godfather to many a child, mainly of women he charmed in his youth. Also, one of the best officers at Scotland Yard and the man with the official credit for solving the case. Alasdair and I had touched on Official Secrets Act related things before, for a case with buried treasure. One might say Room Forty in a new guise."

"One might. And given that we can't be sure that the world isn't plummeting into another conflict with our once allies, then careless talk on the matter could still cost lives."

Toby nodded. "The Landseer publicity machine is—as you can imagine—effective at dissimulation. Fire watching or similar it is."

"Excellent. Now, let's tell that pair either to slow down so we can keep pace or race on ahead and arrange us a pot of tea at St Bride's. There are some practicalities we need to discuss."

"Practicalities?"

"Have you forgotten we have a hundred-year-old murder to solve?" Jonty slapped Toby's back, surprisingly hard. "I know there will be times we work alone or in our usual pairings, but we need to sort out who does what and who works with whom when we're all at the Old Manor. Two's company but four's a crowd."

***

Lowering clouds threatening rain eliminated any further discussion on the hoof. They headed back to the college and Orlando's study, with Jonty going straight to the buttery to plead for hot tea and four cups to be sent up.

"I didn't even have to promise a hefty tip," he said on his return. "They'll be fighting over who gets to meet our guests. It wouldn't surprise me if the tray gets borne by one lass at each corner. Now, have we decided how we split for investigation?"

"We were considering our options." Orlando was warming his backside at a fire he'd just coaxed into life. "Alasdair rather favours going with established pairs, almost on the bridge principal."

"Bridge?"

"That we'd understand each other's bidding habits, as it were, so could work more efficiently," Alasdair said.

Toby cut in. "I'd say there's something to be said for splitting those old pairings. New blood, new thoughts?"

Jonty nodded. "And each pair would in that case have a younger pair of legs to employ, so be potentially less restricted. I won't say they'd also have the benefit of a more mature brain. A more experienced one, perhaps."

Orlando considered the notion and saw that it was good. "Each pair would also have one person with the Stewart connection so would have the key to several doors."

"I concede defeat." Alasdair's eyebrow emphasized his words. "In which case, how do we pair? Blonds together and brunets together? Or should we have a Stewart and Coppersmith together, real and cinematic?"

"Blonds and brunets?" Jonty chuckled. "You might be hard pushed to see the original hair colour in the case of myself and Orlando. The idea of mixing and matching does appeal, though. I'm used to working alongside a tall, dark streak of grumpiness. No offence intended, Alasdair."

"Only in my direction." Orlando harrumphed. That banter hadn't changed in fifty years and would probably never do so. "It might be better to have Alasdair and I together, simply so that he can observe me in investigative action and further develop his portrayal. As can Toby with this scamp." It would also ensure that Jonty wasn't with the type of young man that he might just fancy. The more Orlando studied the actor, the more Alasdair seemed ideally suited to portray him in his younger days. The likelihood of any attraction consequently developing into anything else was remote if not non-existent, yet the old Orlando couldn't help but raise his jealous head sometimes. He cast a surreptitious glance at Toby, seeing some hint of the young Jonty there, especially in the natural tendency to smile. Yet he couldn't say that the actor made his heart glow the way that the incumbent pest of *Forsythia Cottage* still did.

"I'm sure Landseer will be delighted about the close collaboration." Alasdair nodded. "So, a plan of action. A visit to the Old Manor and an inspection of the scene. What else?"

"As I said, I'd be interested to see if my father made any notes about the matter," Jonty said. "We could search through all the material he left."

"Nothing relevant has turned up in all this time?" Alasdair asked.

"Not that I'm aware of, although not everyone in the family has our inquisitive nature. George rather grew out of the phase where he wanted to be a detective and turned to prosecuting criminals rather than finding them. I keep hoping my great nephew Jonny will fully take up the baton when we're ready to pass it on. Sorry, digressing." Jonty rubbed his forehead. "The moment was lost when such papers might have been rooted out. As you can imagine, the loss of my parents hit me very hard and once the turmoil at the end of the war had settled, I really didn't want to have much to do with Papa's things for a time afterwards. I couldn't even bear to look at his handwriting because it brought him back to me too quickly and close."

"Are all his papers intact?" Toby's voice dripped concern and sympathy: exactly so had it sounded in their newly released royal romance, when he'd comforted Alasdair at the point it looked as though he'd never win Fiona.

"I believe so. My sister Lavinia insisted nothing should be lost for future generations. Going through everything will possibly be too big a job for one weekend, notwithstanding four people doing it, although Papa was fond of order and method so I'm hopeful we can narrow things down either chronologically or by subject." Jonty nodded. "Any other bright ideas?"

"I could ask my godfather to see if he can find anything in the official police records about the case but I'm not hopeful, especially if it wasn't formally investigated. Shouldn't ignore the obvious, though." Toby turned to Alasdair. "Anything we've missed that we could be getting on with?"

Alasdair spread his hands. "Not that I can think of, apart from background. Mugging up on the Great Exhibition, what was shown there and where it came from? The exact dates it was being dismantled?"

"I'd add in looking for any mention in the newspapers in the aftermath of the event, concerning missing persons named Drayton. Perhaps something in the personal adverts?" Orlando added.

"Splendid idea. 'Peter, please contact your mother,' or the like. This is where we miss Bellingham. He was the librarian here," Jonty told their guests. "Died in an air raid during the war, when visiting friends in London. He was a

56

dab hand at turning out obscure information. Still, we can always set the present St Bride's librarian on the trail. He'll enjoy the novelty."

Toby, who'd been studying the fire, said, "Sixty years is an awfully long time for somebody to be unaccounted for, unless they had already run away from home and so were out of both sight and mind. How was he dressed, by the way? Any clues about him from that?"

"We never saw the body but Papa reckoned he was kitted out like a senior clerk might have been at the time. I can't recall if the letter he had on him contained his address. Can you, Orlando?"

"Your father believed it was directed to the sort of property which might have consisted of rented-out rooms. Nobody was bothered about chasing up where he'd been living, given it was so long after the event and with other business at hand. I suppose people do take off into the blue and after a while the landlady or whoever assumes they've gone off to seek their fortune and re-lets their room." Orlando warmed to his theme, thrilled to find the game well and truly afoot, even if there didn't appear much possibility of scoring a winning goal. "A clever killer might have sent a note to that effect to whoever Drayton left behind, the contents of which would have explained his disappearance and forestalled it being reported."

"He—or she—would have had to have nerves of steel. Or be sure that the Stewarts wouldn't open that crate as soon as it was returned. Which begs an obvious question." Toby raised an eyebrow in Jonty's direction.

"It does. Involvement on our part. I think we can eliminate the household as it was in 1851 from suspicion, because why bring trouble to your own doorstep when you could have sent it elsewhere? Still, there's a chance whoever put Drayton in that chest knew there'd be a good chance he'd simply be stored away. Choosing *us* meant the killer would gain themselves time." Jonty sighed. "A person who had some knowledge of our ways."

"Which reduces the field and gives us a speck of hope that we could solve this problem." Wasn't this a positive thing? Orlando couldn't fathom why Jonty should look so glum. "You don't seem convinced."

Jonty slowly wagged his head. "Oh, I wouldn't put it that way. Unhappy rather than unconvinced. I should be delighted that we're a step further towards a solution but now I'm wrestling with the notion that someone we knew, perhaps welcomed as a guest and showed those vaults, betrayed our trust by using us as a dumping ground for their victim."

"Perhaps you could look at it in a more positive light," Toby suggested. "Providence ensuring that the dead man turned up where people would bother to make a fuss. A place with in-house investigators who wouldn't take the easy option of simply going with the official verdict. Who'd ensure he had justice, no matter how many years after the event, as they'd done with the Woodville Ward."

"I like that idea. I've often said there's a destiny shaping our ends." Jonty rubbed his hands, although whether to warm them or in anticipation of the thrill of the chase—or both—wasn't clear. "Perhaps it drew us all together."

"The four musketeers?" Alasdair suggested. "The four cardinal virtues?"

"That would be better than the four horsemen of the apocalypse." Orlando chuckled. "Why not the four suits of cards? Clubs and spades for you and me, Alasdair, as we're dark. We'll fight the forces of darkness and delve for truth."

"How marvellously poetic." Jonty's good humour had clearly returned. "Hearts and diamonds for Toby and me—

the former for obvious reasons and the latter…well as hard *and* as beautiful as diamonds might sum us up."

On which pleasant note they could turn to the serious and more challenging business of consulting diaries and finding a time they could visit the Stewarts' ancestral home together.

Chapter Four

Toby had seen a picture of the Old Manor in a book he'd found about the lesser-known stately homes of England. Impressive as the photograph had been, it couldn't prepare him for the reality of a property that not only retained its very old unfinished parts but appeared to wear them as a badge of honour. *Our original builder may have lost his head and his fortune*, they seemed to say, *but we carry on undaunted*.

It was plain from when the building hove into view that the finished parts of the property were beautifully maintained, as were the grounds, and Jonty had promised them that the house would lack nothing in the way of modern comforts. Not even a week since they'd met him and Orlando in Cambridge, yet those days had seen plenty of discussion between Toby and Alasdair about the mysterious Victorian death. Plenty of research, too, although they didn't have much to show for it.

The two Cambridge dons were waiting to greet the actors at the great door, perhaps the Stewart household running so well that the timing of the car journey from station to house could be predicted to the second. Or maybe they'd simply been watching from a window, with the servants on standby to be assembled quickly. Either way, the visit began in a flurry of handshakes and introductions to the staff—the female members of which bobbed and curtseyed as though they were greeting royalty. No evidence here of the difficulties some folk were having at recruiting domestic help. Toby suspected the Stewarts were good payers and treated their retainers well, so had their pick of what was available.

The actors smiled and spoke charmingly to all concerned, although they were relieved to be whisked off to their rooms, ostensibly in order to avail themselves of the bathroom facilities. Difficult to concentrate on the matters in hand—cinematic or investigational—when you had to turn on the magic. Once they were refreshed, they could be taken on their much-anticipated tour of house and grounds.

Alasdair had with him his trusty notepad, as ever in his pocket when taking on a new film. He'd brought cameras, to boot, while Toby would simply rely on his memory, and also on persuading his lover to jot things down on his behalf. They quickly got their bearings inside, being shown such important locations as where to report for a pre-prandial drink, before they headed outside. Here, after a circuit of the immediate area, they ended up in the walled garden. This delightfully laid-out space, with its mixture of flowers, espalier fruit trees and little alcoves containing what appeared to be wicker beehives, potentially provided a beautiful area for a couple of significant scenes in the film. Assuming both Sir Ian and Fiona could persuade Thomas to let them utilize such a private patch.

"It must have been wonderful to be a child here," Alasdair observed, once they'd done a circuit of the paths. "An ideal place for hide and seek."

"It was. We had hours of fun playing all round the grounds. A shame we're not likely to have snow over the next few days as I'd still fancy tobogganing and chucking snowballs." Jonty and Orlando shared a grin, perhaps in recollection of having indulged in such delights as adults. Or maybe some other delights indulged in here which were less admissible in public. "Now, we should make our way to the vaults. I don't suppose I've been down there since 1914. No call for it. Thomas assures me nothing much has changed, except he's had the lighting re-wired."

Jonty led them back into the house, through the magnificent hall and down a corridor at the end of which he stopped, turned to the actors and smiled. "Here we are."

Toby looked from left to right, seeing only panelling and a sturdy baize-covered door typical of this kind of house. "Do we enter through the servants' quarters?"

"Heaven forfend. There'd be a riot if people kept invading their part of the manor." Jonty shot the others a wink. "Try again."

"A hidden door. Behind the woodwork." Alasdair gave a panel a robust tap, then tried another. "I assume it's been made difficult to find by merely searching for a hollow sounding part or else it would be too easy for anyone trying to locate it."

"You assume correctly. No point in a hidden door that unhides itself to all and sundry. That fact alone pretty well eliminates any theory that a stranger could somehow have manhandled a body into the house and then simply located the vault by chance before utilising it." Orlando rapped his knuckles against several different areas. "As you say, Alasdair, the way this has been constructed means the door sounds the same as the real panelling. If one generation of the family were to be obliterated and the secret hadn't already been passed on, it might lie unfound for years."

"It must be marked with something, surely, although I can't see a tell-tale wormhole or knot or the like in the wood." Toby scrutinized the panels. "Is it to do with the pictures? Although they seem to be part of a set rather than having one odd man out."

"Well done. They are a set. There are always matching pictures here, although not always the same ones. You merely count the third from the left." Jonty pointed to the watercolour in question. "And now…" He placed his hand on the top of the picture, moved his fingers up the panel to the nearest piece of carved wood and ran them along that. He then measured a hand's breadth perpendicularly from where the design turned through ninety degrees, before pressing hard on the place he'd located. There was a click, a loud creak and the wood began to move, clearly on a hinged joint. The outlines of the door had been effectively hidden by the intricate designs on the panels. "Thomas had the place opened a couple of days ago, to ensure that we'd have no problems accessing it. In the days of my grandfather the hinges could get rather stiff, because the mechanism wasn't as well maintained as it might have been. Thomas also made sure—aha!—that the lighting works. Electric now, of course, rather than the torches you'd have had in the olden days."

As Jonty spoke, he operated a switch on the inner wall, flooding the void with light. A staircase led steeply down from the very threshold of the door.

"Is that intentional, having the flight begin so close to the entrance?" Alasdair asked, pointing to where the steps plunged away. "It could catch anyone unawares."

"Yes. Part of protecting the hidden space. Anyone from outside expecting to find a priest hole or the like would *not* expect to go straight downwards. Potential of a broken neck if you don't take care, even if you *do* know about the stairs. Make sure you use this." Orlando patted the handrail which began about a yard down the left-hand wall, perhaps deliberately placed a tad too far to be helpful to anyone suddenly falling.

"I feel we should offer to go first," Toby said. "Provide a soft landing if you lose your footing and all that."

"While I'd have contested your offer up until a few years ago, I'll not do so now, especially as it's nearly forty years since I trod these steps. The Stewarts have done their best to make them safe but the staircase is not to be tackled blithely. Please take care: Sir Ian would never forgive us if we hurt his biggest stars." Jonty stepped back, to allow the actors room to enter.

The stairs weren't as perilous as they first appeared, the flight being straight, the treads broad and the risers not too deep. Toby had been expecting a spiral staircase, the sort which led up to their guest bedrooms but on reflection, he saw that such a design would have been impractical if this area was to be used for storage. Stuff had to be got up and down somehow and without killing the bearers in the process. The secret room itself was as well-lit as the steps leading down to it, reminding him of the vaults under Winchester Cathedral, although it was much drier than those had been when he'd visited. The Old Manor clearly wasn't built on ground prone to flooding.

"There's not much to see," Jonty said. "Papa, much as he'd have liked to have everything labelled and sorted, felt that time was of the essence and some degree of chaos would help with the hiding. He was going to rectify the matter at the end of the war and bring order for the first time but he didn't survive to do so. Perhaps it's as well, given that stratagem of hiding things among the old tat was employed again at the start of the last war."

"Ye-es." Alasdair slowly turned, taking in the scene. "The lack of organisation is definitely out of keeping with the rest of the building, at least the parts we've seen. The Stewarts seem to have a passion for neatness."

Orlando nodded. "They do. Sheridan wasn't that bothered about completing what his father hadn't been able to but Thomas had plans to do so, when the clouds started to gather over Germany and he guessed the hiding place might be needed again."

"And the reason he hasn't carried out his plans, given it's years since the war ended, is the concern we're not out of the woods yet?"

"Precisely, Alasdair. When the Stewarts can be certain this space won't be called on, then it will be the time for order to reign." As he'd spoken, Orlando had edged across to a particular chest, on which he now rested his elbow.

"Could there also have been an intention of preserving the evidence, in case of future investigations?" Alasdair asked.

"Possibly. Although we mustn't discount solid if sentimental reasons for not wanting to clear things," Jonty said. "Thomas's children never knew their great-grandfather. Once we're sure of peace—if we ever can be—then theirs should be the generation to give this place the going over it needs. But not before their great-uncles can extract any information they can."

"This is the very crate where the body was found." Orlando tapped the one he was leaning against and so patently trying to be nonchalant about the fact. "You are welcome to look inside. Indeed, you have licence to rummage to your hearts' content among what's here, although we doubt it will tell you very much. The contents will likely have been disturbed in both 1939 and 1945, as well as back in 1918. Little chance that the scene reflects the situation at the time of Drayton's discovery."

"Some poking around could provide an understanding and perhaps a background atmosphere, though," Jonty said.

"Before we do that, can I ask how often you played down here as children? Once you were tall enough to reach the mechanism, of course," Toby added, with a grin.

"Not as often as we'd have liked to. We never seemed to be able to get past the door without being discovered." Jonty shrugged. "I suppose that's another reason why that body wasn't discovered earlier. Generations of Stewart children never got around to rummaging through things. Not that we would necessarily have been able to open this particular chest, as I'll explain anon."

Toby and Alasdair set to doing what the young Stewarts hadn't been able to, getting a box to use as a step to aid their peering into the chest in question. If they could get the wretched thing open, of course, which was proving as difficult as Jonty had just implied it would.

"No, I give up," Toby said eventually, rubbing hands made sore in the attempt.

"Let us. We were shown the particular knack when we visited hard on the heels of Drayton being discovered." Orlando and Jonty didn't appear to do anything Alasdair or Toby hadn't already tried, yet they got the lid open fairly easily.

Toby's hope that the inside of the chest might reveal a clue was soon dashed. It had been emptied of anything it once contained and apart from some staining, proved a dumb witness to events. He and Alasdair proceeded to poke around among the other items in store, exploring the deepest recesses of the vault, while Jonty and Orlando looked on like indulgent parents. Any vague hope Toby clung onto of turning up evidence evaporated: they should have known that Mr Stewart or his son would have picked up on anything significant at the time the body itself was found.

"Was there no hint that the body was here?" Toby sniffed. The air in the vault bore some degree of mustiness, natural if the place was rarely visited or ventilated, yet it wasn't unpleasant. "No tell-tale odour?"

"Apparently not. At least, not until the crate was opened. Papa said that didn't bear thinking about. Come and see this." Perching on a crate, Jonty fingered the lining of the chest. "You'll observe that the choice of this as a hiding

66

place was either an enormous stroke of luck or very well planned. It's lead lined and hermetically sealed, from the time my great-grandfather used it to transport zoological specimens from foreign lands. None of the more recent Stewarts go in for such bizarre activities, so the crate was simply used for general storage if it was used at all."

Alasdair, who'd drawn out a stone hand axe from another one of the boxes, inspected it in a rather downcast way. "Is this one of those extraneous objects?"

"I believe so." Orlando came closer to view it. "Yes. These were originally in with the body, so Mr Stewart had all of them put into a small chest for evidential purposes. He insisted that no such artefacts had been in store in the vaults prior to the Great Exhibition. If there were such things in the Stewarts' possession back then, he swore they'd have been given to the children to enjoy. I think he rather regretted not having had them to play cavemen with his siblings. Ah yes, here's the label to prove it."

"And you said there was some metal stuff?" Alasdair asked.

Jonty shook his head. "I think you're getting confused. The aforementioned metallic items weren't in with the body. Which is why they went during the war, possibly to make the spitfires you flew."

"So, while there doesn't appear to have been a proper schedule of what was lent to the exhibition, as far as you know," Toby clarified, "your father's memory could have been as good as one?"

"To an extent." Jonty's brow furrowed. "If he knew about an object being legitimately stored here, he'd have remembered it. *If.*"

"You're happy for me to photograph all of these items and the chest where the body was found, for our detection purposes?" Alasdair asked, his camera cases out of their bag and ready in his hands as though to seal the deal. "Then, for the film, perhaps some snaps of the vaults for us to use as an aide memoire when we eventually study the script?"

Jonty nodded. "Of course. I'm sure Orlando will help by holding those hand axes and any other old tat to best advantage under the lights. If you wish to develop your work, there's a dark room here which is available for all to use. Thomas is a keen photographer himself."

"That's very kind, but I wouldn't trust myself not to make a mess of things. I'll get the high quality shots from this professionally developed," Alasdair held up one camera. "For the purposes of this weekend, I have a quicker method."

"It's his Polaroid camera," Toby said with a chuckle. "His newest toy. Turns out photos in a trice."

"I've heard of those, but never seen one." Orlando watched, wide-eyed, as Alasdair unpacked the device.

Jonty flashed Toby a smile, then they stood back while their partners busied themselves inspecting the camera. "Look at that pair. Happy as two children, don't you think?"

"Absolutely. They'll be ages, going into all the hows and whys of that thing's workings."

"We should get beer sent down for them. Or maybe not, as we'd not see them again for the rest of the day."

"It's gratifying, how well they get on. Despite his public image, old Alasdair doesn't always take to people at first meeting and one might expect awkwardness all round when it's someone you're going to portray." Toby tipped his head to one side, in imitation of his host. "Is that it, your thinking pose?"

"Mirror image. Mine goes to the left. *My* left."

"Oh, of course." Amateur mistake. "I'll try it again."

"Better. What were you thinking about? Or was it simply practicing being me?"

"A bit of both, Jonty. I was thinking how alike our two chaps are from the back, even down to the choice of tailoring. The cut of their clothes is almost identical: hide the hair colour by wearing hats and Bob's your uncle. It could prove a hoot for the scriptwriters to work that into the film. Mistaken identity at the college and the like. What's so funny?"

Jonty lowered his voice, although the other pair were unlikely to hear, being deep in conversation about the camera. "Art imitating life again. Something that happened to us once on holiday. I'll tell you when we're alone. Poor Orlando still shudders to be reminded of it."

"I thought *we'd* had our share of adventures but yours continue to astound me. More time together to accumulate experiences or more interesting lives?" Toby would have loved simply to sit with this man and hear that life history expounded.

Jonty briefly put his finger to his lips, then addressed the other two. "We'll leave you to it. You'll find us in the drawing room once you're all done and developed." He nudged Toby towards the stairs, ascended them carefully in silence and only when they were at the top spoke again. "I promised I'd tell you the story of what happened at the end of the war. I think it's time to share that now, because it in part explains why we never got our teeth into this mystery at the point when we perhaps should have done. I'll call for tea to accompany the tale."

Once in the drawing room, Jonty began to relate a story which if it had featured in the pages of a book would have been rejected by the editor as beggaring belief. Orlando had been listed as missing, although he'd actually been captured. This had borne a pessimistic interpretation at the time, many of the missing being dead. In many cases, almost forty years after, still no bodies had been recovered for them. Jonty had been injured, lost his memory and spent the final part of the war living under a different name, another man's body being identified as his. Both Orlando and Jonty therefore believed the other dead. Each felt, in such circumstances, there was little left to live for, especially as Jonty's parents had both succumbed to influenza, meaning even that chance of comfort and healing had gone. Then they'd discovered the truth and there'd been a reunion between the two lovers, both painful and glorious, in a French seaside resort. That had been partly due to the perspicacity of the young George Broad, who had remained convinced throughout that his uncle was still alive despite the evidence to the contrary.

"I've often thought our story would make a wonderful film," Jonty said, when his telling of it was complete.

Toby nodded. "Although your character would have to undergo a change of sex—become a nurse serving at the front, for example—or no studio would get it past the censor."

"You'd also have to tone down much of the storyline or your fans would be screaming that it was too unbelievable for words. Even in the hands of as talented a partnership as Alasdair and Miss Marsden." Jonty sipped his tea, which had arrived at about the point in the story that young George had been insisting on keeping his uncle in his nightly prayers. "You'd have to be cast as my brother-in-law, I suppose. Or perhaps a doctor carrying the inevitably futile torch for Fiona."

"True. Shame we can't complete such a project true to the original, though. It would be the weepie of the decade."

"And the scandal of the century. Aha! The photographers." Jonty waved as Orlando and Alasdair entered the room. "Come and join us. There are four cups and a fresh pot due to arrive imminently."

"What were you talking about? What would be the scandal of the century?" Orlando asked.

"If they made a film about us two at the end of the Great War. I was telling Toby...hold on. That can wait." Jonty jabbed a finger at his partner. "You've discovered something, haven't you? Out with it."

"Would you like a fair chance of spotting it for yourself?" Alasdair's grin lit up his face. Rarely onscreen yet often seen in their private moments, that particular smile never ceased to warm Toby's heart. "We didn't notice anything in situ. Despite the lighting in the vault, we couldn't view the pictures as well as we hoped, so had to take them upstairs into natural light. It was after they developed themselves that we spotted something, because the flash of the camera and the angle it struck had clearly worked its magic. We've not yet been back to re-examine the original item. Didn't want to have all the fun."

"Much obliged to you for including us." Toby watched as the photographs were laid out for their inspection. The arrival of the tea and filling of cups gave him extra time to scrutinize the pictures but even his pilot's eyes were struggling to see anything of note. "Well, you've got me stumped so far. Jonty? Oh." Toby had been concentrating on the photos and, when he glanced up, hadn't been expecting to see a pair of spectacles perched on Jonty's nose. The man hadn't employed them when they'd met in Cambridge. "Do you always wear those for close work?"

"Yes. You'll need to add a pair to your portrayal, in plain glass of course, if you want complete accuracy. Only wear the things for reading, though, not driving or other distance work."

Orlando snorted. "Jonty should use them more often than he does but he's too vain. Now, if we're talking about absolute accuracy, please notice, Alasdair, how I keep my

71

leg well out of his reach when making such remarks. He's liable to slap or kick me."

"It's something about the fair, stocky, scrum-half type," Alasdair said with a grin. "Sneaky acts of violence worked on the opponents, especially on the rugby pitch. I suppose he's a bowler of spin as well? They're a similar proposition."

"When you've quite finished demolishing my character, would you be so kind as to tell us what we haven't spotted?" Jonty pushed the photographs across the table.

"Look at the mammoth tusk. There are straight lines carved on it." Orlando pointed to the area concerned.

From what little Toby had seen, the tusk wasn't the largest specimen of its kind, being only some three feet long and while he'd seen marks on it, they'd signified nothing. They still did.

"What does that remind you of, Jonty?" Orlando asked.

"Ogham. Well spotted. Have you chaps come across the stuff?" Jonty rose, heading for the bookshelves and the line of Encyclopaedias.

Toby, pleased to see that Alasdair looked as puzzled as he was, shook his head. "Never heard of that at all. Is it some sort of code?"

"It's an ancient language. Doesn't date back as far as the time of the mammoths, though. One of the chaps at St Bride's is quite an expert on the subject." Orlando paused, as Jonty brought the relevant volume, already opened at the appropriate page, to lay in front of their guests. "You'll appreciate the significance of those timings?"

"If you mean that the writing can't be contemporaneous with either the mammoth or the hand axes, then yes." Toby nodded. "So, these marks, assuming they *are* Ogham and not simply the gnawing of a sabre-toothed tiger, were added later."

Alasdair, who was clearly desperate to chip in, said, "At some unspecified point, up to and including the time when the tusk was sent here. We aren't sure if this is relevant to the case or a simple coincidence."

Orlando tapped the photo again. "Irrespective of whether it's relevant to us, it may be to our colleague Dr O'Neill. I'm sure he'll be delighted to tell us whether this is Ogham or a mathematician's and man of the sonnets' misinterpretation of the markings as such. If it's genuine, he could attempt a translation and try—this is a long shot—to put a date on when it was inscribed. Assuming we'd be happy to place the tusk into his hands?"

"Of course. Expert opinion and all that. It's another long shot, but he could perhaps also put a name to anyone who might have been familiar with the language a hundred years ago. O'Neill would surely have a chance of knowing who the specialists in the field were back then. If we can connect one of those people to the Stewarts, the trail would surely be getting closer." Jonty reached for the pot. "Shall I call for more tea? Although Thomas keeps an excellent sherry, if people would prefer that. Then perhaps you two could crown your triumph by fetching that bit of mammoth, and the other things in the same box, for us to look at in a better light? Axes and lumps of old slag and all?"

"Of course. I'll call for one of the footmen to help us." Orlando and his lover shared a grin. "More than one, then they can drag that chest up here. We should examine everything for Ogham. Crate included."

***

The last of the tea, a glass of sherry all round and much inspection later, the tusk remained the only object showing signs of any form of writing, ancient or modern, and that was only visible if it caught the light on it in a certain way. In the vaults, no matter how well-lit they were back in 1914, it would have been easy to miss. Or perhaps, if seen, people would simply take the marks as evidence of the great beast having sustained damage in battle with a rival.

At that point the four decided they'd done quite enough detecting for the moment. A break was needed to bathe, dress for dinner and get ready to enjoy their meal. Afterwards, if they had the energy and weren't too full of the suetty pudding Jonty had specifically requested for dessert, they could make a start on going through Richard Stewarts' papers.

Alasdair, who'd dressed quickly as he wanted to catch Toby before the gong sounded, nipped into his lover's room just as the man was attacking his black tie.

"What had you been discussing with Jonty when you were hobnobbing alone with him?" Alasdair asked. "You appeared rather mysterious and furtive."

"Furtive for a good reason. It would be no exaggeration to say I was told one of the most moving and belief-beggaring tales I've ever come across. A great love story that can probably never be told outside of a sympathetic group of people. Not until the world is a far more enlightened place." Toby reached over, to stroke Alasdair's hand. "There's no time now to do it justice, but suffice to say that due to a bizarre sequence of events, they both thought the other dead."

"Jonty and Orlando?"

"Yes, you ninny. Who else could I have meant?" Toby stroked the hand again, evidently revelling in the romantic nature of the tale he'd been told.

"Good God, that must have been awful."

"It was. Reading between the lines, it nearly drove both of them mad. I didn't get every jot and tittle of the story but

74

Orlando returned home after being held prisoner and Jonty went off travelling round France, both oblivious to the truth. Quite miraculously, they found each other again. What a reunion that must have been."

"I can imagine." The enormous shock, their enduring love vying with guilt and recriminations. The physical and spiritual reconnection: if that had been he and Toby, Alasdair could picture exactly how glorious—and how raw emotionally—the reunion would have been. "I look forward to hearing the rest. Now for dinner."

They were halfway to the drawing room when the gong sounded, which seemed perfect timing. The meal proved to be every bit as good as they'd hoped, although when they reached the coffee stage, Orlando suggested they shouldn't sit up too late. "I'd like to make an early start on Mr Stewart's papers, rather than peruse them tonight."

Jonty nodded. "Starting straight after breakfast would suit me, as would going to my bed now. It's been a fruitful day. Orlando has already produced a rather nice tracing of the inscription that should get O'Neill suitably excited. I've suggested we take not just the tusk but all the Neolithic bits to show him. Being an expert, he might spot other anomalies which we haven't. Talking of experts, did your godfather—he of the constabulary—have anything to tell us, Toby?"

"Not as yet, although he found the story fascinating. And highly suspicious. Matthew's nose for such things suggests we're right to doubt the official line." Toby pushed his coffee cup away, evidently replete. "I spoke to him this morning, when he said he couldn't yet find anything directly concerning the Peter Drayton case, although he's had to delegate the matter to his trusty sergeant, Granger, who'll have more time to look into it. Fortuitous, really, because if we're talking of experts, then *he's* the man to go to on all matters Victorian, especially as it relates to crimes.

75

Particularly to murders. It was that specialty which was key to putting the last piece of jigsaw in place regarding the *Grey Assassin*. That's a story for another day and quite possibly one we shouldn't share with you but as you favoured us with confidences, I feel obliged to do the same at some point. Anyway, Granger was very interested and has promised to look into the matter. He said the name Drayton rang a bell but we weren't to get too excited. It might be a dead end in the hunt. To mix a metaphor."

"Very hard not to mix them at times." Jonty edged his chair back. "If you'd like to avail yourselves of the billiard table for a frame or two, I'll point you in the right direction before I head to my room."

"We'll keep that for tomorrow," Alasdair said, also rising. "I need a clear head for inspecting these papers and thrashing Toby at billiards wouldn't help."

"What he means is he'd be too cross at me beating him to sleep properly." Toby chuckled.

"I have one simple request," Jonty said, suddenly uncharacteristically serious. "If you can't sleep or have a bright idea or for any other reason feel the need to go and explore the vaults in the dark, please resist the urge. Someone broke an ankle doing that in the past. I've told you those stairs aren't to be trusted and that's based on experience, albeit other people's."

"I promise we won't be doing anything so stupid." Alasdair used his eyebrow to try to convey a solemn vow undertaken. The story of night-time visitors sounded intriguing, though, given what had lain in those vaults. "By the way, when and who was this?"

Orlando raised an eyebrow, almost as eloquently. "I see the investigator's casual, 'By the way,' and raise you a, 'With the benefit of hindsight.' We *should* take note of any such incidents. Jonty, can you enlighten us?"

76

"It was the year the old queen died, which fixes it in the memory, even though I wasn't here to witness the event. Chap of my brother Clarence's acquaintance who tried to get into the vault as a dare. It turned out to be very nearly the last thing he ever did. He broke his ankle and Mama would cheerfully have broken his neck. He could have lain undiscovered were it not for the fact somebody heard him." Jonty, frowning, tipped his head to one side. "Do you know, I seem to recall Papa saying those steps had also nearly done for some careless body back in the 1870's, after which the handrail was installed, along with some illumination. Davy's arc lamps—we were among the first to have them. Apart from those two chaps, I'm not aware of any other instances of unwanted visitors."

"We won't add our names to the list. I'm not sure the place can tell us anything further." Alasdair stretched. "Perhaps it's time to end the conversation or we'll be having bad dreams about pitching into blackness. I never could abide night flying."

Making their way back to their rooms, the actors couldn't help but discuss what they'd been told. Two people had tried to get into the vaults uninvited while a body lay there undiscovered—coincidental or related to the death?

"I call it highly suspicious," Toby said. "One or both of them could well have been looking for Drayton. I doubt there was anything else they were after."

"Agreed. Hardly a treasure trove, even for a devotee of Ogham." Alasdair grunted. "Could both be implicated, if it was a case of *if at first you don't succeed, try again?* Whatever the motivation to make such a venture, it would have to be strong. You'd need to be totally determined or incredibly dim to be tackling those stairs in the dark."

"There is another possibility. If that cellar was used to store items of incredible importance during two world wars, could it have also been used similarly on other occasions, in between? These people suspected there were untold riches to be found and went on a journey of exploration. Although surely our hosts are too clever not to have considered that possibility." Toby shook his head.

"We'll ask them tomorrow." It would beg another question, though, which was why—if they were looking for the body—the intruders hadn't found it, although in each instance a fall on the stairs might have forestalled any further exploration.

"I keep thinking about that chest. It seems suspiciously fortuitous for the killer to find one at hand that would conceal the presence of a body for so long."

"The killer may only have wanted to hide it for long enough to get it off the premises where the murder happened and get himself—or herself—clear. The presence of such a suitable hiding place may have acted as a catalyst, of course."

"Catalyst?"

Alasdair raised his uninsured eyebrow. "Yes. I'm surmising that x, the murderer, was involved in handling items for the exhibition. If said x had been harbouring feelings of malice towards Drayton the arrival of the chest and the knowledge it would eventually be returned here might have got their mind working. An ideal way to dispose of the man."

"Yes, I can see that. Perhaps it wasn't even knowingly planned. The old sub-conscious grinding out a scheme so that when events came to a head—an argument between x and Drayton, let's say—even if the killing itself was accidental, x was ready to make the most of the opportunity." They'd reached the door of Toby's room where they'd part, not wanting to embarrass the staff by risking finding them together in the morning. "Would our hosts give us the equivalent of a gating for speculating like this? We've created a whole scene based on nothing apart from a dead body and a sealable chest."

"I bet academics do the same. Create a theory from some random facts and then test it." Alasdair risked a peck on Toby's cheek. "Let's hope we get some solid evidence to test it against."

Chapter Five

Over an excellent breakfast—when wasn't the food at the Old Manor top notch?—discussion naturally turned to the case. The first question their guests raised, the matter of the unauthorised vault visitors' motivation, suggested to Orlando that the actors would be worthy investigational colleagues. He'd not confessed the fact to Jonty but he hadn't been able to cast off the thought that the pair might have a touch of the dilettante about them and not apply a proper academic rigour to the situation. Despite some annoyance at *his* not having considered whether Clarence's friend and his predecessor might have been on the hunt for treasure, Orlando had to count the enquiry as a feather in the actors' caps.

Jonty clearly felt the same. "I'd never considered that, which is probably because both those illicit visits predated the Old Manor being used as a government storehouse. I'd been brought up to believe nothing in the vaults was of any worth at all, other than vaguely sentimental value to distant family members. I suppose it's possible that items might have previously been put down there on a temporary basis for reasons unknown and the fact was only privy to one or two people. But if that was so I'm extremely miffed Papa didn't tell me." Jonty's grin suggested he wasn't terribly annoyed at the fact. "However, Drayton himself surely couldn't have been here looking for…"

"Yes? Surely couldn't what?" Orlando recognized the expression on his lover's face. He'd had an idea and not a particularly welcome one.

"I was going to say he surely couldn't have also been looking for treasure because how could he have killed himself and then sealed that crate from the outside? And then I realized we've not really eliminated the option of his having been killed here. We've skirted round the issue and pushed it away." As Jonty now pushed his plate away, half a sausage left uneaten.

"I bet your father considered such a possibility." Orlando said, soothingly. "If he'd harboured half a suspicion, he'd have shared it."

"Sorry to intrude on matters I know very little about," Toby said, acting abilities unable to hide the fact he clearly felt uncomfortable at what he was about to say, "but might your father have suspected, or indeed known, the true intention of one or both of the men who attempted to access the vaults? He would then have covered over the fact in the interest of preserving your family's secret—assuming there was one—and the family's name?"

"He would *never* have buried anything in the sand merely to protect the Stewart reputation. Please don't be upset at having to ask the question because that's simply a matter of thoroughness. I don't take it amiss." Jonty flashed a sympathetic smile. "You didn't have the pleasure of knowing Papa but ask anyone who did and they'll tell you he was a stickler for the truth. I'll grant it was conceivable that he might have wanted to protect somebody else but, in that case, I remain certain he would have told another family member, so the secret was passed on. And he wouldn't have been deluded by a sense of his own immortality. He'd have spoken—or left word in his papers—before it was too late."

"Perhaps he went through the same process we are, when you were both out in the trenches," Alasdair pointed out, "and concluded that the accidents were merely that. Dares gone wrong or the like."

"Quite possibly." Jonty tipped his head in thought. "I now have a vague recollection of Mama making some offhand remark about whether Freddie Heathfield—that's Clarence's pal—knew anything about the dead body but we all dismissed it as one of her quips. She did tend to put her foot in her mouth. It's time we widened the investigation to take in events here as well as in London."

Orlando sipped his coffee. "As I recall, the chap in the 1870's apparently had a reputation in his youth for daredevil schemes. Buckets on the top of the college chapel spire and the like. That's why his venture into the vaults was regarded as merely being a repetition of such exploits, although with added scrutiny, that history could be said to make him a prime candidate for carrying out reconnaissance."

"Was *he* mentioned by your Mama?" Toby asked. "In another of her slips of the tongue?"

Jonty shrugged. "Not quite. I do recall Papa remarking that it was best not to make a joke about the other chap as he thought he'd recently died."

Toby wrinkled his nose, his similarity to Jonty proved a touch unsettling. "What about Clarence's pal? Is he still alive?"

"Freddie? I couldn't say," Jonty replied, "although he struck us as the sort of silly ass who'd manage to escape harm when wiser men found themselves knocked for six. Useful rugby player in the scrum—very close to playing for Wales, I believe—but never seemed to have so much as a scar on him, let alone a cauliflower ear. Charmed life, Mama said. He survived the Great War and must have matured, because he served with distinction. One of Clarence's lot might have an address for him."

"I wonder if these things run in families," Toby said. "There was a Heathfield in my squadron who was a complete ass ninety-five percent of the time but when he was in the air, hardly anyone could touch him. Bagged a ton of kills and emerged from every mission without a scratch, even to his fuselage."

"The ages might work for your pal being a younger son. Your mother did say she was never totally convinced Freddie was as silly as he made himself out to be," Orlando pointed out.

"True, oh ye of great memory and even greater brain. Let's hope Papa made full notes from around that time." Jonty, spirits evidently returning to normal, edged his plate back in order to spear the last piece of sausage. He lifted it as he might a glass to make a toast. "Here's to his papers and all they're willing to reveal."

***

Richard Stewart's papers had been, as expected, kept in good order. A room off the Old Manor's library had been used to store them, alongside other Stewart documents, everything being arranged in such a way to make the exploration of it easy. So long as one had an idea of when the item required had been written, it would be easy to locate, given that everything appeared to be organized chronologically. There were no diaries, because Mr Stewart hadn't really kept one, although he'd made notes of things that mattered to him, accumulating all sorts of scraps from newspapers or the like.

"What a treasure trove." Toby, wide-eyed, carefully flicked through some pages of a scrapbook he'd picked out. "I guess these things must have held a particular significance for him. There's a newspaper account here, of a cricket innings. Trumper scoring three hundred against Sussex."

"Trumper was one of Papa's favourite batsmen. He and Mama attended every day of that game, and also saw him make his century at Lord's." Jonty, peering over Toby's shoulder, smiled fondly. "I managed to see him in 1902, rain notwithstanding. Stunning."

Orlando raised a hand. "Might I request we defer the matter of 1902 until dinner? Alasdair and Toby, you won't appreciate how perilously close you've come to the hearing about the cup final of that year. *How Jonty Stewart saw CB Fry play for Southampton and will gladly take you through it kick by kick.*"

"He's only green with envy that he wasn't there." Jonty chuckled as he turned a few pages over. "Bless the old man. The reason he retained some of these clippings is quite beyond me, though. We could speculate on them for hours and be no nearer a solution."

"Yes." Orlando viewed—albeit from the wrong side of the desk—some of the clippings. "Your father was a man of many interests and talents, but why he should have kept an article about a novel type of artificial limb is enough to keep me awake at night puzzling. Let's stick to the matters in hand and thank the lord that he had method in his organization."

"I knew he would, although one might wish at this point that his character had been slightly different." Jonty swept his hand, taking in the entire room. "By which I mean him cross-referencing his things, which would have been jolly useful but which he wouldn't do."

"Why?" Alasdair asked, scanning the room with a daunted expression.

Jonty snorted. "He discarded the notion, saying what was the point in it? *He* knew where stuff would be if he needed to root it out and if his descendants wanted to go hunting for specific items, why take away the thrill of the chase?"

"I wish we'd had the chance to meet him. He sounds like he had his finger on the pulse." Toby apparently couldn't take his eyes off the treasure trove of papers.

"He was a pearl among men. As was Mrs Stewart," Orlando said, acutely aware of the catch in his voice.

Jonty burst into laughter. "He means a pearl among women. My mother wasn't a chap in disguise."

"Oh, do be quiet and start searching. You and Toby tackle the back end of 1914. It'll be safer if Alasdair and I start with the years around 1901. Less chance of sporting digressions."

They transported piles of material into the library, where the light—both natural and artificial—would be better suited to diligent scrutiny. Orlando, feeling a gentle tweak in his arm as he carried the books, realized that his rotator cuff had actually been behaving itself the last few days. Not that he'd admit the fact to Jonty, because he'd say that the problem had been purely psychosomatic and once Orlando's brain had been given a murder to occupy it, all physical ailments had miraculously disappeared. There was only a grain of truth in the accusation.

At Alasdair's suggestion, the two pairs established work bases at opposite ends of the room, to reduce the chance of distraction. The strategy was clearly the right one, given the amount of earnest murmuring from the Stewart/Bowe part of the library. It didn't take long for that combination to strike gold.

"I knew he'd make a note. And what a note it is." Jonty held some papers aloft, hand shaking, before replacing them on the desk. "It says: *This testimony is given by Richard Stewart. It concerns the events beginning on the fifteenth day of September 1914 and the testator's thoughts regarding the death of Peter Drayton. Should these papers ever be needed in an investigation, I have signed each page as evidence that I thereby swear I have spoken the truth and nothing but.* Come down here, you two, so I don't need to holler. Best we all look at it together, anyway. Bring chairs, as there appears to be a fair amount to go through."

Alasdair and Orlando needed no second invitation.

"I hardly could have dreamed that we'd find something so germane. At least, I hope it's germane, not having inspected it all. Might be a damp squib." Jonty's eager expression and mischievous twinkle in his eye belied the cautious words. He plainly wanted to read the things from start to finish straight away and was reining himself in.

"He wrote a neat hand," Alasdair observed, "if a small one. What are the chances of us all seeing the text at the first time if we look at it simultaneously? Might that not argue for only two reading it and then the others?"

"My English sense of sporting fair play would preclude me doing that, no matter how appealing the idea may seem." Jonty gave Alasdair a wink. "One always, naturally, wants to steal a march on the other half of the partnership. However, we don't all need to see it at the same time, simply be made aware of the contents. Perhaps it would be best if I read it out. I can't quite replicate Papa's deep and dulcet tones—it was such a pleasure to hear him speak, Toby—but I'll do my best. After which, we can take turns to scrutinise the original should we wish. I wouldn't put it past the old man to have sneaked in the odd secret mark or the like."

Toby nodded. "Making the thrill of the chase more thrilling?"

"Exactly. I won't reread the introduction, unless you wish me to." Jonty paused, waiting for the signal to continue. "*Now is not the time to look into such things. A man's death some sixty years ago pales into insignificance compared to the danger our country faces at this moment.*

Should we all survive, then a day may come when we can give this matter the attention it deserves. Which I fear the inquest didn't."

Jonty, whose intonation had got very close to his father's, paused again, clearly overwhelmed.

"Shall I fetch a drink of water?" Alasdair asked, rising to his feet.

"No, thank you. If you could ring down for a pot of coffee, though, I'm sure we'd all appreciate it." Jonty gave Toby a wan smile. "I fear I tried too efficient an impersonation. Made me feel he was here with me." He pushed the papers over to Orlando. "Perhaps it would be best if you…?"

"I suspect the same will happen to me. Toby, your voice doesn't quite possess the right timbre but I believe your natural cadence will convey Mr Stewart's words well." Orlando glanced at Jonty, who bobbed his head in agreement.

"A much-underrated character actor, our Toby," Alasdair said, as he joined them again.

The man concerned cleared his throat, took up the papers and read. "*I wasn't alone in my suspicions that the process had been perfunctory and that an adjournment until the war is finished would have been a better outcome. The official attempts to contact any living family for the dead man also appeared inadequate, to the extent that I put a notice in the newspapers mentioning the inquest. To no avail, as it proved.*

Dr McCoist, who first examined the body, was doubtful that death been due to natural causes alone but he was asked by the chief constable, Geraghty, to tone down his report. Geraghty himself is paranoid that Germany is about to launch an invasion from Brest, despite the fact the town doesn't appear to be in enemy hands. One might speculate that is simply a result of his bizarre Napoleon obsession. The coroner, Armitage, is of the same type of mind regarding the war: too focused on events abroad to consider that events close at hand may also be important. The two men are friendly and will surely have discussed the matter beforehand, although I will not go so far as saying they definitely colluded. I believe it's important for the reader to understand all the context."

"That explains that," Jonty said with a nod. "I remember Geraghty. Ramrod straight, very old school and often telling tales about his war exploits, such as fighting under Gordon when he was a boy soldier. Papa was no more convinced of their veracity than I was. You're doing very well, Toby, by the way. An admirable performance. Please continue."

"*It is true that it was not easy to tell much from the state of Drayton's body, given how long the man had been dead, although the chest was designed to be well sealed and the Old Manor vaults are reasonably dry and free from infestation. At this point I must confirm that since I took over the entail, these vaults have been inspected on a yearly basis although primarily for evidence of damp or other problems. While items have been moved as part of the process, it has rarely involved opening any closed chests. Drayton was found inside one of these, when its suitability was being assessed for hiding certain items as part of the war effort. Had those circumstances not prevailed, he may have remained undiscovered for much longer.*"

"Imagine if we'd found him this weekend," Toby said.

Alasdair chuckled. "I'm not sure your logic works. We wouldn't have been here this weekend had it not been for Drayton."

"Not necessarily." Orlando took the point but there was a flaw in Alasdair's logic, too. "You might have been here purely on film business. Assessing the location while observing us. We'd have taken you to see the vault and maybe opened one of the crates to add to the effect. Et voila!"

"That's told him." Toby gave Orlando a bow of gratitude and Alasdair a smirk of triumph. "I can imagine what would have happened if we had found him yesterday. Sir Ian would have been torn between horror at the distraction—and this location being potentially unusable for a while—and the delight at such marvellously apt publicity."

"The rival studios would have poo-poohed it as a publicity stunt." Alasdair's eyebrow made a knowing bob. "Only Toby's godfather would have taken it seriously. He'd have made sure the matter wasn't swept under the carpet."

"Sergeant Granger would have been all over it like a dose of measles. Unsolved Victorian murder case? He'd have taken up residence in that cellar." Toby raised the papers again. "As your father might have said, Jonty, we digress. Shall I continue?"

Orlando nodded. "Please do."

"*My suspicions regarding foul play were initially raised by the location of the body. However, the police pointed to the objects found with Drayton—item the metalworking waste, the flint tools and mammoth tusk—and vowed he'd merely been loading things into the chest when he was taken ill. As a result, he'd fallen into it and couldn't then open the lid again in his weakened state. Admittedly the lid is both heavy and designed to seal quickly and well, but when I pointed out to the attending officer that there was no evidence from Drayton's hands that he'd attempted to escape, he said the body had probably lain there too long to tell anything for certain. He also stated that if the dead man had suffered a stroke or a heart attack, he could have been too enfeebled to effect an escape. Armitage had the nerve to make a quip about "A mortal pitch that struck him dead",* *which sums up the lack of seriousness with which everything* *was conducted. Armitage has a reputation for being a bit of* *a joker, but I didn't expect him to carry his penchant for* *jokes into his public duty. In short, the authorities, apart* *from Dr McCoist, were not interested in pursuing the case."*

"McCoist appears to have signed this page, too." Alasdair indicated a scrawl at the bottom of the page, next to Richard Stewart's elegant signature. "Were there any doubts concerning this account—and I'm not hinting there are, Jonty, simply stating what anyone might think who didn't appreciate your father's degree of probity—the countersignature would argue for its veracity. Do you remember this doctor?"

Jonty gently drummed the table. "I think we met him the once, although not in his professional capacity. Orlando, would he be the chappie who piped in the new year here, cusp of nineteen twelve and thirteen?"

"I believe so. Mrs Stewart spoke well of him." And not simply because he had such admirable legs for the wearing of his kilt. Perhaps best not to enter into the matter of a shapely male knee or they'd hold up all progress. "What's next in the account, Toby?"

"Both McCoist and I noticed a mark on the back of *Drayton's head that looked like a blow had struck him,* *although not necessarily with sufficient force to kill. The* *police said this mark had been acquired when he fell into* *the chest, most likely when his head struck one of the sharp* *items in there. This was supported by the hand axe seeming* *to have blood staining on it and partly matching the wound.* *This was a conclusion McCoist supported, although he did* *point out that—despite the body's unusual degree of* *preservation—at such a time after the event, one couldn't be* *sure. He and I suggest that it's equally possible this axe*

might have been used to strike Drayton a deliberate blow, to knock him out at the least. It is chilling to consider that he might have been alive when the weapon was thrown in with him and the crate sealed."

The door opened, heralding the arrival of the butler with a tray of refreshments. With innate good sense, he laid it on an unoccupied table.

"Thank you, Goodwin," Jonty said. "While we have you here, might I intrude upon you with a question or two? It concerns an old murder case."

The butler nodded, then adopted a domestic version of standing at ease. "I'll do my best to help, sir."

"The matter dates to before your time here. Just after the Great War started." Jonty paused. "Does the timing suggest what we might be talking about?"

"I believe so, yes. The unfortunate chap who'd lain undiscovered in a case in the vault since the days of Prince Albert. I'm afraid the matter has been much discussed over the years in the servants' hall, so while I have nothing to say directly, I'm aware of it and can relate what I've been told."

Jonty rubbed his hands together. "That's exactly what I wanted to hear. I've always suspected the Stewart staff was as inquisitive as the Stewart family when a mystery crops up and my experience has told me that you tend to be good judges of a situation. Has any word of wisdom been passed down through the ages, among the gossip, that might enlighten us about what happened at the time of the body's discovery or the inquest into Drayton's death? Better still—and this is a very long shot—has any fact been passed down, almost as an heirloom, from the time the items returned from the Great Exhibition?"

"It's a case of trying to right what the present Lord's grandfather believed was a terrible wrong," Orlando explained, noting that Goodwin appeared torn between

91

fulfilling his master's uncle's request and maintaining the privacy of the servants' hall. "Mr Stewart felt that the official verdict of natural causes had been reached too hurriedly."

"I wasn't fortunate enough to meet your father, Dr Stewart, but from everything I've been told, if he believed a miscarriage of justice had occurred, then it likely had." Still a hint of reluctance.

"No names, no pack drill, of course," Jonty said. "We don't need to know who said what, especially if it concerned household members or their guests."

That reassurance appeared to seal the agreement. "I do have some relevant discussions I might relate, sir. With the proviso, of course, that none of this is proof or even—with perhaps one exception—the testimony of an eyewitness."

The four men at the table shared eager glances, each no doubt considering the great possibilities of an eyewitness, even though said person was more likely to be from this century than the previous.

"Is your witness from the 1850's or 1914?" Toby asked. "By which I really mean are they still alive or has their testimony been passed down through the years?"

"From the time the body was found," Goodwin confirmed. "Pardon my boldness, but if this had merely been a case of someone's word being recounted time and again, with perhaps amendments and additions along the way, would that then be eligible for counting as a direct testimony?"

Toby grinned. "I stand corrected for asking such a stupid question. Clearly an exacting rigour of thought extends both above and below stairs."

Goodwin's solemn face broke briefly into a smile. "Thank you. I took no umbrage at your point, though, because I know the difficulties associated with people reporting on things they couldn't have witnessed directly."

"The same can apply when people *have* witnessed it," Orlando said, with a snort. "The truth gets expanded upon and not merely to muddy the waters. The person might be trying, misguidedly, to be extra helpful or they genuinely have come to believe they were in a place at a time they couldn't have been. Perhaps because someone else told them they were."

"I would hope that wouldn't apply in this instance. The person I'm referring to was a gardener's lad back then and he's now the estate manager."

"That must be Cutting," Jonty exclaimed. "I always felt that to be a highly appropriate name for his earlier profession. Might we rustle him up, Goodwin?"

"I'll ring for one of the footmen to locate him. It may take some time, depending on whether he's off visiting some corner of the estate." The butler appeared to be on the verge of adding something and then decided against it. He summoned his messenger while the others waited, a touch impatiently, to see what else he had to tell them. Once the lad was despatched, Goodwin continued. "I'll leave Cutting to say his own piece. I'll simply relate what was told to me about the matter when I first came here, and anything relevant I've learned since."

"We could ask for no more. Alasdair, could you fetch Goodwin a chair, please?" Jonty raised his hand to forestall argument from the butler. "I know it's hardly orthodox but pray indulge me. We can't take your testimony in a way that feels like we're conducting an interrogation."

With reluctance, the butler took a seat, perching on it with evident unease. "I know the circumstances in which the body was found and I'm assuming you won't want me to restate those, given that you arrived here not long afterwards, Dr Stewart. I will say that we've often speculated about when you and Professor Coppersmith might decide to investigate." Goodwin eyed his boots. "Sweepstakes have been held, sir."

"How splendid." Jonty drummed the table in glee. "If such a sweepstake is extant, we'll be delighted to confirm whose guess is closest to when the investigation was born. Please tell us anything you can to aid our progress in it."

Goodwin, potentially tricky confession passed, raised his head again. "The staff who were here at the time were terribly shocked. Mortified at anyone daring to sully the Old Manor in such a way. There's clearly been much speculation as to who might have done so but I fear that would be hardly more than tittle-tattle. None of us are aware of any enemies that the family may have had when the body must have been put there after the Great Exhibition. And, unless domestic matters were run in a sloppy manner in the past, it's simply not possible a body could have been deposited in the vaults in the sixty years before it was discovered."

"Can we clarify that?" Alasdair asked. "You are absolutely certain that Drayton couldn't have been installed there in the interim?"

Had Goodwin been less of an exemplary servant, he might have given Alasdair a withering look. "I couldn't swear to it in a court of law but I have two solid facts to offer. One is that the heavily sealed chest definitely returned with the other items when the exhibition ended. I've checked the inventory."

"Inventory?" Orlando shared a puzzled glance with Jonty. "We've been led to believe there wasn't one."

"There may not have been a list made of the contents, either outgoing or incoming," Goodwin's wince showed what he thought of such sloppiness, "but my distant predecessor made a note of which crates and chests went and which returned. The lists were identical."

"Which begs the question of what was originally in the sealed crate," Alasdair said. "Not that we'll ever be likely to know."

"Indeed, sir. I can say nothing about that. My second point concerns the access to the vaults, which is beside one of the access doors to our part of the house. A well-used entry point, so one of us would likely notice if some evidence had been left of unauthorised egress, such as a scuff on the wall. More importantly, the entrance is extremely close to the butler's pantry and sleeping quarters. If the vaults had been opened at night, one of my forerunners would surely have heard it."

Jonty nodded. "Excellent point, Goodwin. The door may be well hidden but it makes a hell of a creak and the stairs aren't muffled, either."

Alasdair cleared his throat, in a manner Orlando was certain he'd heard him use in one of his films. It had signified an awkward question about to be asked. "I'm not wishing to cast aspersions but in the interests of the aforementioned rigour of thought, could one of the butlers in the past have been not quite the model of the present?"

Toby, with a chuckle, said, "I feel I must translate. My colleague means could said butler have been so sozzled when he took to his bed one night that the four horsemen of the apocalypse could have thundered through and he'd not have noticed?"

Goodwin, who'd quickly suppressed a grin at Toby's translation, shook his head. "While I can't vouch for the probity of any of the previous incumbents, there is another item for consideration. The lighting on the stairs. You'll be aware of the circumstances that led to it being installed?"

"Yes," Jonty replied. "Somebody playing at daredevils and almost getting killed. Twenty odd years after the Great Exhibition."

Goodwin inclined his head, with a gravity befitting a high-court judge. Orlando noticed how close an attention the two actors were paying to him and suspected it wasn't merely to do with his words. Professional research to pass on to an actor in a lesser role? "When the arc lamps were replaced with a newer system, it was decided to take the opportunity of guarding against anyone on a similar jaunt ending up hurt and lying undiscovered. An arrangement was made whereby when they are turned on, lights are also illuminated in my pantry. Then, in 1914, your father updated the system by arranging for the switch on those stairs to link to an alarm in both his bedroom and the butler's. You will appreciate what the heightened security was for."

The four investigators nodded. No more need be said on that topic.

"Is that lighting system how Clarence's pal was discovered so quickly?" Jonty asked. "I mean the chap who went tumbling down the stairs in the year one?"

"So I believe. The butler at the time was able to alert your father—and a burly footman in case of trouble with the intruder." Goodwin risked a smile. "It's all in our *own* records."

"So, we reduce the chances of someone sneaking Drayton—alive or dead—into the vault in normal circumstances." Toby's expression was unusually serious. "What about when the family aren't in residence? On holiday or in London, for example."

Jonty shook his head. "There's always a skeleton staff here and anyway, it would be extremely difficult for a stranger to access the house. It's been kept locked and shuttered when the family aren't here, ever since the burglary incident at the time of Trafalgar."

"Exactly, sir." Goodwin suddenly found his shoes fascinating once more. "That would, of course, not eliminate the possibility of it being what I believe is called an *inside job*. To our shame, we have discussed that in the servants' hall, too.

"No shame in that at all, Goodwin," Jonty assured him. "Robust analysis of an intriguing, yet delicate, situation. What did your discussions conclude?"

"That for such a thing to have happened, there would have had to be significant collusion between family and staff." The butler shook his head at such a thing. "We couldn't credit that theory. Surely no Stewart would commit such an act and, as far as I'm aware, there have been no black sheep among the servants. Again, any employee whose character was in question would have been listed in the butlers' records."

"Those sound like an absolute gold mine of information. I shan't ask to see them, much as I'd wish." Jonty shot Orlando a mischievous glance. Was he, despite his words, hatching some scheme to get his hands on this snapshot of life below stairs?

"Much of it would bore you, sir, although some items would be relevant to this discussion. I seem to remember a reference to the time the items were sent and returned, because it spoke of the disruption and mess the movers caused for the maids. And for the local carpenter, because the reinforced corners of that chest—the one that seems to be the focus of all the problems—scraped the panelling." Goodwin's eyebrow was as eloquent as Alasdair's in expressing disapproval. "Not *our* people who did the moving in that instance. That mistake was not repeated when the vaults were called into use during either war."

A tentative knock on the door heralded the return of the youngest footman, to say that Mr Cutting was in the local town at present on estate business but was due back in the afternoon. A note had been left asking for the man to make himself available.

"Excellent," Jonty said. "Perhaps a pot of tea—or better still a jug of beer—could accompany us to the interview. Much talk will make us thirsty."

"I will arrange that, sir. I could also locate any appropriate part of the butlers' records for you to scrutinize. There may well be a mention of the incidents involving unauthorized access to the staircase." Goodwin rose. "Will that be all, sir? I believe I've told you all I can. And that jug of beer won't organize itself," he added, with a hint of a twinkle in his eye.

Once the butler had been adequately thanked and allowed to leave, Toby said, "Well, that was an unexpected bonus. I'm guessing that neither of you knew about the alarm systems?"

"We did not," Orlando replied, confident that Jonty would have told him about them had *he* known. "Or else we'd have warned Goodwin yesterday that we'd be opening the vault."

Jonty chuckled. "Mama and Papa certainly kept those arrangements quiet, probably so that Clarence and his pals wouldn't have the opportunity to work out some way of disabling the mechanism and thereby leave the field clear for mischief. It was exactly the sort of act of bravado they'd have indulged in. It also explains why, as I mentioned, every time we went down there to play, somebody would appear to make sure we weren't getting up to anything we shouldn't. I always assumed it was Mama's telepathic ability to be able to tell exactly where her offspring were, especially if they were being naughty."

"Goodwin's testimony also seems to clarify, as much as one could ever clarify, that the body came here in the 1850's and not since." Alasdair reached across the table to delicately finger Mr Stewart's papers. "We should finish reading these."

"That's my cue." Toby composed himself with a deep breath, as he might for a key scene. *"After the body was found, I had everything in the vaults thoroughly searched. Nothing turned up that might be relevant to an unexplained death, apart from the objects which were in the chest with Drayton and which were highly unlikely to have ever been Stewart property. These items were properly recorded at the inquest, with an expert in such items—a Dr Parker— verifying their nature. A shame that the coroner should have been so meticulous about some ancient artefacts yet not ensure that a man's death was accorded such consideration. Dr McCoist and I had examined all these objects and asked that they all be properly processed to look for blood. This request was refused, the police even quipping they couldn't rule out any blood coming from the mammoth itself. McCoist suggested we put everything back exactly where we found it so that we can carry on the investigation when peace breaks out again. None of the other prehistoric items seem to bear blood or anything else of note."*

"One up to us!" Jonty rubbed his hands gleefully. "Papa would have been furious had he found out he'd missed the Ogham."

Orlando doubted those incisions would have eluded Mr Stewart's eagle eye if he and the doctor had examined them closely. "I would imagine he saw those marks but simply thought they were a result of our mammoth having a tussle with another one."

"The inquest did correctly record that the storage trunk in which Drayton was found was Stewart property, had been

sent to the Crystal Palace and was capable of being hermetically sealed. I do not recall this chest ever being used, or indeed unfastened, in all my years at the Old Manor, partly because the thing was so difficult to open, requiring force and a particular knack. It was said to be empty, as it had only been used for biological specimens and these had long ago been donated to a local museum, although I can't swear to that fact.

It naturally begs the question of why it had been sent to the Great Exhibition in the first place. I suspect the answer lies with my father, who would have cheerfully taken the entire contents of those vaults and burned them, while dancing round the blaze. Perhaps he sent everything he could away, on the principle that some of it might conveniently disappear. I can certainly remember him being quite disappointed when it all came back, He ordered everything to be stashed away and left for a future generation to deal with. The weight of family history and preserving the past for one's descendants is a great responsibility: it can make one envious for the life of the tinker on the road."

"I bet he never suggested to your Mama that they take to their caravan and roam the roads." Orlando snorted. "She'd have blacked his eye."

"It's apiece with him not using his title, though. None of this surprises me." Jonty ran his finger along the text, perhaps reconnecting with the father he still missed. "We seem to be reaching the end. You've delivered an impressive performance, Toby."

Toby inclined his head in thanks. "An enjoyable role to take. A good quality of script, to boot. Here's the last part. *I have spoken to the two people still living who were in service here during the fifties—both of whom offered their services to the inquest and neither of whom were called—*

and they state that the storage chests were put into the vaults by outsiders. By which they mean men employed by those who ran the Great Exhibition.

"Or people who were said to be," Alasdair pointed out. "I've been thinking about this since Goodwin mentioned the damage to the panelling. If I were the killer and had managed to find such a convenient way to dispose of the body, I wouldn't have risked the thing being discovered too soon. I'd fear somebody here would notice that the chest was the wrong weight or simply didn't feel as it should, then would go and open the thing."

"And what would you do in those circumstances?" Toby asked.

"I'd arrange transport myself. Hire a goods wagon on a train, if they ran here then, and a fleet of sturdy carts if not. With equally sturdy men to lug stuff about." Alasdair drummed the table. "One can only hope that the butler of the time made a note of who organized the transport or who completed the job."

"If they caused damage, I bet he did. Toby, shall we hear Papa out, then we can tackle the other dates on our list."

"All this leads me to conclude there's a very good chance that Drayton was murdered, most likely in London, and his body was sent to the Old Manor in the sealed chest in order that the perpetrator could distance themselves from the crime. A strategy which appears to have succeeded admirably. I give my word that the name Drayton is not one I can recall coming across among Stewart connections and I have no further information to offer about the man or his demise. All I ask is that he is at some point given the due care and intention his sudden end demands. And there you have it." Toby laid the papers on the table for all to see.

Orlando, who'd had an idea he'd been dying to share, could wait no longer. "We did contemplate it being what Goodwin so aptly called an inside job. I fear we've concentrated on the wrong place."

Alasdair wagged his finger. "You referring to the Great Exhibition?"

"No. I'm quite happy with the theory that there, or the environs, are quite likely to be the place where Drayton was killed and encrated, but the inside job part refers to somewhere closer to home."

The other three shared a puzzled look. "Nope, Orlando," Toby said, "you've confused me completely."

"The inquest. With both a coroner and chief constable who were so keen to have the matter done and dusted. And who managed to override some important people to do so."

Jonty rapped the table. "You've said that from the start and I think you may have a point. Gentlemen, we must see if we can find any *other* Armitages or Geraghtys connected to this business. Preferably back in the fifties and still exerting an influence sixty years later."

Chapter Six

The four men continued their searches up to the point where it was decided they'd learn nothing new and their stomachs were starting to rumble. Over a cold collation for luncheon, they shared the little they'd found.

As expected, the papers hadn't date back to Richard Stewart's childhood, so no contemporaneous account existed of items being sent to or from the Crystal Palace. No further reference was made to Drayton between the 1914 statement and Mr Stewart's death, because the man clearly had other matters in mind, including his son's welfare.

"I had to swop some of the documents with Toby," Jonty confessed. "Couldn't read the things. Papa was beside himself when we abandoned our comfy roles in London for the trenches. Not that he said so, but one can read between the lines. All in all, I think that Alasdair and Orlando should meet Goodwin this afternoon to look at what our previous butlers have recorded. Not that I worry about becoming too emotional, because he'd not turn a hair at that, being so well trained. I simply I fear I'm too close, being a sprig of the family. The Stewarts have never interfered with matters the other side of the baize door and long may that pertain."

Orlando nodded. "Agreed. Even though we'd be there at Goodwin's invitation, it might be wiser to suggest he brings the notebooks or whatever they are to the library, as he may prefer neutral ground to his pantry. I'll ring now to send a message." Once that had been completed, he retook his seat at table. "We had slightly more luck in our searches. Nothing directly from the seventies, although thirty years later, Clarence's pal Heathfield's adventures get chapter and verse, including an odd little reference." Orlando consulted his notebook. "*Typical of that family, to cause mischief and make other people think they were to blame. Clarence does seem to pick them.* Does that mean anything?"

"Not offhand," Jonty said, with a shrug. "*The Clarence picking them* bit is clear, because he always had an eccentric range of friends and he did feel guilty about Heathfield's accident. I can't recall anything about the rest of that family, although I didn't know them well. I doubt it was a direct reference to either of our men under suspicion—by which I mean Geraghty or Armitage—because Papa would surely have known of such a connection. Add it to the list of things to follow up. Now, I notice you said there was nothing *directly* concerning the other chap. What do we have that's indirect? And is it the pick of what you've turned up, given the twinkle in your eye and the fact you like to keep the best for last?"

Alasdair, who'd noted the way Jonty had picked up the slight nuance of language and wondered if he and Toby would reach the same almost telepathic connection that the dons possessed, said, "Again, it's a slightly mysterious note but it might make sense in the light of yesterday's discoveries." He produced his notebook. "It's when he's talking about Heathfield. I can't do his voice justice, but here goes. *Only the second person to have insulted our hospitality by accessing the vaults without permission, the other being back in my father's day. He was another madcap, on that occasion furnished with the feeble excuse that he was looking for some secret writing said to be there, although that's all my eye and Betty Martin. The thrill of the challenge, that's what these types want.*"

"Secret writing? The Ogham?" Toby asked, as keen as a hound on the scent.

"It's possible. If he knew the Ogham was there," Alasdair pointed out, "then maybe he suspected there was a less savoury item in the chest. How I wish there was a way to read a man's thoughts from the best part of a century ago. It would help to pick the real trail from the false."

The rest of the meal was occupied with a discussion about how their various experiences had helped them build up the ability to tell a red herring from a genuine clue, although Orlando and Jonty both confessed that they still ended up led astray. Not all the dead ends of the maze could be instantly eliminated. Part of this conversation had to take place in Toby's absence, as he'd been summoned to the telephone to take a call from Sergeant Granger. For the man to be ringing the Old Manor had to be an encouraging sign and Toby had scuttled off eagerly, Alasdair's notepad in hand. He'd returned wearing a massive grin and waggling the notepad like Chamberlain and his papers.

"I have information about Drayton," he said, taking his seat. "Alasdair, could you oblige me with a smidgeon of cheese and a cracker or two? Granger has come up trumps and I need sustenance. Been writing like billy-oh."

"Of course." Alasdair chose what he was certain would be Toby's favourites among the vittles on offer.

"Peter Drayton, to all intents and purposes, disappeared around October or November 1851, although he wasn't reported missing until early in the next year, which is why the highly efficient Granger couldn't put his finger on the chap immediately. The case was, clearly, never solved. Thank you." Toby took his plate and loaded one of the crackers with Stilton. "The delay is explained by his parents believing he was travelling. Drayton was employed on the Great Exhibition, co-ordinating working industrial exhibits, such as the one about cotton spinning, but Granger suspects it was probably all hands to any pump at busy times. When the event was over, Drayton's parents received a letter saying that one of the manufacturers had offered him a position promoting their goods across the globe, effective immediately. He would try to keep in touch but they weren't to worry if they didn't hear from him for a while."

"That sounds like it was sent by his murderer or an accessory after the fact." Orlando helped himself to some Cheshire cheese. "Was the handwriting disguised?"

"It was all capitalized, which didn't raise any concerns because it was his standard way of writing, his cursive script being illegible. A good enough imitation to fool his parents, anyway." Toby consulted the notepad. "And the writer didn't leave it there. Another letter came a fortnight later, from Rome, sending Drayton's love and saying he was heading off to the east to help open new markets. He would write again when he could. His family knew he'd always wanted to travel, so still harboured no suspicions, even when he didn't write again. It was only when his landlady contacted them after Christmas to ask if Drayton wanted to retain his lodgings, because the rent he'd paid in advance would be due again at the end of January, that they started to worry. Although the fact he had apparently taken a trunk of belongings with him still suggested he *had* gone away."

"I know there's no evidence for this, but I bet it was the same people who took the trunk as brought the chests here," Jonty said. "This knocks on the head the inquest's accident verdict, doesn't it? Did the family report him as missing as soon as they'd received the landlady's letter?"

"Granger thinks not. They may have lost some time contacting his friends and colleagues, in case *they'd* heard anything from him. You see, Drayton had a possible reason to make himself scarce." Toby polished off another cracker.

"Tell us, rather than leaving us dangling, you annoying little molecule." Alasdair's eyebrow danced its owner's disapproval.

"You must be a setting him a good example," Toby told their hosts. "*Molecule* would have been a lot less polite were

106

we alone. Drayton had been walking out with a young lady and, while his mother felt that had no connection to the case, his father was sure he'd wanted to disentangle himself because he'd mentioned something about women bothering him. Drayton senior apparently told the police, on the quiet, that he'd always felt it possible his son had taken the opportunity to establish a new life."

"The father's rather lessez faire attitude seems rather harsh on Drayton's mother, though. I mean," Orlando raised his hand, "*we* know why he made no further communication but *she* would have been left wondering for the rest of her life."

"Apparently, Drayton senior concluded his quiet word with the assertion that if Drayton junior had taken a native wife, out in Ceylon or wherever, his mother would have died of shock if she heard the news. It was almost better as it was. It does seem particularly unfeeling, so I daresay that's not the whole story." Toby shrugged. "There's more from Granger, by the way."

"I told you he was an annoying molecule," Alasdair shook his head. "This will no doubt be one of Granger's bombshells."

"I'm inclined to send you out of the room, so you don't hear it first-hand, if at all. Except our hosts are too well-mannered not to take pity on you." Toby consulted his jottings once more. "The police concluded, in a surprisingly frank little note made at the time, that Drayton had probably taken his opportunity of escaping a domineering mother. However, in order to reach that deduction, they'd done a bit more investigating than their equivalents sixty years later. They spoke to the aforementioned young lady—whose name was Mary Proudfoot, which is pleasingly unusual—and she appeared to be rather unmoved about it all. The officer who questioned her said that *he'd* have made himself scarce if he'd had to spend much more time with her."

"A young lady does raise the possibility of a rival in love, rather like in your film," Orlando said. "As well as an avenging brother or the like and we've come across a few of those on both counts. Did the police interview anyone else?"

"Yes. Various men who worked with Drayton at the Great Exhibition. Who said he'd mentioned seeking a new position, one in which he could travel. That rather sealed the police opinion on what had happened." Toby closed his notebook. "I asked Granger if he could find us the names of those men, which he will."

"It sounds to me as if expressing that wish to travel may have contributed to Drayton's death." Jonty crumbled the remains of a cracker onto his plate. "If somebody wanted to get rid of him, it gave them their chance, rather like the sealed chest did. A deadly combination. Who took his trunk, though?"

"Whoever got their hands on the key to his room?" Alasdair suggested. "Did he have a keyring on him when he was found?"

"I don't remember being told and I'm sure Mr Stewart would have noted if he had. We make progress, though." Orlando patted his partner's arm. "We can now have ninety nine percent confidence in rejecting an accident, as well as virtually eliminating any chance of the killing having happened here or later than 1851. Unless Drayton went abroad, sent those letters, slipped back, got himself killed and was put in the crate without anyone here knowing. Which theory I can't accept."

"A case of, 'Once you eliminate the impossible...' Sorry." Toby lifted his hand. "Mea culpa. I nearly quoted *him*."

"You are excused any forfeit, having not finished the quote." Orlando made a gesture suggestive of absolution. "I have always wished I'd written to Conan Doyle to say that some people said rail travel was impossible, because people would be unable to breathe at the high speeds. The seemingly impossible can happen but not, I think, in Drayton's case." He checked his watch. "And now, we must be about our business."

"Talking of impossibilities, there's another we should have mentioned before now," Jonty said, as they pushed back their chairs. "Young Adam, our housekeeper-cum-chauffeur in waiting, knows a thing or two about gardening and he's also an avid reader of books related to murders, real and fictional. He likes to spot when the authors get their facts wrong, so he was most interested when we told him about the rhubarb leaf poisoning plot for your film. Trouble is, he reckons it can't be done. That you'd have to be stupid to eat much of the stuff in the first place and it would need a sack load to kill you. You might want to get your writers to ensure they've got their facts right or the gardeners of Britain will be boycotting the film. And thinking we're a right pair of chumps for coming up with the—albeit fictional—solution."

With which sobering thought, the pairs set off on their separate missions.

"I'd better contact the studio as soon as we've seen Goodwin," Alasdair said, as he and Orlando headed back to the library. "Adam hasn't got a better alternative to offer?"

"Not yet. He'd turn his nose up at anything that smacks of the famous unknown poison from the deepest jungle, though." Orlando snorted, a not unattractive noise that Alasdair would like to imitate onscreen. It could prove popular with his fans, so long as it wasn't overused.

"That's more Holmes's specialty than yours. I promise I'll make my portrayal of you chalk to his cheese."

"Much obliged. *I* don't rely on best guesses dressed up as absolute certainties." Orlando's chuckle sounded as delightfully as his snort. "Now I'm sounding as pompous as him. Let's hope Goodwin doesn't have any strange faces at windows or missing rugby players to regale us with."

The butler didn't appear to be bearing bell ropes that snakes could crawl down or anything else so beloved of the sealed room devotees, simply a selection of heavy bound notebooks which were already laid out on one of the library tables, ready for examination.

"Before we begin," he said, "I must tell you I have mentioned your investigation to the staff, who are most gratified that the Old Manor's mystery—and more importantly, Drayton himself—are being given their due. Dr Stewart might like to know that we've also declared the current sweepstake winner *in absentio*. His lordship's valet was the only person to have predicted an enquiry would start this month."

"What does he win?" Alasdair asked.

"A bottle of port. And bragging rights, not that he'll be the sort to use them when he returns from London." Goodwin grinned, before reassuming his standard, impassive expression.

From the very first reading, Alasdair found the butlers' books full of the kind of clues that any investigator could appreciate. The first surprising information being that the name of the person in charge of transporting the items back from the Crystal Palace had turned out to be false. This had been discovered when a letter of complaint about the damage caused to the panelling had been returned to the Old Manor because the address given was that of a bookseller—

Bryant—just off the Strand. The staff there swore they'd had nothing to do with the matter.

Goodwin moved his finger across the page, as though to draw a line under matters. "I can find nothing further in the subsequent entries, so I assume the issue was simply let drop. I'm sorry to produce such a dead end, sir."

"A dead end maybe, but it accords with our theory that whoever killed Drayton may have hired the men who returned the chest here. Negative evidence can have its uses." Orlando flashed the butler one of his rare smiles. What a charmer the man must have been in his prime.

The charm clearly worked on Goodwin, who sat up taller as he produced his next exhibit. "This is from the eighteen seventies. I have some other information from that time, too, which will need explanation."

The butler then had stated in his notes how a guest had caused great consternation by accessing the vaults and nearly killing himself. The guest's name was Gerald Proudfoot.

"Proudfoot?" Orlando and Alasdair shared a glance. "There's a possible connection to Drayton. He was walking out with a young lady of that surname and it's sufficiently unusual to warrant further investigation."

Alasdair jotted down a reminder to do that very thing. "We'll ask Granger if a Gerald Proudfoot gets a mention in the original investigation. We've discovered more about Drayton, you see, Goodwin. We'd better brief you on what our Scotland Yard sergeant and expert on Victorian crimes had to tell Mr Bowe. Prepare yourself for a tale of letters which may have been forged and a supposed escape from an unwanted lover."

After the summary came to an end, Goodwin asked, "Might I relate this to the rest of the staff, Mr Hamilton? They're taking a great interest in the matter, especially as we have two sets of investigators in action. Although I suppose that technically yourself and Mr Bowe are only acting the part as you do on film?"

Alasdair grinned. "You may tell your colleagues that Mr Bowe and I do more than a little dabbling in the world of amateur detection. It's probably inevitable, given that Mr Bowe's godfather has such notable cases to deal with and some of them touch on studio life." Best to leave it there, because the details of how the *Grey Assassin* case had touched quite so closely weren't to be discussed in public.

They returned to reading the journal entries from the time of Proudfoot's foray but the next few paragraphs, concerning the installation of lighting, provided nothing new.

"You told us there was another piece of information," Alasdair said. "Does it concern Proudfoot?"

"Yes, sir. First, I must explain the context. The cooks here have always kept a record of particular recipes. From household favourites to dishes which have been well received at formal dinners and the like. Dr Stewart's preferred version of jam roly-poly, for example."

"A dish you should try, Alasdair." Orlando raised an eyebrow. "If the studio would risk you putting on a pound or two. Highly addictive."

"It sounds magnificent." As was the fact that the man he was to portray was providing plenty of scope for an authentic use of the heavily insured eyebrow.

"I'll get the recipe copied for you. Or perhaps have a pudding made for you to take home, although it won't travel well. Mrs Stokes, our cook, is a great one for your films so I'm sure she'll provide something appropriate." Another grin from Goodwin, soon hidden. The man's training clearly had to work hard to overcome his nature. "These recipes I refer to are preserved in various volumes, with plenty of

112

space left in between for them to be annotated with successful variations and notes of praise. Queen Victoria was most taken with a particular clear soup, I'm told, and his Lordship is hoping that the present queen will enjoy it, too, when she visits."

"We walk with the great when we walk here. I've still not become accustomed to the idea." Orlando nodded solemnly. "I'm assuming there are notes pertaining to Gerald Proudfoot among the annotations."

"Yes. Again, to fill in the background, the then cook was said to be a bit of a tartar, despite the lightness of her pastry. Her trifle recipe is accompanied by a note saying how Gerald Proudfoot had sent her a message praising it mightily. She then goes on to state that maybe he was searching for the recipe—and others which were unique to the Stewart table at the time and which have been kept secret—when he took his tumble."

"Oh." This was how a balloon must feel when suddenly deflated. The intruder may not have been chasing Ogham so much as chasing tiddy oggies or something similar. They turned their attention back to the butler's journal.

"There is another reference to the intrusion, though." Orlando's finger hovered over the page. "The then lord—Dr Stewart's grandfather—was furious at his hospitality being so abused."

The account also stated he'd been angry that the servants had been put to the unnecessary trouble of carrying Proudfoot up the stairs and having to go for medical help. *His Lordship apologized for venting his bad temper in front of me and made a quip about antiquarians and how they didn't care a jot for people, only old inscriptions and a burned bit of ash that might be a votive offering.*

"Does that suggest he was searching for the metal slag, or even the Ogham, do you think?" Alasdair asked. "That's a sort of ancient writing, Goodwin. On the mammoth tusk."

"Ah, I see, sir." Goodwin clearly didn't see but was no doubt too polite to mention it.

"Let's look at events in the new century and Freddie Heathfield's abuse of Stewart hospitality, if we may," Orlando said.

Goodwin showed them the relevant volume, remarking that it was the stuff of household legend that Clarence had been known to have some over-enthusiastic and not particularly sensible young friends. So while Heathfield's tumble down the stairs had been just as disruptive as Proudfoot's, it had also been generally winked at as youthful high spirits. This view was supported by the journal text, which referred briefly to the previous invader of the vaults and said he'd been old enough to know better. More—very elliptical—support for him having been a contemporary of Drayton's?

The most interesting thing was a reference by the then butler, Hopkins, to Mrs Stewart tending Heathfield and the chap rambling, which had made her fear he'd sustained a head injury. Something about Guinevere, which made no sense at all. The doctor who'd been called later confirmed that the young lad had merely suffered a touch of concussion, nothing worse than he might have experienced on the rugby field. Although the doctor had also issued a stiff warning to Heathfield that he'd got away lightly with a broken ankle and that events could have turned out far more seriously. Heathfield's people had soon come to take him home and everyone in the house, above and below stairs, had been given another reminder that the vault was a dangerous place for the unwary.

"What a shame Heathfield wasn't going on about looking for dead bodies rather than tales of King Arthur or whoever he had in mind with Guinevere." Alasdair rubbed his forehead. "Which brings us to 1914. Was it the same butler?"

"It was," Orlando chipped in. "Hopkins. Splendid chap and a great reciter of Kipling. I recall one magnificent entertainment involving all the household, with Lavinia's husband giving us Gilbert and Sullivan and Dr Stewart performing a rendition of *Hearts of Oak*."

"Would that be the time you told the ghost story, sir?" Goodwin asked, with a hint of a twinkle in his eye. He tapped the book. "That gets a splendid write-up too."

"Perhaps best to get back to the matter in hand. I shan't be giving an encore." Orlando couldn't hide his delight at the mention. "What does Hopkins have to say about the body being discovered?"

"Not as much as could be hoped." Goodwin replaced the 1901 volume with the one of thirteen years later, where he'd bookmarked the relevant pages. "His concerns were mainly about his charges, who were extremely upset. One of the kitchen maids had hysterics at the thought she'd been in the same house as a long-dead corpse. By the time he'd managed to get everyone back on an even keel the body had been examined and taken away."

"Where was Drayton buried?" Alasdair asked. "Was he returned to his family?"

Orlando slowly shook his head. "I have no idea and if Dr Stewart knew I'm sure he'd have mentioned it. Our minds were otherwise occupied, as you'll appreciate."

"That's another question for either the redoubtable Granger or the St Bride's librarian, then. There would surely have been a mention in the newspapers." Alasdair studied the volume once more, then pointed to a particular line. "Look at this."

I never saw the body nor wished to do so. This man's death is now a matter for the proper authorities.

"That shows a faith in them they didn't deserve," Alasdair remarked.

However, I cannot say I am surprised that something so disturbing was discovered. I have not mentioned this to Mr Stewart as he has enough to deal with given both the dead man and the imminent arrival of items of great importance which we must preserve for the nation. However, I feel I must make it a matter of record for my successors.

"As well he did. Would I be right in saying Hopkins was one of a number of people in the household who succumbed to the influenza, Goodwin?" Orlando asked.

"Yes, sir. A terrible swathe it cut through us, as you and Dr Stewart know only too well." The butler nodded, eyes fixed on the page.

My predecessor, Henson, told me that he believed there was something hidden in the vault which perhaps not even Mr Stewart's father knew about. Henson believed it to be treasure, possibly dating back to the civil war when the vault was constructed, but possibly from later. He had as evidence the fact that someone had accessed the place without permission back in the seventies, coming a cropper in the process.

"Have you come across any rumours like this?" Alasdair shot a glance at Orlando, who shook his head, evidently as surprised as he was. "Goodwin, has anyone else in the servants' hall ever mentioned a similar suspicion?"

"Not a word, sir. It has always been emphasized that while the vaults have been used for storage in periods of national crisis, at all other times since the days of Cromwell the contents have been of little worth. As far as I know, when they have had their regular inspections and airing, it's all hands to the pump—gardeners as well if muscle power is needed—and no hint of secrecy. Which latter one would expect were treasure really to be there. And plenty of staff know how to open the access door, in case of an emergency."

"It certainly beggars belief that the incumbent title holder wouldn't know that his vault contained a treasure worth risking one's neck for." Orlando stroked his chin. "How could Henson know what his master didn't?"

"That strikes me also, sir. Most implausible sounding. Perhaps too many ghost stories and the like influenced people's thinking." Goodwin returned their attention to the text.

In my opinion, it is possible that Drayton also managed to access the vault, back in the days before proper lighting was installed. He had an accident and ended up entombed there.

"Oh." Alasdair let his eyebrow practice an Orlando-like show of disappointment. "I was hoping there'd be something related to Hopkins thinking his death was murder. Were these notes written after the inquest?"

"They may possibly have been added as a postscript." Goodwin bent over the writing. "I can't tell. Do you think the verdict influenced him?"

"Possibly. We have the circumstantial evidence of those letters to suggest it couldn't have been an accidental death. Evidence that the police could have located amongst their own records in 1914, if they'd been bothered to do so." Orlando took another scan of the volume, then offered it to Alasdair who did the same before closing it. "Thank you for your time, Goodwin. Dr Stewart and I must remember to keep you up to date with what we discover."

"A summary of your eventual conclusions would be sufficient, sir." The butler inclined his head and then ran his fingers gently over the books. "There will be speculation enough about what's been discovered here."

"We'll make sure you have one. Although if anything further turns up, or somebody shows a brilliant piece of insight, please let us know. The more ideas the merrier, eh, Alasdair?"

Alasdair nodded, even if he was unsure whether this would be a case of many hands making light work or too many cooks spoiling the broth.

Once Goodwin had departed with his arms full of his invaluable journals, Alasdair said, "So, at least one person had suspicions about Proudfoot's motives, even if she appears—to our eyes—to have gone down the wrong road. Still, we must assume there's a good chance this Gerald Proudfoot chap is linked to Drayton's Miss Proudfoot. She who was said to be abandoned by Drayton but who wasn't necessarily."

"Ah yes. You've considered that story could be a lie?" Orlando beamed his approval. "Whatever Drayton's father said to the police or their opinion of the lady, there's no really solid evidence that he meant to walk away from her. Only hearsay and perhaps not even that. I can imagine that those left behind when someone disappears would be trying hard to rationalize the event, attempting to find a reason for the person's going. They could easily end up persuading themselves of the wrong one, because it was convenient or comfortable. I can also imagine the anguish of Drayton's family, having no proof of what had happened to him." The smile had vanished, Orlando clearly remembering his own similar experience.

"It doesn't sound as though anyone suspected Drayton's disappearance could be laid at the feet of a particular person or surely that accusation would be in the records Granger found. Records which, as you pointed out, the inquest didn't bother to look for, which I'd say is more circumstantial evidence of the process not being carried out properly."

"I agree on both counts, Of course, if the person the Draytons suspected was one of influence, the name might have been deliberately omitted from the official records. One shouldn't rule out a scenario in which the 1914 equivalent of Sergeant Granger found exactly what our man has, but that evidence not being used. Or even the files being quietly robbed of anything with a certain name on it."

Alasdair sighed. "Was it this difficult with the Woodville Ward case? Trying to piece things together from hundreds of years ago?"

"Easier, I'd have said, because we had so many relevant papers to hand. *Papers yellowed with their age*, as Jonty describes them, because he can't resist a sonnet. And any persons of influence were much longer gone than in the present situations. You don't need to count that many generations from 1851 to 1914, do you?" Orlando spread his hands. "In both cases all you can do is form a theory around the facts you have and test it against each new one as it emerges. Which they have in droves, today. It'll make for an interesting discussion over dinner, especially if the other two turn up as much."

"Yes. I think I'd like to go away and have a long, hard ponder." Alasdair stretched and yawned.

"I feel the same. A little resting of the eyes would be an aid to organizing one's thoughts." Orlando rose. "I'll see you in the drawing room for a pre-prandial snifter."

"I'll have my ideas ready to air." Although would the most satisfying of naps help to point the way to a definitive answer to why Proudfoot was in the vault? Or how he'd known about it in the first place?

Chapter Seven

As they left the dining room, Jonty expressed his pleasure at the upcoming meeting with Cutting.

"Now that I don't have Orlando to tell me off for indulging in sporting reminiscences, I can confess to very fond memories of a splendid catch Cutting took at long on, off my bowling. He was a mere lad at the time and made an extraordinary leap to save the ball sailing over the boundary, managing to hold on to the catch at the same time. It meant we dismissed the other team's best batsman, to boot. I hope we'll have time to discuss such matters once the murder bits are done with."

"You're very kind to let me tag along," Toby said. "I wouldn't mind if you said you wanted to chat with Cutting alone, so you can touch on old times."

"Nonsense. Your presence will ensure that we don't simply reminisce about bygone days rather than deal with what we should be dealing with. Orlando would upbraid me if he discovered I'd wasted all my time in idle persiflage," Jonty chortled.

"I've been practicing your laugh, you know. I think I nearly have it." Toby tried a chuckle.

"That's pretty good. You'll have to try it out on our man of maths, of course, as he'll have a better opinion. One can't always gauge one's own voice and it never sounds the same when recorded than inside one's head."

"Indeed. I had a terrible shock when first I heard a playback of myself speaking. I was all for going to a voice coach to change the timbre but the studio insisted it was already more than acceptable. It doesn't sound quite so bad coming from the screen, or perhaps I'm simply used to it.

I—" Toby cut off as they turned a corner and a man hove into sight, waving brightly as he spotted them. If this was Cutting, he wasn't quite as old as Toby had first expected, but then he'd have been younger than Orlando and Jonty at the time of the body's discovery. If he was a mere lad then, he would be in his late forties or early fifties now. Not old enough to have seen action in the first war although no doubt he'd have done his bit in the second. Toby couldn't imagine that any Stewart employee would have neglected their duty.

"Mr Cutting!" Jonty shot his hand out. "What a pleasure to see you again. This is Mr Bowe and we're both most grateful for you taking time to see us."

"Pleasure's all mine, sir. It must be fifteen years since we last met."

"It is and that's far too long. I confess I haven't been coming here as often as I should. It doesn't feel the same without Papa and Mama, no matter how well Thomas runs things."

"No, indeed." Cutting's sympathetic smile reflected his own evident affection for Jonty's parents. "And might I say how thrilled my daughter will be when she learns I've met Mr Bowe? I didn't dare tell her or my wife that you and Mr Hamilton were staying this weekend or she'd have insisted I engineer an accidentally-on-purpose meeting between them and you."

"I'll send you a signed picture, to pass on to her, if you want." Toby paused, envisaging what Sir Ian might suggest was appropriate in the circumstances. The studio head always had an eye for promotional value. "Actually, if they don't live too far away, we could find five minutes for a little chat between now and dinner? Assuming that could be easily arranged?"

"We're at the lodge, sir and have a telephone for estate business, so if Dr Stewart wouldn't mind me making a call, when we're almost done, I could ask my wife to come up. My daughter will have to miss out but that serves her right for moving to Stoke Poges."

"It does indeed." They entered the office—where both beer and savoury biscuits were waiting for them—then took their seats before Jonty continued. "Wasn't Stoke Poges where the cricket team came from, against which you took the catch of the century?"

"I'd hardly call it that, Dr Stewart." Cutting blushed. "Although I confess I'm still proud of it. Yes, the team were on tour. Happy days, those. I'm sorry if we're boring you, Mr Bowe."

"Not at all. A privilege to hear all these stories." And solid background research. He gestured towards the refreshments. "I feel thoroughly spoiled."

"You can pay by pouring the beer," Jonty said. "Mr Cutting, as Goodwin no doubt mentioned, we're interested in the discovery of Peter Drayton's body, back in the year war broke. Unlike us, you were here at the time, so are the only living witness we're aware of."

"I could well be. Poor Mr Drayton. My Bessy—Mrs Cutting—makes sure he has fresh flowers on his grave at the anniversary."

"His grave?" Jonty's glass juddered in his hand, although he was clearly expert enough to ensure no beer was spilled.

"Yes. Didn't you know he's buried in the local graveyard?" Cutting jabbed his thumb over his shoulder, in the general direction of the parish church.

"That's barely a stone's throw away, Toby, and I had no idea he was there." Jonty took a sip of beer. "I can

122

understand nobody telling us, given what else was going on but I'm surprised Goodwin didn't mention it this morning."

"He no doubt thought it would be my place to share the information, given Bessy's particular involvement. Not a man to steal anyone's thunder, Mr Goodwin."

"You're probably right. He did seem to be about to mention something this morning and then thought better of it." Jonty gave Toby a shrug. "I think we should take the opportunity to pay our respects at the grave after we leave here. Perhaps Mrs Cutting could join us there to ensure we're not wandering around helplessly trying to find the correct plot?"

Toby nodded agreement at the excellent idea. An opportunity to get one up on Alasdair, for a start. "How did Drayton end up being buried here?"

"As I understand it—and I've pieced this together from what I heard here at the Manor and what the old vicar told Bessy—the coroner released Drayton's body to the parish, because they couldn't locate any family for him. The vicar reckoned they hadn't tried that hard, so he and your father put an advert in the papers. When nothing came of that, they assumed the Draytons had died out or recent generations weren't aware of their distant relative and how he'd disappeared. We've always wondered whether he was ever looked for."

"We can shed some light on that." Jonty gave Toby a nod. "Sergeant Granger is *your* police contact, so it should be your story."

Toby gave the estate manager a summary of what Granger had told him about Drayton's family, their concerns and the business of the letters, ending with, "So it would appear that somebody tried to cover up his disappearance. Effectively, as it turned out."

"That's one mystery solved, then. Bessy's often wondered why nobody claimed him when he was found. She'd concluded he was an orphan. Sad for the family though, never to know." Cutting drank some of his beer. "Good brew, this. Almost pre-war quality. Although we'd better not get talking about ale or we'll forget our duty. After nobody came forward in response to the newspaper appeal, Mr Stewart paid for Drayton's burial and a nice headstone. A shame the man had nobody close to mourn him but your mother laid a lovely wreath and plenty of us turned out to give him a proper send off."

"I wish I'd known and I'd have come, if I could. Although we were rather pre-occupied at the time. I'm glad Papa did the right thing, although I'm peeved that neither he nor Mama mentioned it to me. Not at the time and not in his notes, that we've been looking through today." Jonty shook his head. "Although they did keep the odd thing close to their chests if they thought it appropriate. I got a terrible shock when I discovered Mama had been involved in a secret meeting in Cambridge at some point before the war. Landseer should make a film about her, Toby. Fiona would be perfect casting for Mama in her pomp."

Cutting nodded. "That's spot on, Dr Stewart. She was a beautiful woman, your mother. Hidden depths, too, if I may be so bold."

"You may indeed. I suspect we'll never get to the bottom of them. I suppose Papa, who was always inclined to hide his light under a bushel, didn't want a fuss made about his charitable action in organising the funeral. I do know he felt a responsibility for Drayton."

"So does my Bessy. She was taken with the story from the first time she heard it and wanted to play her part by making sure Drayton's kept decent. I suppose I feel a duty to him, too, having been there when the body was found."

Now they were coming to the crux. Toby asked, "Were you on shifting and carrying duty down in the vault that day?"

"I was. Do you remember Ramsey, Dr Stewart?" Cutting asked.

"Who could forget him? He was head gardener at one point, Toby. My brothers and I called him the *Ancient of Days*, while my sister Lavinia said he was *Old Father Time*. Remarkably lithe and strong for a man his age, though." Jonty raised his glass, clearly toasting the man's memory. "Or was he simply younger than he looked, Mr Cutting?"

"A bit of both, Dr Stewart, although I wouldn't have asked him his age to his face. I had the back of his hand for sauce more than once."

"I think I had the same. I'd have had my leg slapped from Mama as well, if she'd known I was cheeking the staff. She wasn't averse to laying out some corporal punishment even when we were adults." Jonty laid down his half-empty glass. "I'm guessing he'd have been helping, too. I seem to recall he was one of those who'd been instructed in the arcane art of getting that wretched chest open."

"Yes. I think it was passed down from head gardener to head gardener. It meant Ramsey was the first to see the body. We were opening that chest together—we had the muscles as well as the knack, Mr Bowe—and it was a hell of a shock. I admit I felt so ill I couldn't make it to the stairs before I was sick. Then I was sent to find somebody to give me what I needed to clear up the mess I'd made, as we didn't have water or a mop to hand, so I missed the crucial bit." Cutting drained his glass, perhaps still affected by what he'd seen that day and either unaware of the effect the magic words "crucial bit" would have on his hearers or milking the moment. "There was something Mr Ramsey saw, or believed he saw, and which everyone else missed—he reckoned—so afterwards they told him he'd imagined it."

This was better than Toby could have hoped. When Jonty subsequently said that he couldn't envisage Ramsey imagining *anything* it simply added to the anticipation.

"I'd agree, Dr Stewart. Ramsey was never a man for flights of fancy. He swore there was something in the dead man's hand. A dried-up flower. Ramsey reckoned it was probably a rose but when they moved Drayton's body, whatever he'd had in his hand crumbled and joined the mess in the bottom of the crate. Not just the bits of flint, but something that looked like very old petals, maybe. The sort of things you might get in an old flower press, only all crushed up."

"How interesting." Not as significant as Toby had hoped, though. "Were they mentioned at the inquest?"

"Not as far as I know. Ramsey was called to give evidence about the body being found but when he started to talk about the rose in Drayton's hand, he was hurried on, because the coroner said it wasn't relevant. He was livid. Ramsey, that is."

"I *can* picture that." Jonty sipped his beer again. "Did he have any theory about why a man would clutch a flower while he was being killed? Assuming Ramsey was on the murder side of the fence, as it were, as opposed to thinking the death was an accident."

"Oh, he believed it was murder, all right. We all did." Cutting stuck out his lower lip in thought. "Those dried up flowers got a lot of discussion among those of us who worked on the grounds. They still do when Bessy's in the mood. Ramsey thought they may have been given him by his sweetheart or he was on his way to give them to *her* when he was struck down. Bessy tends to favour chance. She says perhaps he was killed when pruning them in a garden or more likely when he was indoors, putting the things in a vase, given that you wouldn't want to have to move the body too far. Drayton would have been distracted then and not aware of his killer either creeping up or suddenly attacking him."

"Either of those are possible. What do you think, though?" Jonty asked. "There's something in your voice which suggests you don't agree with Bessy's ideas."

"I'm no Sherlock Holmes. Oh." The estate manager put his hand to his mouth. "Begging your pardon for mentioning him, given that Professor Coppersmith doesn't like the man and Mr Hamilton makes his living portraying him."

"No offence given or taken," Toby assured him. "I'm sure you use your eyes, ears and brain as much as he did."

"Thank you, sir. I try. You might find my theory as outlandish as I find Bessy's, though. You see, I wondered if he was lured into his place of death. Let me demonstrate." Cutting stood up. "It's a tall old thing, that crate. Up to here." He laid a hand at rib level. "Another reason why I don't think an accident could be that plausible an explanation. Drayton couldn't have inadvertently tipped himself in. He wasn't a small man, though, so if he was killed elsewhere, it would have been quite a job to move him. Especially if he'd started to stiffen."

"Most logical. You underestimate your own powers of reasoning," Jonty said. "What's this outlandish theory?"

"That the flowers were somehow used to entrap him. Imagine this is the chest." Cutting stationed himself next to a filing cabinet which was about the right height. "My enemy, which is what we'll call him or her—and this would allow a woman to both kill him and get his body in there— gets their hands on this bouquet and chucks it in here, perhaps as a sort of joke. Flirting, you know." Cutting mimed the action. "Drayton wants to rescue the flowers, or

127

is asked to by the woman, so he climbs up, using something to stand on."

"Yes." Toby nodded vigorously. "We had to use a crate to get a good look inside the original."

Cutting fetched a small pair of steps from the other side of his office, placing them next to the cabinet before standing on the lower rung. "He climbs up, all unsuspecting, then gets bashed on the head. While he's dazed, he has his legs pulled up so he overbalances, is tipped in and the lid shut." He mimed the action, much to Toby's amusement. Had the man a penchant for amateur dramatics? "Although I have another explanation to offer, which might be better. Imagine he has actually climbed into the crate to fetch the flowers."

"He'd have to, surely, unless he had some device to grab them with," Jonty pointed out. "It's a deep chest and his arms wouldn't have been that long."

"Exactly. He'd have then had to bend down to pick them up. When somebody does that, it usually involves his head rising quickly as he straightens up again. As his head comes up, he gets whacked—either knocked out or killed outright—so he falls back in, rose still in his hand."

"That would eliminate any need at all to get the body into the chest, because it's already there." Jonty nodded, evidently impressed. "You then simply seal your victim in and, if he's still alive, leave him to suffocate. Or you make sure of things by getting in there too and finishing him off."

"How would the killer get out again?" Toby asked. "He's on the wrong side to use the steps, although I suppose he could haul himself up and over."

"He could have clambered up. Or used poor Drayton to stand on—if you're the one who murdered him, you'd not be bothered about doing that." Jonty finished his beer. "I think you may have something there, Cutting. I like an explanation that is neat, simple and lacking in obvious discrepancies. I suppose it would be beyond our wildest dreams to hope that you might have anything else to tell us?"

"Well, sir, I do but it's rightly Bessy's story so if we're going to meet her, I'd be best leaving it to her. If I may?" Cutting retook his seat, hand hovering over the telephone.

"Please do. I'll just have another of these little savoury morsels. Toby?"

"Just the one, Jonty, thank you." Just as well they were only at the Old Manor for a few days. Any more hospitality and his seamstress would have to let out all Toby's costumes.

***

The stone on Drayton's grave was plain yet dignified. It bore his name, year of death—the latter with a *c* for *circa* in front of it—and the simple statement, "Known to God".

"It reminds me of the graves of my fellow soldiers," Jonty said, gently fingering the stone. "I see my father's hand in this."

The churchyard was as well tended as it had been in the days he had come here with his parents, sometimes with Orlando in tow. Every time Jonty saw the place he was filled with fond recollection of the occasion when a particular Christmas Eve service here had played a vital part in his lover getting his memory back after a period of amnesia. A drastic loss of memory which had caused them both great hurt. Funny how that period of their lives had also led to a graveside, at the culmination of the *Woodville Ward* mystery, the solution of the case sealing their fame as detectives.

129

"It's a truly lovely location." Toby turned his face to the sun. "God's little acre indeed."

"You'll have to visit the church, if you can, Mr Bowe," Cutting said. "Will you be here for evensong tomorrow?"

"Alas we'll have left by then. Matins might be possible." Toby, glancing at Jonty, tipped his head to the side.

"It will indeed. I'll come with you. We might even persuade Professor Coppersmith to attend, heathen that he is." Jonty tipped his head, too, with a wink. "Ah, is that Mrs Cutting?"

They turned to see a well turned out woman coming through the lych gate and heading in their direction.

"That's my Bessy. Dressed in all her finery which she wasn't earlier, Mr Bowe," Cutting added softly.

"I'm honoured." Toby gave her a wave.

Jonty let Cutting make the introductions, both he and Toby insisting that Bessy not call them "sir" although she balked at the very idea of addressing either man by his Christian name.

"That wouldn't be proper, Dr Stewart," she said, with a shy smile and the hint of a curtsey. "Now, you want to know about Mr Drayton?"

"Yes. We're trying—and it's much overdue—to find out exactly what happened to him. I had no idea he was buried here." Jonty patted the gravestone. "Nor so well looked after."

"It's a lovely stone. The old vicar wanted it to have the verse about not one sparrow falling to the ground without God's say so but your mother apparently dug her heels in. She said that would be lacking in taste, seeing what the official verdict of the inquest was."

"That he'd fallen into that chest by accident? She was right, of course." Jonty gave Bessy a sympathetic nod and a chuckle. "Rather ironic, given her own propensity for verbal

130

faux pas, that she'd have picked up on someone else's. She'll be looking down from her cloud—resting from her proper work of checking all the angels have clean handkerchiefs—and feeling grateful for your consideration towards a man that none of us knew."

"Bless you, it's her tradition I carry on. Always fresh flowers on the anniversary of the day he was found."

"When your mother passed on," Cutting explained, "Master Sheridan's—sorry, his late lordship's—wife carried on the tradition, although we suspected her heart wasn't really in it. A duty rather than a pleasure, if you get me."

"I do indeed, Cutting." Jonty knew she'd have done it with a smile, but one she'd have forced herself to wear. "I'm so pleased you volunteered to take over. Especially as I hear you have something particular to tell us."

"About the flowers left here," Cutting said, when Bessy looked perplexed.

"Oh, yes, Bob. Silly me." Bessy nodded at her husband. "It would have been in the early thirties, when three years running flowers were put on the grave. It was mid-November—I can pin the date down because it was close to Jenny's birthday. Jenny's our daughter, Mr Bowe, and she'll be mortal envious of me having met you. And you not being a disappointment." Bessy's hands flew to her mouth. "Oh, I'm so sorry, sir. Mr Bowe. I didn't mean anything by saying that."

Toby gave her the smile with which he lit up the screen. "I'm sure you didn't. I'm both unoffended and delighted I'm not a let-down. Clearly people have been in the past."

"They have. During the war we met Ivor Novello, after we'd seen him in *The Dancing Years*. I can't say why, but I wasn't impressed." Her brow crinkled. "He was shorter than he seemed on stage and nowhere near as handsome."

131

"Truth be told, based on a similar experience and strictly between us, I would agree with you. Which I would never have been brave enough to admit at the time." Toby flashed her another smile. "Anyway, if we manage between us to crack this case and work out what happened to poor Drayton, I'll treat all three of you to dinner at the Savoy. In fact, I'll do that anyway, in gratitude for you tending his grave so well. We'll see if we can drag old Alasdair along to keep us under control. Or perhaps we'll be controlling him."

As both the Cuttings thanked Toby for his offer—in the process making a clearly half-hearted attempt to tell him he needn't put himself out—Jonty was struck by the fact that *he* tended to make similar quips, accusing Orlando of untold excesses when the reality was that *he* was usually the source of mischief. Would Orlando be finding similar resonances with Alasdair?

"We should get back to the matter in hand," he said. "I can imagine Mama on that same heavenly cloud shaking her head and telling me to keep to the point."

After a flurry of apologies, Bessy recommenced her tale. "After the flowers appeared I asked both the vicar and the verger if they knew who'd left them but neither of them could tell me. None of us had done it and we never did get a name, even though we asked around. Mr Smith, the vicar, felt the time of year could be significant, because the Great Exhibition had been officially wound up in October and would have taken time to dismantle."

Jonty nodded. "This mysterious person who left the flowers having taken a guess at roughly when Drayton would have died, maybe."

"Or having inside knowledge of the exact date, something they had perhaps only just discovered, given how long their visit was after the burial," Toby pointed out. "Or it might be that the location of the grave had only recently been learned about, given the gap in years."

"Yes. It was all very puzzling. You see, no more flowers—or indeed anything else—appeared on his grave over the next few months and we almost forgot about the incident until the next year when exactly the same thing happened at around the same time. One afternoon I came down here and there they were. Bronze chrysanthemums, same as had been left on the grave the previous year. This time I went straight to get Mr Smith and the verger and together we decided on a plan. We made a note of the date and we all put it on our calendars to make sure we each kept a special eye out for our—what did you call them, Dr Stewart?"

"Mysterious person?"

"That's it. An eye out for the mysterious person. When the time neared, I reminded both the vicar and the verger, although it turned out neither needed me to, because they were as ready and eager as I was to find out more. As it happened, Mr Smith was the one who saw her, on the day we'd predicted, leaving a bunch of bronze chrysanthemums." Bessy looked down at the headstone. "That was the final time. When the flowers didn't appear the next year, I got some from the gardens at the Old Manor and brought them here so he'd not miss out. I've carried that on, since. The family always make sure I have what I need."

"Did Mr Smith talk to her?" Toby asked.

"Yes. He passed a few words with the lady, as he would with anyone he met in the graveyard. It all went well when he was on the usual, 'Isn't it a lovely morning?' kind of thing but when he asked if Drayton was a relative, she became quite agitated. Poked him with her umbrella."

Toby laughed, then swiftly stopped himself. "Sorry, no laughing matter."

"You're all right, Mr Bowe. The vicar saw the funny side. A big, tall man like him being set upon by a tiny old lady." Bessy mimed stabbing her husband in the leg with an imaginary brolly. "Mr Smith reckoned she was perhaps losing her marbles as a result of her age, if that's not too crude. She was going on about how Drayton was her husband, but the vicar didn't think there's any way he could have been, unless she was around a hundred and he didn't think she was *that* old. In her eighties at the most. Anyway, a chap and a woman—both in their twenties, he guessed—came up the path at that point. The woman wrapped a blanket round her shoulders—the mysterious person's—and managed to calm her down. They apologized for the attack and explained that while their mistress was normally quite capable for her age, when she got upset she ended up confused and a bit unpredictable. The woman was her nurse and the man her driver, because she needed accompanying everywhere."

"Did either of those say whether she'd visited the grave before?" Jonty asked. "And could they furnish Mr Smith with any information about how she was related to Drayton?"

"When he tried to get information, the mysterious person got agitated again, so the woman took her off to the car. The driver stayed behind, as he said he felt the vicar was due an explanation. He told him that this was the third time his mistress had come to leave flowers and each occasion left her more distressed. The nurse, Miss Dacres, hadn't wanted her to come that November but her mistress had insisted she had a duty to perform. Mr Smith asked if Drayton really had been her husband or if that had been her confusion talking, not letting on he knew that situation would be almost impossible." Bessy studied the headstone again. "The driver said his mistress wasn't Drayton's wife, although she was a close relative. She'd apparently only discovered two years previously that he was buried here."

"And a name?" Toby asked eagerly. "Did Mr Smith get a name for her?"

Bessy slowly shook her head. "I'm afraid he didn't. He told me that he did ask, very courteously—Mr Smith was a very polite and pleasant chap, wouldn't have offended anyone—but the driver immediately said he had to go. Scurried off down the path like a cat who'd heard a gun go off, was the way Mr Smith put it. I'm sorry I can't be more helpful."

"You've been very helpful," Jonty assured her. "Solving a case is like completing a jigsaw puzzle. If you only had a handful of pieces, you couldn't tell what the finished picture would turn out to be. The more pieces, the clearer it becomes. Wouldn't you agree, Toby?"

"Absolutely. Even if some of them are missing, you can guess the end result." Toby gave Bessy's hand a squeeze. "Who knows if you haven't given us the vital part on which the whole depends."

***

"Do you really think we've just been given a vital part?" Jonty asked, as they walked back to the Old Manor. "Or were you simply being charming?"

"A bit of both, probably." Toby, who'd picked up a walking stick as they'd left the house, swished it at some long grass. "Did you habitually carry one of these when you were my age?"

"Not often. But if you wish to use a stick in the film for effect, be my guest. A handy prop, I'd say."

"Yes, like our pipes when we play Holmes and Watson. Plenty of capacity to use them for gesturing."

135

"I was amused that Mrs Cutting prefers you to Novello, a verdict with which I can't disagree. I saw him on the stage and found him something and nothing."

Toby flicked his cane again. "Well, if you saw him—or she met him—after he'd had his stint behind bars for petrol coupon misuse then it's no surprise either of you were disappointed. I've spoken to people who knew him before and they say that prison was hard on him. Although he only had himself to blame."

"Indeed. Not what he might have been in prison for, I hear." Jonty gave Toby a knowing glance. "He was lucky he wasn't caught doing something that might have completely ruined his reputation."

"Aren't we four in the same boat? Discretion having permanently to be our watchword." Unexpectedly, Toby chuckled. "Novello tried to seduce me, you know. Under the guise of an audition. I barely escaped with my virtue—and trousers—intact. Perhaps we should get back to discussing the case, or I risk you hearing all my secrets. You shouldn't be such a sympathetic ear."

Jonty snorted. "We'd better discuss this mysterious person with the flowers, then."

"Old Alasdair won't believe she existed. He'll think we've constructed the story to get one up on him. Actually, I'll correct myself. He'll probably believe in her—he's an old romantic—but he'll find the bit about the rose in Drayton's hand too far-fetched."

"If that's what Ramsey said he saw, then Alasdair had better trust in his word. Mr Smith's, as well. I didn't have much to do with him but I know of his reputation from my family. If he was right about our mysterious person's approximate age, she *couldn't* have been Mrs Drayton, unless she was a baby when she was married. What the driver told him backs that up."

136

"She could have been a much younger sister of his, though, or a cousin." Toby nodded slowly, clearly working things out as he spoke. "Close enough to feel it important she paid her respects, even if she wasn't always sure how she was related to him."

"The confusion about his identity makes sense. I had a great aunt who often, when I visited, thought I was my father. When she wasn't convinced I was *her* father." A situation that had been tricky to deal with, picking the right path between Jonty assuring her of his correct identity and simply pretending to be the person she thought he was.

"Oh! Now, I wonder..." Toby tapped his walking stick on the ground. "Miss Mysterious could have been Drayton's *daughter*. That opens the possibility of why people assumed he'd made a swift escape from his previous life. Had he got some poor girl up the duff? Such a child could have been in their eighties at the time the flowers started to be left. In which case, Miss Mysterious would have grown up having no idea that her father lay dead here."

"Yes. In that case, a mother might pretend that the father had died, which would in this instance have been both ironic and rather neat, a convenient lie actually being the truth. It would be quite a shock if Miss Mysterious—I like that name, by the way—later discovered said father was actually supposed to have run off. And a double blow when she realized his body had been found in strange circumstances." Jonty considered for a moment. "For her to discover that, she'd have had to be told her father's identity—maybe by her mother making a dramatic deathbed confession—and she'd then have either found the report of the inquest or been informed about it. A shame Mr Smith couldn't charm her name out of that driver."

"Said driver's reported reaction suggests that there might have been a particular reason to keep her name secret, doesn't it? Over and above not wanting to upset his employer. A particularly private person, perhaps? Afraid of the scandal of being illegitimate, even after all those years?" Toby suggested. "Or somebody who had become famous and didn't want folk to know she was born the wrong side of the blanket?"

"If so, she wasn't someone Smith recognised and as I recall he wasn't the type of clergyman who has no use for the world at large. He'd have recognised a famous actress or singer, for example. Still the notion holds if it was, for instance, a woman who'd married into a notable family." Jonty patted Toby's arm. "I'm speculating too much on too little evidence, of course, but it's an old man's privilege, and I'll extend that particular umbrella over you."

"Much obliged, although I have nothing much to add at present. How do we get a name for Miss Mysterious? I suppose we could go through all the death records between the last laying of the flowers and when the next one was due, if we can pin down the exact years. It would be a hell of a lot of work, though and we'd be relying on finding a name that signified something. If she'd married, we'd likely be sunk."

"I'd discard it as a wild goose chase anyway. She might not even have died between one visit and when the next was due but simply become too infirm—physically or mentally—to carry on what she felt was her duty. We need to find another way into the problem."

Toby halted, giving Jonty a puzzled glance. "Any suggestions as to what that might be?"

"Finding Miss Dacres. She might have been registered with a nursing agency so we could contact some of those or we could simply put an appeal in the newspapers. Unless— and please God this doesn't apply—she was killed in an air raid or something equally nasty that cut her off in her prime, the chances are Miss Dacres would still be alive. She was described as young in the thirties."

And with the smug satisfaction of having got one over the younger generation, Jonty picked up his pace, heading for his ancestral home and a nice long bath.

Chapter Eight

Relaxed and refreshed after his bath, Jonty fairly trotted off towards the drawing room for a pre-prandial something or other. He'd tapped on Orlando's door en route but found the room empty. A note, left conspicuously in the middle of the floor and addressed to him, suggested an explanation had been left for his absence.

Gone to make a telephone call. All will be revealed later.

Jonty chuckled. At their age, all rarely got revealed—if one took the phrase in the physical sense—although when it did, the experience was still blissful. Perhaps when they got back to Forsythia Cottage, a game of "What the naughty professor said to the expert on the sonnets" would be called for.

When Jonty reached the drawing room, the two actors were ensconced on the settee, hands notably empty of refreshment.

"You should have helped yourself," Jonty said, sweeping his hand towards the array of drinks of the sideboard. "Shall I?"

"We're happy to get a drink now you're here. It would have felt impertinent to help ourselves." Alasdair joined him. "Where's your partner in crime?"

"On the telephone. I have no idea to whom or what about." Jonty poured himself a sherry. "Shall we punish him by discussing this afternoon's developments before he arrives?"

"You will not." Orlando, grinning, appeared at the door. "All should be fair in love and investigating."

"You're in a chipper mood." Jonty generously handed Orlando the glass of sherry he'd poured for himself. "Useful telephone call?"

"Yes. Although it would be logical if I leave reporting on what it concerned until we've discussed the afternoon's developments or it might not make sense." Orlando took his seat. "Would you like to go first or shall we?"

"You first, please," Jonty said. "Technically, Goodwin takes precedence over Cutting."

He sat back and listened while Orlando and Alasdair recounted the various butlers' theories about treasure and those—including the remarkably and surely not coincidentally named Gerald Proudfoot—thought to be in search of it. They also shared some of the little asides, which Alasdair had noted because they might be useful for enabling the scriptwriters to produce an authentic tone.

"I think we must lay aside any notions of hidden treasure as a distraction," Orlando concluded. "If your father had the vault contents thoroughly examined in 1914, anything valuable would have turned up."

"I agree," Jonty said.

"Unless, of course, Proudfoot considered the Ogham as being beyond price." Toby scratched his head. "What do you think of the 'looking for the recipe' story?"

"I'd guess it may have been one the chump quickly thought of to explain why he was in the vault," Alasdair suggested. "Maybe not divulged to Jonty's grandfather but mentioned to whichever servant had the valeting of Proudfoot, in the expectation the story would get back to the cook. The surname alone would suggest a connection, irrespective of whether he was looking for Ogham or Drayton. As does the fact he was described as an antiquarian. However, what I'd like to understand is how Proudfoot ended up attempting the vault? I've been thinking about this ever since Goodwin showed us those books and have several questions. Starting off with why Proudfoot focused on the Old Manor, including how he was aware of

141

the vault's existence, through to him having learned the way of opening the door, which isn't at all obvious."

"I have some thoughts to offer on the first part, but I'll defer to Jonty for the other two." Orlando did so with a bow.

"I have the easy questions, then." Jonty took a sip of sherry. "That the vault exists is no secret. Several books making reference to the Old Manor mention it, especially if they deal with the time Cromwell was knocking things 'abaht a bit', to quote the song. As for getting through that door, it's inside information, again. All you'd need is the equivalent of Clarence—and I'm sure every generation would have had one—who'd gleefully take you to the entrance and demonstrate the mechanism without a second thought as to the consequences. We only took a family decision to be much more circumspect about who we shared the secret with after Heathfield when arse over tip. Just as well we did, considering events of the next forty years."

"You didn't consider trying to erase mentions of the vaults in those books? I guess it might be possible to alter later additions." Toby asked.

"There would have been no point if the earlier ones still were in circulation. And to attempt a change when war broke out would have drawn attention to them and us, when we wanted folk to be looking the other way." Jonty turned to his lover. "Orlando—part the first of Alasdair's questions?"

"Why did Proudfoot come here? We need to consider whether the Old Manor was his only port of call or if he had a list of places to search. While it might seem highly unlikely he would work his way around all the places which had loaned items for the exhibition, many of which could be factories, it's odd that he didn't come here until twenty years after the event. That would suggest something had delayed him, which might have been working through other

142

locations." Orlando spread his hands. "Or merely trying to discover where to search."

Alasdair nodded. "Yes, I'd concluded Proudfoot didn't know enough about where to look until he'd done all his research. Add to that allowing time for him to cultivate a friendship with the Stewarts, then getting himself invited here, although I find it hard to believe it had taken him since the fifties to achieve that."

"There are other explanations which would explain Proudfoot knowing where Drayton had gone much earlier than when he came here," Toby pointed out. "He could have been in prison or had been relocated abroad with his work, so had no opportunity to go looking until he'd respectively been released or returned home. He might even have been looking for Drayton in the countries where he was said to have gone. Far-fetched, I know, but we should consider all options that fit with what few facts we have."

"I agree," Alasdair said, "which brings me to my next questions."

Orlando raised his hand. "Sorry to cut you off, Alasdair, but I hadn't quite finished my answer. I'm most grateful to Toby for giving us his ideas, because it would be easy to forget there are other interpretations for the twenty year delay and that bears on what else I wanted to say. We must seriously consider the possibility that Proudfoot knew about the sealed chest and where it had come from because Drayton himself told him. Or told Miss Proudfoot, who passed the information on to Gerald, if he was her close relative. One of our few facts is that Drayton was involved with the exhibition and could have been directly responsible for handling what came out of the chest originally. It's equally possible that Proudfoot—the antiquarian, remember—was also on the staff. Alasdair, your other questions?"

"Firstly, have we grounds to eliminate Proudfoot as the murderer, vexatious as that would be?" Alasdair asked. "Circumstantial evidence to support that theory being that he would have known when and where Drayton had gone, so wouldn't need to look for him. Why go to look for the body anyway, if it hadn't turned up in all that time? Why not sit tight and not draw attention to yourself?"

"Inability to believe his luck or that it would hold?" Jonty suggested. "Not everyone has the strength of will to ignore what they've done. Like picking a scab on your knee when you were young. You know you shouldn't but you have to keep doing it. Proudfoot's age would work in favour of his having been around in the fifties, too, given that Papa spoke about him having been a bit wild in his youth which implies he no longer was. Young or wild, I mean."

Alasdair considered the answers for a moment, nodded and then moved on to his next question. "If Proudfoot was innocent of complicity in Drayton's death and was merely looking for him because he suspected he'd been killed and his body had been unlawfully disposed of, then why not tell the man's family what he supposed? If he had, they'd surely have mentioned such a thing to the police. Or he could have told the police himself."

"Perhaps he didn't want to upset the parents, if all he had was a theory about what had happened. Especially if Drayton senior was convinced his son had made himself scarce." Jonty glanced across as the door opened. "Ah, Goodwin."

The butler arriving to call them in to dinner seemed fortuitously timed and not just because Jonty's stomach had begun to rumble. Toby, mouth opening and shutting like a fish, only to find one of the others had begun to speak, seemed like he was about to burst. Most likely with the need to share what the Cuttings had told them.

"What did you two learn this afternoon?" Alasdair asked, as they took their seats at table. "Will it turn all our speculation on its head, in which case we'll look damned silly for having prattled on about our stuff without considering yours?"

"I think they chime rather nicely together. Although be prepared for something that sounds like it's from one of your films. I can see Margaret Rutherford in the role of Miss Mysterious, can't you, Toby?" Jonty spread some pate on his toast and left the actor to take centre stage.

Toby's account was a masterpiece of impromptu acting, unless he'd been practicing up in his room in order to polish the presentation. The show included reproductions of both Cutting's demonstration of Drayton going into the chest and the vicar being attacked with the umbrella. All Jonty had to do was corroborate any points and to suggest that trying to find Miss Dacres could be fruitful.

"Well, well," Orlando said, when the performance concluded. "If only the vicar could have discovered if your Miss Mysterious was called Proudfoot."

"Or Armitage or Geraghty." Toby set about his food, which had been neglected. "We mustn't forget *them*."

"You're quite correct to remind us." Orlando inclined his head. "Yes, that would create quite a different kettle of fish. The coroner or chief constable might well want the matter dealt with brusquely if they had a female relative whose reputation they wanted to preserve. Especially if they knew that Drayton was the reason it had been sullied in the first place. What say, Jonty? Jonty?"

"Oh, I am sorry. Off in a world of my own, as so often. There's been something nagging at me from earlier and what you've just said has set it off again," Jonty said, drumming the table furiously. "Oh, Lord. Yes, that's it. I should be stuck in a pillory for being an addle-pated idiot."

145

"What are you going on about?" Orlando asked. "He always does this sort of thing, Toby, so make sure it finds its way into your script."

"Noted. No doubt he does it to provoke such a reaction." Toby gave Jonty an understanding grin.

"You must visit us again, Toby. It's nice to have somebody in my corner. Anyway, what's just struck me is the remark the coroner made about Drayton falling. *A mortal pitch that struck him dead.* I'm sure that's a quote from one of the sonnets. Although I'm blowed if I can put a number to it offhand." Jonty tapped his fingers together. "I should have noticed at the time but I recall being a bit overcome by the closeness to Papa."

"Understandable."

"Thank you. Anyway, it's not from one of the earlier pieces—I know them all pretty well by heart, dealing as they do with old Will being besotted with a beautiful young man. Not that they teach you that detail at school. Or what Wilfred Owen wrote about young men who sell their favours to chaps."

Toby's jaw dropped. "Never. I thought he only wrote about war."

"You need to read *Who is the god of Canongate*, young Toby. Quite an eye opener." Jonty smirked. "And *Shall I compare thee to a summer's day* takes on quite a different hue when you consider it's a man writing about a man."

"We must try and work *that* into one of our scripts," Toby said, gleefully. "You could read it to Fiona, Alasdair, while I stand in the background and adopt a series of significant expressions. Not in the film about you two, I hasten to add."

"Much appreciated. There must be a book of sonnets somewhere here for me to consult." Jonty eased out of his chair.

146

"Don't you carry one about your person at all times?" Orlando quipped.

"Surprisingly, I don't. Make a note of that for your performance, Toby. I'm off to see what I can root out. See what conclusions you can come to in my absence."

When Jonty returned, book in hand, it appeared that no progress had been made on the case, mainly because the other three had apparently been reciting favourite bits of poetry over the last of their pate.

"Did you find anything?" Orlando asked.

"Yes. I located the relevant sonnet without too many difficulties and it's given me an idea, one which may sound quite daft." Jonty took his seat at table once more. "It assumes that the coroner, for whatever reason, wanted to make a private joke that only he might find funny. The mortal pitch line comes from a sonnet which begins, *Was it the proud full sail of his great verse*. Note the word proud. Then consider that sonnets are written in iambic pentameter or feet."

"Proudfoot!" Alasdair exclaimed. "Was he giving a subtle hint about the truth, knowing that nobody would get the reference? Rather like how Toby and I look at each other in the Holmes and Watson films?"

"Papa did say that Armitage was fond of jokes." Jonty closed the book, laying it carefully on the table.

"Why give anything away, though?" Toby asked. "Especially when you were going to whisk the inquest to a favourable conclusion."

Orlando shrugged. "Being a smart Alec? I can think of a case of ours where a murderer—albeit one who didn't appear to be all that mentally stable—seemed to be determined to see how far he could push things. As if he were trying to prove he could get away with whatever he wanted and not be suspected."

147

"I remember *him*." Jonty shivered in recollection of a particularly nasty piece of work. "The same could very well apply in this instance. Armitage could drop the hint and nobody would pick it up, because who'd suspect that the coroner himself could have any kind of link to Drayton's death? They'd just think he was being frivolous in an erudite manner, as Papa did. If the old man hadn't been so upset at Armitage's flippancy, he might not have preserved the remark for us to pick up on."

"If Armitage did have prior knowledge of the situation," Alasdair said, "I can imagine he'd have been cock-a-hoop to be given responsibility for this district. So that if Drayton ever did turn up, he'd be in a prime position to cover things over."

"And I can imagine my father showing one of his rare tempers if he suspected Armitage of such underhandedness. Papa had high and quite particular standards, both of his own behaviour and in his expectations of people around him. One of the reasons he never trusted our present queen's great-grandfather. He certainly didn't trust—or like— Armitage, so perhaps he picked up on some subtle sign suggesting shenanigans. That's not easy to say after a glass of oloroso, so don't have it put in the script, Toby." Jonty sniggered.

"You father was a man of high intelligence, one who liked a puzzle and a code," Orlando said, "and he'd have been wary of the law of libel, too. In both the spirit and the execution."

Alasdair, picking up some subtle sign himself, asked, "What do you have in mind by that, Orlando?"

"I was considering the possibility of Armitage not actually having quoted that sonnet and it being Mr Stewart's own insertion into his journal. One he knew his son would pick up on." Orlando looked to Jonty for comment.

"That's possible. If Proudfoot was still alive, Papa may not have wanted to make the link explicit." Jonty's brow crinkled in thought. "In which case, were there any other messages he left in his notes? I don't think it could have been anything like the first letter of each line, because he'd have thought that too obvious."

"Yes, he'd not have wanted to leave a message that anyone could pick out. He was perhaps writing with half a mind that his words would be for the benefit of those who came after him, perhaps fearing—for whatever reason—that he might not see the end of the war." Orlando gave his lover a sympathetic smile. "In which case, he'd have surely been inclined to include things that he'd know we'd spot but others wouldn't. And while we haven't picked them out yet, they may make sense in the course of time. It may be unprofitable to go searching for them at the moment."

"Agreed." Jonty nodded. "Let's stick with the one reference we think we've identified, whoever left it. Proudfoot. I'm going to state my belief that today we've had our first hint of a motive. Drayton gets somebody—Miss Proudfoot would be the obvious assumption—with child but doesn't do the decent thing and marry her. As a result of which, her brother or father or would-be-suitor decides the cad has to pay the ultimate price. It's even possible the deed is done by Miss Proudfoot herself, using the method Cutting demonstrated of getting a victim into a chest when he's bigger than you."

"Speculate away, but I'm going to be devil's advocate." Orlando said. "Why would she kill the father of her child?"

"Because he refused to marry her," Toby suggested. "He'd had his fun and didn't want to pay for it all his life. So, he ends up paying with his life."

"Or, to turn that on its head," Alasdair said, "he *did* want to marry her and she didn't want to be stuck with him. She's

149

an independent woman who believes that living with shame is preferable to a life with a wife beater or whatever about him puts her off. Or she's met somebody she prefers and who'll take her, unborn babe and all. Someone who might even have good reason to think the child is his."

Toby lifted his glass in evident approval. "I like that idea. Her preference being somebody of wealth and influence, to boot. Miss Proudfoot, later Lady Whatever, may well be performing rotations in her grave at this point as we slander her, but those roses in the dead man's hand and the chrysanthemums so lovingly put on his grave imply romance is involved somewhere."

"Miss Proudfoot could also be the injured party in another way, just as Drayton's father suggested," Jonty pointed out. "He gets another woman pregnant and wants to do the decent thing by *her*, leaving his previous girlfriend in the lurch. Not the native wife as mooted by Drayton senior, although that reference in itself suggests that he knew his son possessed what one might term a wandering streak. That would make Miss Mysterious no relation to the Proudfoots—should that be Proudfeet?—but provides a further motive for Drayton's death. I can envisage just such a scene in one of your films, perhaps with the lovely Miss Marsden playing in it, where Drayton—that would be you, I'm afraid, Alasdair—had bought those roses for his new sweetheart and the sight of them drove his previous one to clonk him over the head."

"Except that Fiona would never be allowed to kill Alasdair on screen," Orlando said. "What next in such a scenario? Mary Proudfoot shuts the chest, walks away and takes her chances?"

"Possibly. Unless she has a willing accomplice in the man we assume is her relative, Gerald." Despite the arrival of various staff to clear the table, Alasdair didn't pause his answer. "She either turns out to be extremely fortunate when nobody immediately discovers her crime or has help to keep it undiscovered. The employment of other bits of subterfuge, such as Drayton's supposed letters, are decided on after the event. We must remember that those communications in themselves tell us that his killer wasn't a stranger or had an accomplice who knew the victim well."

Jonty nodded, in silent appreciation of their guest carrying on the conversation. Quite right to let the staff hear, given how much help those below stairs had already provided to the investigation. Would they be having, or have had, a similar discussion over their meal? If so, he hoped the best ideas would eventually be reported back to the family's side of the baize door.

"I keep thinking about roses and bronze chrysanthemums," Toby said. "The remains of the flowers in the chest and the ones left on the grave—is there's any significance in the particular species chosen? It wouldn't be so easy to buy roses in late autumn, so had Drayton gone to special trouble to get hold of them?" A plate appeared before him, laden with fish pie. "Oh, my favourite. Did you know, Goodwin?"

"The cook is rather a fan of yours, Mr Bowe. She'd read somewhere that you're fond of the dish and so insisted you have it tonight." The butler smiled. "If I may be so bold, I doubt you'd get a better fish pie anywhere in England."

All conservation about the case stopped while they were being served. In the hiatus, Jonty cast a glance at Orlando, then smiled. His partner was wearing a familiar expression. If it had borne a caption, that would have read, "I know something the rest of you don't and the more we talk, the smugger I feel."

"Orlando," Jonty said, cramming a wealth of meaning into how he spoke the name. "Your telephone call. Are you being devil's advocate because it turned up a juicy fact that you're hiding from us?"

"I'm not hiding anything. I merely haven't wanted to interrupt the flow of information." Orlando quickly hid a grin.

"You rotter. I apologise for the professor's behaviour in breaking the proper rules of investigational conduct. He'll get a jolly good telling off in a moment." Jonty gave a startled maid a wink, then waited for the staff to leave before carrying on. "Admit it, you swine. You've been sitting there having a great time, potentially letting us go down all sorts of blind alleys, waiting to shine illumination on our mistaken endeavours."

"A man is permitted a little fun. And I'm not sure you *have* stumbled too far away from the truth. Perhaps the alleys bifurcate and come back together." It was a compliment to their guests that Orlando evidently didn't feel the need to explain the word "bifurcate". "I spoke to Dr O'Neill, our expert on Ogham, having rung St Bride's yesterday to arrange a chat with him. I didn't mention it in case nothing came of the plan. He says he's delighted to help us and is very excited about seeing the inscription. He confirms that there's almost certainly a mismatch between when the animal died and when the writing was done. If the tusk had been inscribed within a short time of the mammoth being alive then either the history of Ogham or the zoological timeline would have to be rewritten. It would be that momentous a discovery."

"So far, as expected," Jonty said. "Have some pie and then get to the important bit."

Orlando, for once, did what he was told. "I asked O'Neill if he had any idea who the Ogham experts were in the mid nineteenth century. After some beating around the bush—how it reminded him of some chap called Macalister but couldn't have been because he was barely out of short pants, if actually born, at the time we're interested in—O'Neill came up with a couple of names. One was Williams, who was based in Wales. O'Neill said it would be easy enough to find out more about him given his academic reputation but I'm suggesting we park the chap to one side for the moment."

Alasdair, evidently as eager as Jonty to hear why they should ignore Williams, a reason which was sure to be significant, nobly sacrificed his curiosity on the altar of Orlando's stomach. Not fair, as he said, for the excellent pie to get cold. They could wait; it couldn't.

Once they'd almost cleared their plates, they returned to experts in Ogham.

"The other man O'Neill referred to was a young Oxford don," Orlando said. "Name of Maximillian Armitage. Yes. The same as the coroner although we have no evidence—as yet—that they are related."

"See? He's an absolute rotter." Jonty shook his head. "I'll forgive you, for bringing that name, though. Was there anything else O'Neill had to say about him?"

"Two things. Apparently Armitage wasn't actually one of the great experts in the field of ancient languages but he was a first class man where large extinct mammals were concerned. Ogham was his side-line. Not unusual for the Victorians to have a range of academic interests, dabbling or serious."

"Extinct mammals indicate our pal the mammoth." Toby pushed away his plate with a contented sigh, the pie having been—as he'd vowed while eating it—the best he'd ever tasted, pre or post war. "Had Armitage been combining his two interests with said tusk?"

"The relevant dates don't preclude it. There's more, though. O'Neill told me Armitage was named as a

153

collaborator with another man on an excellent paper, one that investigated a connection between the origin of Ogham and the church. The man he wrote the paper with had an odd name, which O'Neill couldn't bring readily to mind." Orlando's delighted grin appeared again. "I asked if it might be Proudfoot."

"And was it?" Alasdair asked.

"He said it might well have been. He'll check for us and let us know when we're back in Cambridge. I can see that vexed expression, Jonathan Stewart, and I'm ignoring it. If the man had definitely been called Proudfoot I'd have said earlier."

"You are forgiven, although only by a mere hair's breadth. Like a last-minute kick that seals the game but only gets over because of a deflection off the posts." Jonty grinned. "Toby seems less pleased at the response."

"That's because I'm a bit vexed. I feel we have Proudfoots and Armitages coming at us from all directions and can't shake off the sensation that some of them are either mirages or wild geese. I'm not explaining myself very well." He turned to Alasdair. "Do you follow me?"

"Yes, I believe so. A suspicion that we're being served up a surfeit of them. Although isn't that what we wanted? The genuine link." Alasdair shot another hopeful glance at his plate but it was as bare of pie as every other one round the table.

"We did want a link and I suppose I'm being over suspicious because it's not like there can be an orchestrated campaign to point us in the wrong direction." Toby picked up the volume of sonnets. "If this book were called, say, *The Case of the Undiscovered Corpse* and it detailed our investigations so far, it would strike me that the author was ramming these families down the readers' throats. And then it would turn out that the lady at the grave was actually called Miss Geraghty and the only reason she was leaving flowers was because she didn't approve of the way her father had treated Drayton's death so dismissively. Actually, we'd better make her *Mrs* Geraghty, with the chief constable as her husband, as that might work better with what I'm guessing was his age."

"You are quite right to warn us against making rash assumptions," Orlando agreed. "We do keep ignoring the only person who's been referred to in the journals as being a bit peculiar."

Alasdair nodded. "His 'bizarre Napoleon obsession'. I think that was the description used. Although the ages wouldn't work for him to be Drayton's killer unless he was a dodderer in 1914."

"He wasn't," Jonty said. "Hence our doubts about some of his war stories. It's a good point not to forget him, though, because he's also the only person among those mentioned in our enquiries—apart from Clarence's potty pal—whom one of us has met."

"With the benefit of hindsight, which is reputed to be the clearest sight but which can get tainted with knowledge accrued in between, does he strike you as the sort of man who might bend the law to cover up a family scandal?" Alasdair asked.

"Quite possibly. I can state that he believed people had a duty to country, family and justice in that order, because he told my father so." Jonty steepled his fingers to his chin. "Can we go back to O'Neill and the strange name that may or may not be Proudfoot? It's noble of our colleague to go searching for him, because unless he has all the papers to hand it'll be a lot of work."

"Not necessarily." Given Orlando's fleetingly smug expression, he had at least one further revelation to come. "You see, O'Neill has the elusive real connection that we've been looking for. One stronger than yours and Geraghty's. He knows, from his student days, Armitage's grandson. The man was in charge of some of the digs O'Neill worked on."

Jonty slapped the table. "A hit. A palpable hit. I should be cross at you for your continued hiding of information—a bit too much like your arch-enemy Sherlock Holmes, so you might want to amend your ways—although you could redeem yourself by providing an address for said grandchild."

"I'm on the trail. Or rather O'Neill is, for reporting on when we see him." Orlando closed his notebook, which he'd probably only had open for effect as he'd barely consulted it. "One of the reasons I've been dilatory about sharing all the information is that I'm trying not to get too excited about what O'Neill has said. It could turn out that we haven't actually stumbled across a relation to the coroner and that the Ogham man is from another Armitage family. Or his academic collaborator was called Trayfoot or Pecksniff or something equally outlandish."

"Proudfoot itself sounds like it comes from a novel," Alasdair said. "Almost too daft to be true."

Orlando snorted. "No more so than Coppersmith and I can assure you that's real."

Alasdair's face fell. "Sorry, Orlando. Should have thought before I spoke."

"You're forgiven. Those of us who have to live with unusual surnames become accustomed to it. I've been known to have to explain to students that it's genuine rather being some identity I've assumed for investigating." Orlando seemed amused rather than upset at the fact. "I think they're quite impressed that it can be traced back to an Italian worker of copper who came up in the world. That would make an interesting film, as well, if slightly near the knuckle."

"Yes. Signor Artigiano del Rame made his fortune by, um, satisfying the requirements of a royal lady when her husband was unable to," Jonty said, with a quick glance at the door. As far as he knew, those exact details hadn't been shared with the staff.

Toby, wide eyed, said, "You should write a book about your lives. Or get someone else to do so. Don't let all these incredible stories be lost."

"Don't encourage him. He'd talk for hours about us and the college and his family." Jonty rolled his eyes. "His poor biographer would either be worked to a frazzle or bored to tears. And everybody we know would be getting the book for their birthday or Christmas and he'd be visiting them so he could expand on every incident as they read it. Let's get back to the case. Orlando?"

The professor blew out his cheeks. "I have nothing more to reveal and, to be frank, I think we've done all we can at present. Much more speculation will make me mad."

"Agreed," Toby said. "I want to go away and sleep on everything. I feel as if I've been in a hail of informational bullets and can't tell where I should point my Spit's nose next."

"A perfect analogy." Alasdair smiled. "Especially as I'm feeling like I used to when I had the inkling there were bandits coming up behind me but I couldn't work out where."

"Or a sniper ready and waiting across No Man's Land whose presence you merely feel. Yes, I understand that." Orlando nodded. "Jonty would call it a thought buzzing around his brain like a fly that he's aware of but unable to swat."

"I would indeed. A less poetic comparison although cheerier. By which I'm guessing that we're all feeling as though there's something we've missed today in the welter

157

of new information? A tiny fact that's gone unnoticed." Jonty scanned the others. "I wonder if it's the same one for each of us or whether four of the little sods have slipped through."

Chapter Nine

Sunday Matins proved a most pleasing service, with a sermon that was little short of revelatory. If Orlando hadn't counted it as being highly unlikely that the vicar had inside knowledge about the four guests from the Old Manor who were in his pews, he'd have thought one or two lines had been specifically aimed at them. And in a surprisingly positive way.

The text had come from Matthew and the main body of the homily had concerned the sanctity of marriage. The vicar—a pleasant old bird called Jones, which nicely chimed with his predecessor being called Smith—had included in his talk a later passage from the same gospel. In this Jesus had outlined, without condemnation, the three kinds of folk who couldn't get wed. Jones had explained what each of those categories meant, boldly in the case of those who had chosen not to have a partner for the sake of their faith and rather coyly when it came to eunuchs. His reference to the third type, those who'd been born unable to marry, had brought the revelation. It carried a distinct, if elliptical, hint that the passage could indicate those who preferred their own sex.

Jonty had clearly had the same thought, because he'd jabbed Orlando's leg at the time. There would be much to discuss later, away from prying ears.

The presence of the two actors in the congregation had produced, from the moment of their arrival, a small and very English style of sensation. This manifested itself mainly in nudges, whispers and people deliberately not looking in the men's direction if they were likely to be spotted doing so. Once Matins had finished, that decorum started to fray, with direct smiles aimed at both Toby and Alasdair, and one or two people being brave enough to approach the pair in order

159

to compliment them on their films. Jonty too had been nabbed, by a couple of people who remembered him from previous visits and wanted to have a chat. All this left Orlando free to observe the scene with amusement, up until the point he was approached by two women, one of whom quickly introduced herself as Bessy Cutting.

"You must be Professor Coppersmith," she said. "I wanted to thank you, as well as your friends, for looking into Mr Drayton's death. I'd love to ask you if you've discovered anything else since yesterday, but potatoes won't cook themselves and I have to get back home right now. This is my friend, Mrs Hammersley. We were chatting before the service about poor Mr Drayton perhaps getting justice at last and she says she might have something of interest to tell you." Bessy flashed a smile and left them.

Mrs Hammersley had to be older than Orlando, with a face like a wrinkled apple yet eyes as bright and sharp as a woman a third her age. "I hope you don't mind me catching you, sir, but when Bessy told me you were looking into Mr Drayton's death, I wanted you to know that I remember him being buried here."

"I don't mind at all being caught, especially when you can tell me about the funeral." Would it be hoping against hope that Mrs Hammersley would have a tale about a stranger who'd turned up to see the body interred? Or a floral tribute which had appeared, bearing the name of the sender?

"It was a lovely service. Quiet and dignified, but that's what you'd expect from the Stewarts, A few of us locals had been asked by the vicar to make up for a lack of the unfortunate man's own family and friends."

Collapse of Orlando's hopes. He still managed to smile encouragingly. "No strangers appeared to see Drayton off?

160

No roses or chrysanthemums appearing at the graveside from persons unknown?"

"I'm afraid there was nothing so exciting. Mind you it was all a bit of a nine days wonder and something to take our minds off events elsewhere. Sad to say that about a man's funeral, isn't it?"

"It is, Mrs Hammersley, although I do understand what you mean." It was easy to forget what a turmoil there'd been back then, the elation and the belief it would all be over by Christmas 1914 already dissipating in sensible quarters. "I also know it may appear odd for us to be so concerned with the death of one man when so many were lost in those years but it feels important to discover the truth, if we can."

She nodded. "I do so agree. Which is why I wanted you to hear this. I've always helped do the flowers in the church, from when I was barely more than a girl. Especially at Easter, when I've brought white lilies from my garden, and not just to signify the empty tomb. I want to remember those who've gone over the past year and are awaiting their own resurrection. That seemed particularly important during wartime."

"I would imagine it did." Orlando felt a frisson of excitement, spawned by a twinkle in Mrs Hammersley's eye that signalled the crux of her tale wasn't far away.

"Well, Easter of 1919, I had a lovely crop of lilies to put by the altar. I was in the church on the afternoon of Easter Saturday, putting them in the special tall vases we have, when I heard someone come in. I didn't look round, as I was at a fiddly part and anyway, you don't want to be nosy. When I'd done and was starting to clear away, I glanced up and saw a man I didn't recognise in one of the pews. He had his head bent, like he was praying or thinking."

"How very interesting." Orlando smiled encouragingly. Please let her finish the tale before one of the others

161

appeared to hear the disclosure also. Although, after the telling off he'd had last evening, he'd better be careful how he shared this new information—if he played the "I know something you don't" card too carelessly, he might find all bedroom privileges at Forsythia Cottage being withdrawn. Which, even at their age, didn't bear contemplating.

"When I'd done with my flowers and made my way down the aisle, I noticed this chap was in tears. Not unusual, at that time, given what had happened the previous few years. I wouldn't blame any man for crying if he survived and his friends didn't. Sorry, I'm going off track and you won't have all day to listen to me witter on." Mrs Hammersley flapped her hand. "I asked him if he was all right and if he wanted me to fetch the vicar. He said that was kind but no, he just wanted some quiet. He'd lost a good friend and had only just discovered where he'd been laid to rest. For some reason—I'd say it was God giving me a jolly good nudge—I felt I had to ask him if it was Mr Drayton he was talking about. He was that stunned he couldn't reply, only nod."

"He must have thought you could read his mind." A man, though, looking for Drayton's grave. Connected to Miss Mysterious or another thread to follow?

"I told him an angel must have whispered in my ear." She seemed to be welling up herself, in recollection of what must have been an emotional conversation. "I asked if he'd found the grave, which he had, and told him I'd been at the funeral. How we'd given Drayton a decent send off. He asked about that and how the body had been found and I told him all that I knew, which wasn't much. Not much for certain anyway, because a lot of what had been going around was just idle gossip. I suggested he contact the Stewarts but he said he'd decided against that. They had their own grief to deal with."

162

In spades. "Did he give a name?"

"No and I didn't think it right to ask. I could guess at how old he was, though. Similar to my age now, and wrinkled as a prune, although his mind appeared to be all there."

"Like you, Mrs Hammersley. Apart from the wrinkles," Orlando added quickly.

"Bless you, I've plenty of those. My mirror doesn't lie." The blush on her cheeks showed she'd appreciated the compliment, however. "Anyway, I left this chap to it. There was a motorcar waiting outside, one I didn't recognize, so I guess it was for him. Flowers on Drayton's grave, too."

"What sort?"

"Roses. They must have come from a greenhouse or the like because it was too early for them."

"Thank you, Mrs Hammersley. You've been very helpful." Orlando shook her hand, then watched her head off in the direction of what might be Mr Hammersley.

"What was that all about?" Jonty's voice sounded at Orlando's elbow. "Are you chatting up the ladies of the parish?"

"I'll tell you later when we'll all together. I'm not holding anything back but I do need to think it through. And no, I wasn't chatting up anybody, as well you know."

"Glad to hear it. I have a reputation to maintain here and association with a known lothario would besmirch it." With a gleeful grin, his lover scuttled away to have a quick word with the vicar, leaving Orlando to wonder if Jonty would ever grow up.

He also wondered if the mystery of Drayton's death would ever get clearer, instead of becoming ever more complicated, which is what it appeared determined to do.

163

Chapter Ten

"I'm feeling distinctly maudlin at leaving," Toby confessed, as he and Alasdair waited for the car to come round. They were all heading to the station together, to catch the same train to London. The extraneous items from the vaults had been carefully packed away to be borne in the luggage van along with their cases. The four had enjoyed a light lunch and each been given a wrapped portion of cake, should they become famished on the journey. As though they were schoolboys heading back for a new term, rather than grown men. "I've had a smashing few days."

"We'll be back here though, even if it's only for filming purposes." Alasdair glanced over to where their hosts were taking a fond farewell of the staff. "We mustn't lose touch with that pair. When filming's over *and* after we have a solution to the mystery, I mean. I'm not simply suggesting that so we increase our chances of being invited back here. There's a lot I still want to ask them about, concerning their lives."

"I agree. Much we can learn from them on all counts. I'm rather envious they'll be seeing the Ogham chappy without us. While taking Sergeant Granger out to dinner will be both entertaining and instructive, it won't be quite the same as wandering in the groves of academe."

"Don't discount the possibility that the names he can provide from a hundred years ago prove the key to everything." Alasdair's eyebrow somehow managed to convey how smug that would make him. "Ah, here they come."

All discussion of the case was put on hold until they were on the train and safely tucked up in a carriage they had to themselves, one which would allow the frankest discussions.

"I've two things I'd like to share with you," Orlando said, as the train got into motion. "The first is a thought, the second some unexpected information that only turned up this morning. I will give them chronologically as they occurred."

Alasdair noted the grin Jonty was trying so hard to hide. Was *he* as verbose at times and did Toby take equal delight in it?

"That sermon got me thinking," Orlando continued. "There is a possible element in Drayton's death we've all avoided discussing, either because it's so unlikely we've each dismissed it out of hand or it hadn't occurred to us."

"Are you referring to the bit in the sermon about those who are born unable to marry?" Toby asked. "Yes. I noted that. Rather broad minded of the vicar, I felt."

Alasdair, who'd not been paying as much attention as he should have done to the sermon, because he'd been intrigued by a memorial to a young soldier who'd died in Cawnpoor and had got into wondering what said chap had looked like, realized he must have missed something significant. He'd have to get Toby to explain, later. Because if he asked now, he'd look a right chump.

"Exceptionally broad minded if he meant what we clearly thought he did. Taking that hint, let's imagine that either Drayton or one of his pals was so inclined. He was given those flowers that he clutched in death, but by a man." Orlando glanced round his companions. "Miss Proudfoot, who might simply have been his young lady for the purposes of camouflage, got wind of his true nature and became riled. Then this loving gesture from Drayton's boyfriend to him was the last straw. She committed violence on him."

"It could be." Toby raised an eyebrow at Alasdair. "*We* have a succession of young ladies to provide us with

165

camouflage, and while none of them have yet resorted to belting us in anger, at least one has become rather annoyed when it's become plain that there's no romance in the offing. It might also be a motive for one of Miss Proudfoot's champions—family or friend—to take revenge on him for toying with her affections."

"Or Drayton may have been the one giving the flowers and the young man he fancied wasn't interested," Jonty said. "He thrust them back into Drayton's face and thrust *him* into the chest while he was at it. Determined to rid himself of unwanted advances. So many possibilities, all of which are grand ideas, but the vicar's sermon, illuminating as it was, and our personal natures aren't evidence. We have no indication that another man was involved. Oh, you swine." He slapped Orlando's arm. "That's part the second, isn't it? I bet your fancy woman from church provided this chap for you on a plate."

"Is that the very smiley lady you were speaking to? She reminded me of my granny." Toby, who'd been slowly opening his packet of cake, broke off a small piece and consumed it. The rest might not last long, given his immediate delight at tasting it.

"Mrs Hammersley. Yes. She had quite a story to tell and I haven't been hiding that fact from you, merely setting the scene for you to receive it." Orlando regaled them with a tale of an unnamed Easter visitor, some possibly angelic inspiration and the link to roses being left on Drayton's grave. "So we *do* have a man in the case, one who was around the same age as the deceased and in tears over him, not long after he was found. Whether his leaving roses, as opposed to another flower, bear any significance I can't tell."

"A Mr Mysterious to add to our Miss. Definitely not young enough to be his son, though, if your girlfriend was

166

right in guessing his age." Jonty pursed his lips. "Another time lag for us to explain, albeit a shorter one. The inquest and the funeral were some years before. If Mr M had read about them in the newspapers, why so long to get to the grave? He couldn't have been otherwise occupied out in France or Belgium."

"What about him being ill?" Orlando suggested. "Or not finding out that Drayton had been discovered until the spring of 1919, so he got here as quickly as he could?"

"Whatever the reason, I'd say we're safe in assuming he didn't share the information with Miss Mysterious back then, or why would it take her so long to pay her own respects at the grave?" Toby said. "Another person we need a name for. Would he by any glorious chance have written it in the visitors book, if the church had one back then?"

Jonty narrowed his eyes. "I believe it did. Or certainly had previously. There was quite a scandal one year—before we met, Orlando—when some young scamp made an entry which was inappropriate. The rapscallion was never run to ground although I'm fairly sure a Stewart wasn't involved. They'd have spelled the rude words correctly, for one thing. I'll ask either—or both—of Bessy Cutting and Dr Jones to get on the trail."

"I wonder why Bessy didn't know about the flowers being laid previously?" Alasdair asked. "I suppose if it was merely the once and not the time of year flowers were normally laid there, she might not have noticed."

"Tending the grave wouldn't have been under her wing back then." Toby broke off another piece of cake, although it appeared to be an automatic action. Something was clearly bothering him. "Will names help us, though? While the appearance of a new lead is exciting, I've been increasingly struck by the likelihood of our not reaching a definitive conclusion to this case."

Orlando leaned across to pat Toby's arm. "Never say die. Think of the progress we've made this weekend alone. Lots of information, yes, but we'll refine out the dross and narrow it down."

"Orlando's right. We've never been defeated yet and we don't intend to be now," Jonty said. "Too early in the business for despair or anything like it. Let's see how the cards lie in another week."

"Back to our four suits analogy?" Alasdair smiled, glad of some levity to raise his lover's mood. "What did you say clubs and spades would do, Orlando?"

"Fight the forces of darkness and delve for truth." Orlando nodded in satisfaction, those evidently being two things he valued greatly. "I'd say we've done that quite well so far. Certainly the latter. How have the hearts and diamonds fared?"

"Well," Jonty said, "I think we've also been diamond hard when needed. I confess to a wobble or two over the old man's papers, but Toby rescued me when I could easily have left you three to read them. Then there's the matter of beauty and charm, which we could never not display. You should have seen how young Toby worked his magic on Bessy. I suspect if he'd been one of those types who are all charm on the screen and obnoxious in real life, we'd have made much less progress with her. Bessy not being one to suffer fools or dilettantes gladly, I'd have said."

"You're beginning to sound like the Landseer publicity department, although they'd be more subtle about the kind of actor you allude to with the 'charming on screen but obnoxious off' part." Toby, spirits clearly lifting, toyed with some more cake. "I think we need a plan of action. Are we to report information as it turns up or wait for a conference over the telephone, say a week tomorrow when things may have moved on?"

"I'd say only immediately report things which prove we're on the wrong tack or take us off on a new one," Orlando said. "Best to deal with the questions we have so far rather than lay on more. There are plenty of those."

"Of course, we don't have a deadline looming on this," Jonty pointed out. "We have world enough and time to make sure we get it right. Although should Orlando and I get knocked down by a runaway lorry on our way home then we'll expect you to take up the challenge."

"The same applies to us," Alasdair said, with a fond glance at Toby. "Only we're more likely to be trampled to death beneath a horde of admiring fans."

"It's a deal." Orlando nodded. "One way or another, we'll make sure Drayton isn't abandoned again."

***

By Wednesday, Alasdair could look back with satisfaction at the last few days.

For a start, there'd been a successful meeting with the wardrobe department to begin kitting him out with appropriate Great War era costumes, both academic and everyday. He'd rather enjoyed swishing around in a black gown and had felt his appearance compared favourably to a picture of Orlando from a similar time. Then there'd been a potentially tricky meeting with both Sir Ian and the chief scriptwriter to mention the delicate matter of rhubarb leaves. They'd eventually agreed to look for another means of killing the main character, the neatness of the plot being overridden by the fear of appearing foolish. Landseer pirates may dress as no man who ever took to the high seas dressed but their plots were always watertight.

Now he had a midweek dinner with the admirable Sergeant Granger—and Toby—to look forward to. From the police officer's happy yet enigmatic response to the invitation, he must have further information to share. As Granger stated, he'd be singing for his supper and the song could prove worthwhile.

They'd arranged to meet at a small restaurant few people knew about and which, according to Alasdair, could knock the Savoy's catering into a cocked hat, making a small selection of items go a very long way due to the sheer excellence of the cooking. Once assembled, the three men wasted very little time on pleasantries. The actors were desperate to bring Granger up to date with everything they'd learned at the Old Manor, not least because they valued his astuteness and reckoned that his independent eye had a good chance of either spotting something they'd missed or leading him to a fresh insight on the mystery.

"It strikes me," Granger said as they concluded their account with the tale of Miss Mysterious's final visit to the grave, "that you've got too much information on one hand and not enough on the other. Strange writing on an old tusk, lumps of old dross, a sealed chest in a hidden vault, lots of different people either popping up mysteriously or trying to pop down into that vault, and yet you've not got any real, proven connections between the different parts. All of which won't be news to you."

Toby pursed his lips. "It isn't. We were hoping you might help us find one or two of those links. Produce a highly influential Geraghty or Armitage whose descendant would do all in their power in the way of protecting the ancestral reputations."

"Or a Gerald Proudfoot, although Toby isn't going to be happy if you throw him at us. Especially if you bear new people of that surname," Alasdair added with a grin.

Granger returned the smile, used by now to the banter between this pair. "Well, I have neither of those surnames

170

listed for the three colleagues of Drayton who were interviewed after his disappearance, although that's not to rule out men called Armitage or Geraghty being involved. As Mr Firestone says, absence of evidence isn't evidence of absence."

"Our new friends from Cambridge would appreciate that. What were these three men called?" Toby asked.

"Gray, Southerton and Williams. Are those any use to you?" Granger took a draught of beer.

Alasdair shrugged. "Williams might be. Remember the old writing on the tusk? One of the experts in Ogham back at the time of the Great Exhibition was called Williams. We'd parked him to one side because the other experts presented a better chance of a link to the case, given what we knew last Saturday. Perhaps we'd better unpark him."

"We'll get the Cambridge connection onto that," Toby said, "it being more a job for academics than policemen."

"I'm glad he might be helpful. In terms of their statements, Hugh Williams's was the most interesting, I have to say." Granger took another swig of ale. "The other two said pretty much the same as each other, that one day Drayton had upped sticks and gone. He'd left a note to say he'd been made an offer of a job that started immediately and he was very sorry to leave them in the lurch. While it was annoying, they didn't think it suspicious because Drayton didn't leave anything personal behind and the note appeared to be in his handwriting."

"Everything adds to the notion of his death being covered up from the start," Alasdair said. "By somebody who could imitate his scrawl and had access to his effects both at work and at his lodgings. I've had a chilling image come to mind of somebody standing calmly producing a forged note while leaning on the chest itself wherein Drayton was either already dead or slowly suffocating."

"Aye, well murder's a nasty business, Mr Hamilton. I know there's a thrill from running the culprit to ground and I'm as bad as anyone, with the old, unsolved crimes I can't help going back to and wondering about." Granger stared ruefully into his beer. "But we must always remember the victims, both those who died and those left behind to mourn. Or, in this case, those never to find out what happened to their son or sweetheart."

"Before we turn to Williams's statement, can I ask if you ran across any mention of flowers?" Toby asked.

"Like the ones Drayton was supposed to have been holding?" Granger shook his head. "Not a word."

"What about a heartbroken male friend, like the man who was crying in the church at Easter? Oh," Alasdair paused. "We didn't mention him, did we?" Possibly because of their natural reticence to touch on matters that could potentially come too close to their true relationship.

"Not that I recall." Granger sat back, nursing the remains of his drink and ready to hear the overlooked piece of information. When the actors had related the tale of Mrs Hammersley's lilies and her angelic nudge, the sergeant gave a satisfied nod. "Now, I can't prove that man in the pews was Williams, but there's what you might call a certain resonance with his statement. Like the others, he had no idea where Granger had got to but he was more troubled about the fact. Drayton was his best pal, he said, which I'm broad minded enough to recognise might have been a euphemism for more, although I'd also take it at face value. If my best mate disappeared without telling me face to face where he was off to, I'd be upset. I'd smell a rat, as well."

"Williams smelled one, too?" Toby asked.

"You can read between the lines and come up with that, yes. He asked to be kept abreast of any developments because he didn't know Drayton's family well and wouldn't

172

hear directly from them." Granger shrugged. "I know times were different then and what was 'done' and 'not done' among the posh folk seems laughable now but surely he could have dropped them a line and asked them? Especially if he was their son's close pal."

"That certainly seems odd. As though he didn't get on with the family." Which might weigh on the "romantic relationship" side of the scales, although were plenty of potential reasons why the Draytons didn't get on with him. Something as simple as a disagreement over politics, for which little verification would likely still exist. "It also might argue against Williams being implicated in the death."

"Or be a clever ruse to make it appear so," Toby pointed out. "Notwithstanding any of that, he's a feather in your cap, Sergeant Granger. Shall we order pudding in celebration?"

They chose a lighter option than the Stewarts' famous jam roly-poly with which to end a meal which had been on the robust side so far. Alasdair had been certain his waistband had been groaning as he'd finished his last potato: water and lettuce for the next fortnight might be the best strategy.

Granger beamed, eyes wide, when the meringue and fruit confection arrived at their table. "This is the best part of any meal, for me. I've been burdened—or blessed—with a sweet tooth since I was in nappies." After a few mouthfuls, which clearly didn't disappoint, he continued, "Now, you asked me about a Gerald Proudfoot. I can state that he's not someone whose statement was taken when Drayton was reported as missing, unless it was taken and misfiled but I doubt that. Nor is he mentioned by name in any of the relevant documents."

"I think I'm quite relieved about that," Toby confessed, carefully demolishing a tricky bit of meringue. "I feel as though fate has been thrusting Proudfoots at us willy-nilly and I've begun to think they're all smoke and mirrors."

Granger chortled. "Sorry to disappoint you, but it looks like fate's been doing it again. I've found him elsewhere in our records and I wouldn't have done if some eagle eyed and efficient officer of ninety years or so ago hadn't left a note right at the bottom of the Drayton file, pointing to the coincidence of names with the missing man's sweetheart."

"A shame they didn't take it further than noting the coincidence," Alasdair said, "although I suppose we should be grateful for their action."

"I guess it's only with hindsight—especially with what you've been telling me earlier—that you can see a potential link." Granger gave his spoon a surreptitious lick. "There was a complaint made against a Gerald Proudfoot for damage, allegedly accidental. He'd been a house guest at a place up in Shropshire and was found trying to access their priest hole. His family helped smooth it all over, saying that he was a sleepwalker and known to do odd things while he was actually out like a light, things he'd have been horrified at when awake. He'd pleaded that much himself when he'd been discovered by the butler, who'd heard a noise and gone to investigate. Proudfoot said he had no idea what he'd been doing at the concealed entrance nor how he'd got there."

Toby, after sharing a knowing glance with Alasdair, asked, "If it was smoothed over, why was a complaint lodged and how did Proudfoot not come to be charged?"

"The complaint was lodged by the eldest son of the house, after Proudfoot had left, because he'd felt his hospitality had been abused. He'd been the one to invite the chap there, you see. His parents were more pragmatic, there being minimal damage and the reparation was paid for by Proudfoot's father, alongside a handsome donation to the local church. An institution which the lady of the house was deeply involved with." Granger raised an eyebrow. "All done and dusted, but my predecessors kept a note about it. Just as well."

"He wasn't reported for doing the same anywhere else?" Alasdair scooped up the last of his dessert.

"Not as far as I know. Are you thinking he might have been going round various places looking for Drayton and never struck lucky because he was caught in the act at the Old Manor?"

Toby nodded. "That's exactly what we've been speculating on, sergeant. Proudfoot didn't use the sleepwalking excuse at the Old Manor, which might suggest it had little truth in it. If he had tried elsewhere than there and Shropshire he wasn't caught and if he'd got a reputation for these midnight ramblings it didn't stop him being invited as a house guest

"Did his family know what he was up to, I wonder?" Alasdair asked. "Maybe, if he's related to Miss Proudfoot, she or they may have put him up to it. We don't by any glorious chance know if the family at whose home the alleged sleepwalking took place had any involvement with the Great Exhibition?"

"I thought you'd want to know that." Last scoop of pudding consumed, Granger pushed his plate away and sat back contentedly. "I could claim that I've been doing lots of work to get an answer but that would be a lie. It was in the original complaint, how the son of the house had first got to know Proudfoot when they were involved with the New Zealand exhibit. It was a particular interest of his family. We know no more than that and without an extensive search of the records from the time—if they exist—I doubt we'll pin anything else down. Shame we can't have a record of people's thoughts and motivations."

"Vast as they'd be, they'd certainly help you with your unsolved Victorian murders. As to our unsolved Victorian murder," Toby gave an embarrassed grin at the link, "while we're working with circumstantial evidence, we should be grateful things keep coming back to Hyde Park and antiquities. A couple of times we've compared detecting to completing a jigsaw and it's good that none of the pieces we've turned up seem to be from a different picture."

***

In the cab they caught from outside the restaurant, the actors decided that what Granger had told them didn't warrant contacting their Cambridge colleagues. Williams was a common enough surname and that may not have been the name of the man in the church, anyway. Still, things were moving in a positive direction.

The icing on the cake was to arrive home and discover that a letter from Cambridge had been delivered to Alasdair in the second post. Not, thank goodness, notice of a significant development in the case—thunder stolen wouldn't be gratifying—but a message to say that young Adam, Jonty and Orlando's factotum in training, had a suggestion for a poison which could be used in the film plot. A poison that nobody had used in any fictional setting, as far as he was aware. He was apparently afraid of being presumptuous but Jonty had insisted that his clever idea should be shared. More detail would be forthcoming when the lad had double checked that his idea was viable, especially as he'd been the one to warn against the rhubarb leaves murder, so didn't want to fall into the same trap.

"Not the terrible unknown poison favoured by authors?" Toby asked, having been reading the communication over Alasdair's shoulder. "You know, one that allegedly originates with the Amazonian Indians, who'd probably never come across the stuff?"

"I doubt it. Given Orlando's antipathy to the Holmes stories, he'd surely veto such a suggestion."

"Let's hope that Adam comes up with his wonderful idea before the script rewrites get too far." Toby flopped into a chair, sprawling himself attractively.

"He's got a fair chance of doing so." Alasdair draped himself in the chair that faced his lover, hoping he'd appear just as alluring. "The last thing I heard, the writers were scratching their heads for an alternative method of killing so had put the details of the murder on hold while the rest of the script is constructed around them. After all, the specific how is less important than the why and who."

Toby chuckled. "Less important also than the vehicle for me suffering nobly, you brooding with unrequited passion and a triumphant ending in which you get the girl."

"Will they still be using that formula when I'm Orlando's age? Trying to win a geriatric Fiona from the arms of her current admirer?"

"I don't think even Landseer would envisage that. They can keep us as Holmes and Watson almost in perpetuity but there'll be newer and younger combinations of stars to delight the audiences. Which could work out beautifully, as we might be allowed to fade into semi-retirement, to keep a little house together where you can write detective novels and I can tend bees."

Alasdair raised his uninsured eyebrow. "I didn't know you had apiarian ambitions."

"I don't. I was thinking of Yeats and his bee-loud glade. Only I wouldn't want to be living alone, nor indeed having a cabin made of wattle and clay." Toby chuckled. "You can have nine bean rows, though. I like beans. I wonder if Jonty grows them in that idyllic garden of theirs?"

"We'll have to ask. Purely for research purposes." Alasdair, yawned, stretched, then went to perch himself on the arm of Toby's chair. "I know that we're in a situation with this film where art is being encouraged to imitate life but it would be most gratifying could the reverse apply as well. By which I mean it would be a triumphant ending to this evening were I allowed to secure the love interest for myself."

"You don't need the benefit of a Landseer script to do that." Toby got up then extended a hand to pull Alasdair in the direction of the bedroom. "We'll improvise this scene as we go along."

Chapter Eleven

Dinner at the O'Neill's house, on the Friday after Jonty and Orlando's return from Sussex, was an event deserving pleasurable anticipation. Mrs O'Neill's cook was said to produce a wonderful curry, something Derek O'Neill described as a marvel of ingenuity given the current situation regarding food supplies.

The expert on Ogham had come to St Bride's at the end of the war, after distinguished service in Burma. That was a time in his life which he refused to discuss with anyone, other than stating he was glad the Gurkhas had been on the side of the Allies and not against us. He, too, had committed the sin of sitting in Orlando's particular chair in the Senior Common Room, exactly as Jonty had some forty years previously, although the eventual outcome hadn't been the same. O'Neill had a wife, Alice, and two delightful children. However, he and Orlando had formed a friendship based on their love of bridge, although their bidding styles were sufficiently different to prevent them playing as a pair.

Friday would see not just a good meal taken in good company, but a chance to discuss all matters Ogham related. Alice, being a biologist, had her own expert opinion to offer.

"That's a fine mammoth tusk," Alice said, as they sat in the conservatory enjoying a pre-prandial sherry in the rays of the westering sun. "Not as big as the average, so either from a relatively immature individual or—more excitingly—from an as yet unknown species of pygmy mammoth. There is great debate about whether a third species of elephant exists at present, one that is significantly smaller than its relatives, so if this is a mature tusk..." She shook her head. "Sorry. One of my favourite topics, speculating about species which may or may not exist."

"We all have our pet subjects." Orlando gave her an encouraging smile. "Could this be part of a tusk, one that's been broken at some point either in life or post-mortem?"

"I'd say not. It's quite complete." Alice passed the item to him. "I'd also say no carnivore made those scratches on it. Quite unlike the marks a predator would leave. At a pinch, one might consider them consistent with the process of de-fleshing, but ivory doesn't need that done to it."

"Ogham it is, then?" Jonty asked, dandling a small and sleepy O'Neill upon his knee.

"I believe so, although not original, at an educated guess. A modern replica." Derek had their other child snuggled next to him, happily reading a picture book and cuddling one of the hand axes. Orlando and Jonty had met young Sebastian before, when he'd come to see a rugby game at St Bride's and had proved very interested in the rules. Not all of which were being observed on the field of play. "There have been many experts in the field of Ogham—it's history and interpretation—and a fair few dabblers. I'd say this was the work of either a better-than-usual dabbler or a slightly off form expert."

"Why would you say that?" Orlando turned the ivory in his hand.

"I've inspected the lines closely and their formation strike me as lacking in confidence, if that makes sense and isn't just me reading into them what I want to see. As though they'd been laboriously—if accurately—copied by the writer, rather than them having the confidence to do such a thing naturally."

"That makes perfect sense," Jonty said. "Does the writing, though? Can you translate it?"

"I've tried my best. With some input from a colleague at Trinity." O'Neill took the tusk back, fingering the marks as he spoke. "What they appear to mean may not, of course, be what the writer intended them to mean. It could be referring to a place. The place where the ash tree was burned and purified. Does that help?"

"Not particularly, although in my wildest dreams I couldn't have hoped it said, *I, Maximillian Armitage, intend murder.*" Jonty adjusted the position of his charge, the child having fallen asleep on his lap.

"Funny you should say that, because Armitage was one of those I had in mind as the writer. I suppose it was his interest in animals that made him spring to mind, especially as I knew—from his grandson, Clive—that he collected fossils, bones and the like. Couldn't resist a piece of large mammal. I'd also seen an example of the older Armitage's reproduction Ogham, if we can so name it. In fact, I can state that I've seen it in action." O'Neill grinned.

"In action?" Orlando said. "I don't follow you at all. What had he put Ogham on?"

"A couple of things to amuse his smaller family members, apparently. Clive had a cricket bat which his grandfather gave him as soon as he was old enough to wield a full size one. On the back it had some scratches that were supposed to signify both the willow tree—from which the bat was made, obviously—and steadfastness. Appropriate for a batsman like Clive, who had a touch of the Trevor Bailey about him. He blocked my bowling on more than one occasion."

"I can understand and greatly admire the reasoning behind the cricket bat but what about the tusk?" Jonty asked. "Why would he write on it? A mere act of whimsy or did the thing, like the bat, have a deeper meaning?"

"I would first consider the option that it's merely a label," Alice said, rising to take the child from Jonty and no doubt whisk her to bed. "If he found the tusk near an ash tree and it—or bones with which it was deposited—showed burning or cleansing. Such as might happen if the meat had been stripped off with a scraper before or after cooking. As is quite possible, had the creature formed a tasty dinner for one of our ancestors. Terribly prosaic and not the answer you'd want, I know."

"If it's the truth," Orlando said, "then it matters not what we want." Once his hostess had left the room with her charge, he asked O'Neill, "Do you think it's merely a label?"

"I most definitely doubt it. I never met Maximillian Armitage but from what I've heard about the man, I'd say that would be too mundane an explanation. Clive thinks the same: it would have meant something particular, although he can't shed any light on what or for whom. You also wanted to know about Armitage senior's collaborator on the paper, didn't you?"

Jonty nodded. "Yes. He of the strange name which we're hoping will be Proudfoot."

"Then you're in luck. G R Proudfoot. Funnily enough, like Armitage, he wasn't primarily an expert in this field. That's one of the reasons Clive could tell me something about him, because this pair had put the academic cat among the pigeons, writing so lucidly about an area that wasn't theirs." O'Neill sniggered. "Some Victorians liked a touch of the polymath, though."

"What *was* he an expert on?" Hopefully something that didn't take them off down another track. Orlando mentally crossed his fingers.

"Early metal working. Prior to the time of Ogham and later than the era when that tusk was roaming around as part of its shaggy bearer. But he also wrote papers on volcanic activity in the Mesozoic era and a possible meteor strike in China, the best part of a thousand years ago. Do any of those help?"

"They might or might not. The man's initials are certainly suggestive that it's the same Proudfoot—Gerald—who tried unsuccessfully to access the Old Manor vaults eighty years ago. Perhaps he was after the iron slag, if he was an expert in metal working, although it seems an awful lot of effort to get that back even if it were his in the first place. If the two lumps were huge gold ingots, that would be a different matter. Real treasure, as some of the staff believed was hidden there." Jonty blew out his cheeks. "Irrespective of any such theories of secret riches, the only thing we can think of that would be worth such a midnight foray is locating Drayton's body."

"If Proudfoot thought Drayton was in the vault then why not ask the police to search it? Ah, no, stupid question." O'Neill raised his hand. "You wouldn't want to accuse such a notable family of hiding dead bodies unless you were sure of your grounds."

"Exactly. While the Stewarts aren't the sort to raise a huge stink about being falsely accused," Orlando gave Jonty a nod, "their standing and connections would still make anyone reluctant to do so."

"Did you ask your pal Clive Armitage whether he's related, however distantly, to the Armitage who was presiding over inadequate inquests in 1914?" Jonty asked.

"I did and he is. Not that closely—cousins several times removed or second cousins or whatever it's called. Fortunately, he's the keeper of the family bible and the long line of who begat who is preserved." O'Neill rose, in order to deposit his son, now asleep but with his hand clasped around the axe, on another chair. He tenderly covered the boy with a blanket.

Orlando, moved by the paternal love on display, said to Jonty, "Can he keep the axe, at least for this evening?"

"I'd say let him keep it in perpetuity. The Stewarts have no claim on the thing in the first place and until the real owner steps forward—which is most unlikely—it's as safe in young Sebastian's hands as in any." Jonty's nod sealed his approval. "He bears a nice Shakespearean name, as well, so that's fitting."

"Thank you. It might prompt an interest in the subject. Too easy as parents to ram your enthusiasms down your offspring's throats, so better to let them develop their own passions." O'Neill patted the boy then took his seat again. "Sebastian strikes me as being very taken with you two, so he'll regard Uncle Jonty's present as an absolute treasure."

"Tomorrow you should tell him that, if he's good, his nice pal Professor Coppersmith will come round one day and play cavemen with him. He's had plenty of practice at make believe with various generations of my young relations. As a result, he's almost as accomplished at that as he is at bridge."

Orlando harrumphed, secretly delighted at the prospect of playing an avuncular role. "If we may turn our attention from troglodytes to the Armitage family, what's the exact line of relation between Maximillian Armitage and the coroner?"

"The coroner was the grandson of Maximillian's brother, Horatio. Who'd a penchant for big game hunting, apparently."

Jonty whistled. "That close?"

"And—" O'Neill paused as his wife re-entered the room, to propose they should go in to eat while all was calm children-wise. "Gentlemen, there's one last thing I have to tell you but having opted for a cook instead of a nurserymaid, we daren't keep her offerings waiting."

"Indeed. Food can spoil but facts won't." Orlando gave a little bow as he rose, although he couldn't help wishing

184

Alice had arrived a couple of minutes later. Perhaps this was fate's way of punishing him for the times recently he'd been holding back information until the last moment.

Once they were settled, plates laden with a curry that looked—and smelled—every bit as good as they'd hoped for, Jonty said, "That 'and' of yours, Derek. Pray continue with it."

"It concerns something I wouldn't have thought to quiz Clive about, had it not been for the further questions you'd been asking and, I confess, my own growing interest in the case." He loaded a spoon of chutney onto his plate. "I enquired about Horatio's wife's name. It was Mary Proudfoot, they were wed in 1852 and she was the sister of the Proudfoot who was co-author of the paper."

"Game, set and match." Jonty rapped the table. "I refuse to believe that we have two women of that name. It has to be Drayton's young lady."

"Was Horatio his rival in love, do you think?" Alice asked. "I confess it goes against my sensibilities as a scientist to jump to such conclusions without evidence but this detection lark is quite addictive. The more I've learned, the more I want to make connections."

Jonty, who'd just taken a mouthful of curry and was clearly enjoying it, said, "Think of it like discovering a fossil. You might only have a few bones to start with but you endeavour to reconstruct the entire beast. You're guided by your own experience and knowledge of similar animals."

"That's a reassuring analogy. Yes, I see that." Alice's nose wrinkled in thought. "If you then turn up another bone that suggests you've got your reconstruction wrong, you revise it. Sometimes, of course, the odd piece is from another animal entirely and has merely been redeposited among the rest. You have to eliminate it. I suppose it's the same for you when you're investigating a case."

"It is." Orlando, the aroma from the curry having sharpened his appetite, scooped up another forkful.

"I wonder if you've got an anomalous bone in the Drayton affair?" O'Neill asked.

"Quite possibly." Jonty shrugged. "Although my feeling is there's a genuine fragment that somehow has eluded us. Still stuck in the aggregate because we passed it over."

Alice smiled sympathetically. "Because you thought the part that protruded was merely a pebble?"

"Something like that. It happens, doesn't it, Professor?"

"It does. To extend the analogy, it's often the passed over bone fragment that turns out to be the key to the whole construction." Orlando warmed to his subject. "The same thing happens in mystery stories. The detective is presented with a handful of clues, then he—or she—pursues some of them, convinced they're the important ones. Only to find it was the unconsidered trifle they should have been paying attention to."

"The Professor has quite a good track record of spotting them when he's reading," Jonty said gleefully. "A great shout of 'Eureka!' pierces the air. He's not yet succeeded with this case, though."

O'Neill chuckled. "Please let us know when he has. We're hoping this will be another triumph in the style of the Woodville Ward."

Orlando inclined his head graciously while Jonty assured their hosts that a full report would be made. Yet he couldn't help wishing that it was as simple to spot the relevant clue in real life as it was between the pages of Agatha Christie or Marjory Allingham.

**

186

Saturday morning, a quarter of an hour before the agreed time for the telephone conference, Jonty was chomping at the bit. He'd wanted to ring Toby or Alasdair as soon as they'd got home from the O'Neill's house, but Orlando had pointed out that despite actors probably keeping more outlandish hours than academics, it wouldn't be a good idea to assume they were available to talk. Who knew what that pair would be getting up to, given that they were relatively young, apparently virile and clearly besotted with each other. Jonty had to admit that the chances were their activities would be something not suited to the eyes and ears of their fans and that the new information could wait.

There was plenty of it in addition to what they'd learned at the O'Neill's, including the contents of a letter which had just arrived from Mr Jones, the vicar, providing a name for Mr Mysterious. Add to that Adam's idea for the Landseer poison having been verified in the most gratifying way by the St Bride's librarian, and any man would be eager to share his cornucopia of news. If the actors had anything like as much to share, between the four of them they might be able to start formulating their first real theory. Although the actors were going to be disappointed on at least one front.

"Will you stop prowling?" Orlando said, from behind his newspaper. "At ten o'clock you can ring Toby and not a minute before."

"Not even at five minutes to the hour? I feel sure that he and Alasdair will be ready and waiting themselves."

"Or they may not be and you'll get them flustered. Go for a walk round the garden. Or reread your notes. Have some patience."

"Patience my arse," Jonty said, then headed for the garage where Adam was washing the car. He'd provide a sympathetic companion for ten minutes or so.

187

As it turned out, Adam was so sympathetic about car-related matters that Jonty was almost late in making his call, re-entering the house with a hurried, "Sorry, been chatting about the best kinds of polish for the bodywork," before haring into his study to pick up the telephone. Orlando could listen in from the instrument in the hallway in a similar arrangement to the one which was apparently going to be used chez Bowe. It was a strategy which they'd employed before, even if in the past they hadn't needed a chair to plonk their backsides on should the call last over a few minutes.

They got straight through to London, shared the usual pleasantries, then tried to find a logical order in which to address things, given that everyone said they had important information to share.

"Let's get Adam's poisonous plant out of the way," Orlando suggested.

"Fire away, Orlando," Toby said. "Alasdair is ready to take notes."

"Adam's suggestion is a nice—if one might call such a thing so—specialised garden species that his great uncle Andy warned him against when he was helping the old man at a big house where he tended the grounds. It's called *Gelsemium*."

Alasdair cleared his throat. "Never heard of it."

"It's not in any way spectacular, apparently," Orlando replied. "A bit of a collector's piece. However, it can be deadly if taken in too large a quantity and the victim has a vulnerability to its effects. Is that unusual enough to fit the Landseer bill? All the facts have been verified by Dr Howe, the keeper of the St Bride's library."

"It sounds spot on. Could you impose upon him to send all his notes to me so I can pass them on to Sir Ian?" Toby asked. "Academic verification always welcome."

"Of course," Jonty said. "Howe's hot as mustard about anything that needs tracking down."

Orlando cleared his throat. "I confess I had my doubts when first he arrived at St Bride's, because he seemed so young. Then everyone seems to be so young, these days. Nevertheless, he helped me track down an obscure paper on Euler's formula in a quick and efficient manner."

Not wishing to risk a ten-minute long lecture on Euler—who'd seemed a bit of a lad, if a clever one—Jonty pressed on. "Sir Ian will also appreciate a rather splendid connection to the Hamilton/Bowe pantheon, if not to the film about us. Young Howe dropped in on Thursday with an article he fished out, one which has had us all dancing with delight, young Adam included. Our old pal Conan Doyle administered *Gelsemium* to himself, in a clinical experiment, which he subsequently wrote up for the British Medical Journal."

Alasdair's harrumph down the line sounded just like one from Orlando might. "Never. You're pulling our legs, surely?"

"We are not," Orlando said, with a harrumph of his own. "It was back in the days of the old queen, so you could work that into the script if you wish. Lots of potential for your eyebrow doing its most annoyed jig when you're in role. I'd have been vexed if I've discovered it."

Toby chuckled. "The scriptwriters are apparently having plenty of fun with your Holmes antipathy. They appreciate the scope for making little jokes."

"I'd take his vexation with a pinch of salt," Jonty said. "He's quite chuffed, really, because old Sir Arthur self-administered this stuff in increasing doses and made himself quite ill in the process. Sort of thing Holmes himself would have done and which sensible detectives like we four never would."

189

"We'll pass all of this on as soon as we can. Please thank Adam and Dr Howe for their efforts," Alasdair said.

"We can do better than give our thanks," Toby cut in. "We'll ensure they both have seats for the premier, alongside you two, of course."

"Adam will be thrilled, thank you. He'd have been content simply in the knowledge his idea was used." So far so good. Time to turn to Drayton. "Now, rather than you sharing your evidence and then us, it might prove more efficient to group it by subject. I suggest we start with all matters Proudfoot. Orlando, want to open the batting?"

"Gladly. And I'll hit the first ball to the boundary. Armitage's collaborator on his paper about Ogham was an antiquarian called G R Proudfoot."

"We'll do the same with the second delivery," Alasdair said. "There's a Gerald Proudfoot who, prior to the incident at the Old Manor, tried to access a priest hole at another house. It was all smoothed over by his family, who backed up his tale that he'd been sleepwalking. Sounds awfully like it's the same chap cropping up each time, especially as the other family involved had loaned things to the exhibition's New Zealand exhibit."

"This is turning into quite an over." Jonty chortled. "I rather think I'll loft the next one for six. Ogham Armitage—Maximillian—had a brother called Horatio, who married a Mary Proudfoot in 1853. G R Proudfoot's sister and probably, although not to a hundred per cent certainty, Drayton's young lady."

"We can't beat that." Alasdair's voice dripped with admiration.

"I can," Orlando said. "Horatio and Mary were the coroner's grandparents. So, assuming that we haven't conflated different people simply because of their coincident names, we have a link to the botched inquest. Sorry to spoil your theory about the Proudfoots being red herrings, Toby."

"I think it's spoiled itself," Toby admitted. "This new information also puts a spanner in the works of Miss Mysterious being an illegitimate child of Miss Proudfoot and Drayton. Unless Armitage was happy to take both her and her child."

"Not necessarily," Alasdair said, "if the child predates the wedding and was perhaps hidden away in some manner. Portrayed to the world as being Miss Proudfoot's newly arrived little sister. That sort of 'happy accident' to an older mother is a strategy families use to cover such situations."

"That point's well made. Anything more on Proudfoots or do we face the bowling from the other end? Tackle other matters Armitage, I mean?" Jonty asked.

"We'll nudge the first ball for one and let you face the rest, because we've nothing new to say. You clearly have," Toby added.

"We do," Orlando said, "and it's no doubt what prompted my learned colleague to use the cricketing analogy." He regaled the actors with the tale of the Ogham inscribed bat and how O'Neill thought it likely Maximilian Armitage had similarly inscribed the tusk, in which case the message probably carried a meaning for somebody. "One can imagine some wag having that on display at the exhibition, wondering if anyone would notice."

"*The place where the ash tree was burned and purified.*" Alasdair spoke the words slowly, as is probing them for that hidden significance. "I can't link it offhand to anything or anybody in the case."

"We may never understand what it signifies," Jonty admitted. "Mrs O'Neill thought it might simply refer to where the specimen had been found but for all we know it refers to nothing other than some scrape the intended

191

recipient got into at school. One of those tedious in-jokes which are hilarious for those involved and which leave everyone else cold because they don't know about the incident with the cigarettes behind the cricket pavilion that nearly set the place ablaze. In which case, let's turn to another person altogether. Orlando, as this was originally your thread, will you update our cinematic pals on our communication from Mr Jones?"

"Gladly, although we fear this may prove a disappointment." A rustle came down the line, suggestive of Orlando organising his notes. "The vicar was very sympathetic to our request for information, especially when I told him Mrs Hammersley's story about the Easter visitor. I get the impression she's one of his favourite parishioners and not purely because of her light touch with pastry. There is no *Mrs* Jones, by the way, so the ladies of the parish supply him with all sorts of baked goods."

"I bet there are fights in the pews about whose angel cakes he prefers." The constant plight of the eligible clergyman, although Jones's marital status had led Jonty to some interesting reflections on that sermon they'd heard.

Orlando continued. "Mr Jones is also very fond of a mystery—a reader of Sayers and Lorac so he has good taste—which meant he was delighted to be able to help progress our investigation in some small way. Fortunately, there is capacity in the parish church to store all sorts of old records, visitor books included, and because he had a year and a specific day, he could locate the relevant volume quite easily and pinpoint our chap. He was called Williams and while we don't have his Christian name, he signed his initials, H W."

"That's no disappointment," Alasdair said. "We have a Hugh Williams who's turned up. One of the people from the Great Exhibition who made a statement at the time

Drayton's family were worried about him having seemingly disappeared. Williams was particularly concerned. He asked to be kept up to date with developments, which suggests he didn't know what had happened."

"Or that he knew exactly what had happened and wanted to see how much the police had found out." Bluff and double bluff—Jonty and Orlando had run across that, too. "Your Williams may be our Williams, given the initials and approximate age, but he's not the Ogham expert Williams. He was an Ifor, according to O'Neill, who gave us a copy of the notes he'd been making relevant to our case. That's our lot at present. We have nothing else that's turned up trumps."

"Neither do we, Jonty," Toby said. "Apart from the fact that Alasdair has been using his charm with some nursing agencies and I've put an advert in the paper, so we await developments on the Miss Mysterious's nurse's front. Orlando, you said something along the lines of academics making a theory and weighing it up as each new fact emerges. I'd say that we've gone from no facts—apart from the finding of Drayton's body—to a plethora of them. Do we have enough to construct our first theory or do we need more thinking time?"

"I'm happy to start the ball rolling, if I can mix our sporting metaphors." Alasdair gave an amused snort. "I'd already got an idea and nothing I've heard today necessarily changes it. Proudfoot was after the contents of the chest, but not the slag. I think he was after the tusk which his mate had inscribed for him as a joke."

"That's possible," Jonty conceded, "given that Armitage the Ogham man had already left a personal message scratched onto a cricket bat specifically for the man wielding it. It would be logical that message on the tusk was for his pal whom he wrote the paper with. Even if we have no idea what that message meant."

Alasdair continued. "The tusk ends up sent to the wrong place after Proudfoot had loaned it to be exhibited. He obtains a list of places where it might have gone so gets on the hunt."

"Why not simply write to all these people and see if they've been sent it by mistake?" Orlando asked.

"He's a madcap. Wants the thrill of the chase, which is something your father would have appreciated." Alasdair's reasoning sounded thin, although people did do things for the strangest reasons. "He's not so madcap as to go hunting for the tusk if it's with a dead body, so that possibly eliminates him from the role of murderer."

"Unless he's scared that the body will be found and the tusk alongside it. That Ogham may mean very little to us now but it's possible that a hundred years ago it would have pointed straight to Proudfoot. A clue worth risking your neck to retrieve…" Jonty paused.

"Hello?" Orlando said. "Where have you gone?"

"Sorry. I was struck, yet again, by the feeling that I've seen or heard another hint—more than one, the nagging little voice the back of my mind tells me—and not recognised them for what they are. Carry on while I rack my brains."

"What about Armitage as the killer, he being a rival for Mary Proudfoot's affections?" Toby suggested. "He visits Drayton to have things out with him—the Victorian equivalent of a duel over her hand or a challenge because he has besmirched her virtue. Then he sees the roses Drayton's bought for her, gets enraged, and goes into the whole bashing and tipping sequence."

"That could work but where would Williams come in?" Orlando asked. "Purely a very good friend who mourns

Drayton as we might mourn Dr Panesar should his plane have crashed, or was he something closer? I'm not suggesting he killed him because he discovered his love could never be requited, although that might sit nicely with him visiting the church at Easter. Contrition and shriving as he neared his end. If he knew about the roses in Drayton's hand that might have influenced him in his choice of flower for the grave. Roses would have taken some acquiring at that time of year, which suggests a significance."

"Sorry to have to ask, but what if Drayton wasn't murdered?" Toby said. "What if it was a case of manslaughter? He gets hit on head in what my blessed mother would call a fracas, then the chap he fought with goes off, unaware how badly injured Drayton is. Perhaps our victim doesn't realise, either, so carries on as normal, packing stuff away. Comes over dizzy and ends up in that wretched crate. He's so disoriented that he seals himself in while trying to escape. Nobody knows where he's gone."

"At the risk of yet another sporting metaphor, that horse falls at the first hurdle." Alasdair didn't sound too upset at shooting down his lover's theory. "The hurdle being the letters which were sent after his death."

"They'd already been written. By Drayton himself, which is why the handwriting was convincing. He was already planning his own disappearance, so he'd told folk he was looking for a new job and they weren't surprised when he went." If Toby was extemporising this idea, he was doing so with aplomb.

"Why did he want to disappear, though?" Alasdair asked. "To run away with his secret lover, whoever he or she was? Williams, perhaps?"

"Or to escape from threats issued by the person who eventually killed him, whether that act was intentional or not. The killer or their accomplice found the letters and used them to cover their tracks."

That last suggestion of Toby's was intriguing, and Jonty appreciated the bouncing of ideas between the two men. "There may be some merit in the theory that Drayton wrote the letters, particularly the first one. In which case, Toby, would Armitage be the killer? Which is why his great-nephew swept everything as far under the carpet as it would go?"

"Much as it sticks in my craw to admit the Proudfoot connection, Armitage seems the most likely. I still can't help thinking Williams comes into it somewhere, although I feel I'm confusing personal feelings with solid facts. Imposing my preferences on Drayton's, which can't be good, rigorous thinking."

"It isn't, Toby, although it's excellent that you recognise the trap before you fall into it. I wish all our students could think so maturely," Orlando added. "Some I've had to deal with would take the place where the ash tree was burned and be sure it was to do with smoking furtive cigarettes behind the cricket pavilion because that equated with their experience. Speaking of hidden messages, have you pinned down what you thought we'd been missing, Jonty?"

"I feel I'm getting nearer. It's an incongruous phrase, although only slightly out of place, as the coroner's words were that we linked to the sonnet and Proudfoot. They seem even more significant now that we have the family connection." Jonty sniffed. "It's a shame our Ogham inscription doesn't read as the place where the coroner was birched."

"Didn't the full translation include something about the tree being purified?" Alasdair pointed out. "Although I'm not sure if that's any help. I can't think of any references to purification. Sounds like a religious rite of some sort."

196

Religious rite. A tingle shot up Jonty's spine. "Alasdair, could you consult the notes you took about what was in the butlers' journals? I've a notion that's where the annoying item might lie. I'm now confident I didn't read it for myself."

"Of course. Let me just find the pertinent pages." The only sounds down the line were suggestive of paper being flicked through. "Jonty, you're a legend. Here it is, although I'm not quoting verbatim. It's a report of a remark your grandfather made about Gerald Proudfoot, that antiquarians didn't care much for people, only bits of burned ash which could be a votive offering."

"That's it!" Jonty beamed in delight at his memory still being pretty sharp. "That now begs the question of whether it was a happenstance remark or whether Proudfoot himself had used that phrase in conversation. Referring to the Ogham in the knowledge his words wouldn't mean much to anyone else."

"More likely used to see if they did spark a reaction," Alasdair said. "Let's put ourselves into Proudfoot's shoes. If I were trying to establish whether my hosts had unearthed that Ogham and knew what it meant, I might casually let those words drop over dinner and see what transpired."

"That's possible. So, our net tightens around Proudfoot and his motives, but does that bring us any closer to having Horatio Armitage as the killer?" Orlando asked. "There's the Mary Proudfoot connection and that's all. We mustn't get so wrapped up in the doings of his brother that we forget that Maximillian isn't Horatio."

That would likely put a dampener on everyone's spirits but Orlando was quite correct to make the point. "Toby, can you remind me of the names Granger gave you for the other two men, as I failed to make a note of them?"

"Gray and Southerton. Why?"

"I'm taking a leaf from your book and not letting myself be blinded by all the Proudfoots and Armitages. Whoever killed Drayton was surely present when the exhibition was being packed up," Jonty said. "While it's quite possible that Proudfoot, Armitage, Uncle Tom Cobbley and all were also there, we shouldn't discount the other two. Should we get Dr Howe on their trail, Orlando?"

"I think so. Toby and Alasdair, we've turned up another gem in him. Like his predecessor Bellingham, he doesn't always have a piece of information to hand but is jolly good at knowing where to find it." Orlando's tones reflected his admiration for the librarian, an admiration possibly influenced—not that Orlando would ever admit such a thing—not just by the help with Euler but by the man being ruggedly handsome. "He says he'll be able to lay his hands on some relevant information from the time. Things that we couldn't ordinarily access, such as names of the people who were working at the Great Exhibition. We've already asked him to find out all he can about what one might term the usual suspects but we'll add the other two to his list."

"Good," Toby said. "At our end, we'll have to hope either the nursing agencies or the newspaper appeal come up trumps. I had the message put in everything from *The Times* to the scandal sheets."

Alasdair sighed heavily. "I'd rather that any response came sooner rather than later. We've promotional business going on still from the last release and it won't be long before things start to rev up on your picture. Landseer doesn't stand upon the order of its going. You'll have the new term to deal with, too."

"Yes. Old dons do tend to struggle on well past the point others may have retired. Brain work less of a strain on the joints," Orlando said.

"We'll all cope, though." Jonty cast a glance at his already-straining diary then reminded himself that if you wanted something done, it was best to ask a busy person. "You'll have had to work an investigation alongside your shooting schedule and we've dealt with cases in the height of term. We shouldn't forget that we've made more progress towards the truth in the last ten days than has been made in the previous hundred years."

"Jonty's quite correct, even though he'll be smirking at me admitting that." Orlando snorted. "I suggest we plan another telephone conference in a week, unless anything of real note turns up."

"Agreed," Toby said. "Although if another Proudfoot makes an appearance I might have to go and lie in a darkened room."

Jonty could appreciate the sentiment. "And if it turns out we find incontrovertible evidence that Drayton's death was from natural causes, I'll join you."

Chapter Twelve

Tuesday morning brought a response to Toby's newspaper appeal—via his solicitor, Mr Ludlum, who was handling the matter. A Miss Madeleine Dacres, with the married name of Mrs Newman and living presently in Kent, had been in touch and had answered Ludlum's questions of identification to his satisfaction. No point in wasting anyone's time if the Miss Dacres concerned had nothing to do with visiting Drayton's grave.

Ludlum informed Toby that the woman had married the same chauffeur the vicar had spoken to on the Sussex visit and was happy to receive the actors at her home, if that was amenable to them. "She says she's been reluctant to travel far since the war. Lost her brother when the bus he was in got hit during an air raid and it's knocked her confidence about going too far from home. She says she knows that's silly."

"Not silly at all. One can never judge how events affect people. Not everybody can return to normal life without batting an eyelid."

An appointment was proposed, soon agreed upon and written into Toby's diary with glee. Events were on the move again.

The following Saturday, when he and Alasdair arrived at the house a few minutes ahead of the scheduled time, they found a tall, handsome chap—surely Mr Newman himself—pottering in the front garden.

"Sorry, gentlemen," he said, standing upright and easing his back, "I've got a bit behind with this. I won't shake your hands at the moment, as mine are filthy." He spoke with a Geordie lilt, one that had seen any rough edges knocked off.

200

Toby gave the hint of a bow. "Our fault for being early. Punctuality is the politeness of princes and all that but being over-punctual can bring its own problems."

Mrs Newman had emerged from the house, to welcome them with great and clearly genuine warmth. She was a striking woman, her hair barely touched with silver and blessed with a face that seemed naturally ready to smile. She ushered them in and settled them at her fireside, arranging for refreshments with the minimum of fuss. In all of this, she gave the impression of being the type who'd make an ideal nurse, ready to deal with any eventuality in a calm, competent manner while emanating an aura of common sense.

As she departed, Mr Newman reappeared, in a change of clothes and now clean enough to offer a handshake to his guests. He must have been stunning in a chauffeur's uniform, or indeed in whichever one he'd have worn during the war.

"I'm glad to meet you, Mr Bowe, Mr Hamilton. Maddy and I love your films. I was an aircraft mechanic myself, so I have to say I prefer the war stories you make over the other ones you're in. I know they're much closer to reality than some of the movies from other studios."

"We try our best. Or I should say Landseer tries. We're mere players," Alasdair added, with the merest flick of his insured eyebrow.

"Hiding your lights under a bushel, as Maddy would say. Anyway, we're pleased to be able to help you."

"We very much appreciate it," Toby said. "As I'd hope your late mistress would appreciate your co-operation, given that she appears to have had a close connection to Drayton. Mr Ludlum will surely have told you we're part of a team investigating his death. Which has led us here."

201

"As it should. We'd better wait for Maddy before we get down to business or I'll be in trouble for jumping the gun. Or telling you things and missing something important." Newman broke into a huge grin. "Assuming anything we can tell you *is* important."

"I hope we'll all end up better informed," Maddy said, as she came through the door bearing refreshments. Alasdair leaped up to help her with the tray but was soon shooed away. "You're our guests, so there's no need to pitch in."

Newman mouthed, "Very independent," behind his wife's back as she poured the tea, then he said aloud, "We've wondered about Drayton on and off over the years, haven't we, Maddy? What really happened to him."

"Yes. Quite a mystery there." Maddy laid a plate of biscuits on the table and then fetched the actors their drinks.

"You're not alone in discussing it," Toby said. "The staff at the Old Manor—that's the big house near the churchyard where Drayton is—have also been speculating about it for years, apparently."

"That's where he was found?" Newman asked.

"In a chest in the vaults. You probably know that already."

"We know what was said at the inquest, although we didn't find that out until the thirties, from some old newspapers that Mrs Sterne-Lewis had come across. Or, to get it right, her solicitor had found for her after she'd got him on the trail." Maddy settled herself next to her husband, cup and saucer in hand.

"Mrs Sterne-Lewis was your mistress?" Alasdair asked. "The woman who visited Drayton's grave on three occasions, each of them in November?"

"Yes. Elizabeth Sterne-Lewis. She died the first year of the war, bless her, still not knowing what really happened to him."

"I don't think we know what really happened. Yet," Toby added. "We're getting closer, though. Mr Stewart, who was lord at the Old Manor when the body was found, seemed quite convinced that Drayton's death was no accident. A view supported by the doctor who first examined the body. They believed that either the coroner or the chief constable made sure the inquest was merely perfunctory. The case for foul play is strengthened by the fact somebody sent letters home supposed to be coming from him, but probably after he'd died."

Newman nodded. "She suspected something dodgy had gone on, although to be honest, she was probably past the point of doing much about finding out what. Unfortunately, her solicitor put her viewpoint down to her losing her…sorry, I was about to say, 'marbles' but that sounds cruel."

"True, although you knew her well, so your assessment is really valuable to us." Toby, who'd already slipped a biscuit onto his plate, took a sip of tea. "*Was* she losing her faculties?"

"On and off, yes. Like many old people, one day she could be sharp as a pin and others…" Newman shrugged.

Toby, moved by the devotion clearly on display, decided to edge round that subject for the moment. "We've spoken to the lady who keeps Drayton's grave ship-shape and *she'd* spoken to the vicar whom you met. Mr Smith. He felt you were very protective over Mrs Sterne-Lewis—although clearly none of us knew her name until today."

Maddy, with a hint of welling up, said, "She was a lovely woman and the sort of considerate employer it's hard to find. We wanted so much to protect her at the time, although now she's gone we can speak freely."

"Bessy Cutting, who tends the grave, puts flowers there on the anniversary of Drayton being found. Your mistress laid flowers in November. Was that because it accorded with the time she believed he'd died?" Alasdair asked. "And is there any significance in her leaving bronze chrysanthemums?"

"Only that they were her favourite flowers," Newman said. "She'd have had them in the house all year round. She chose the date to be as near as possible to the time he might have fallen—or been pushed—into that crate."

Toby and Alasdair shared a look. "She suspected he might have been pushed?"

"Yes, Mr Bowe, and that wasn't her age speaking. It had upset her greatly, only discovering where Peter Drayton was buried so long after he'd been found, because she could have gone to his funeral. Her husband was gone by then and there were no children to consider. Her twins had died in infancy and no more followed." Maddy cast a fond glance at a family photograph which showed her and Newman with what must be their own offspring, given the likeness.

What she'd said suggested they might be on the right track with the family-scandal-that-had-to-be-hidden theory. "What was Mrs Sterne-Lewis's connection to Drayton? We know that she told the Mr Smith that Drayton was her husband but that surely can't have been so."

"That was her age speaking. When the vicar met her, she was becoming increasingly frail mentally, although she lived on a number of years afterwards. So sad when the body outlives the mind but she was a fighter." Maddy lifted her teacup, no doubt a signal that she wanted her husband to take up the tale.

"She wasn't up to visiting the next year," Newman said. "She was well down the path old folk tend to tread, mixing up family members. Sometimes she thought Maddy was her mum or her cousin Rose, both of whom were long gone. One thing she was always determined about, though, confusion or no confusion. She wanted reputations to be preserved. That's why I wouldn't tell Mr Smith anything, no matter how bad I felt about keeping him in the dark."

Conversation paused, as all present drank some tea and nibbled at the delicious—and fortifying—biscuits. The couple must have been so used to playing their cards close to their chests that they'd not answered the key question. Time for a nudge. "I'm no clearer on Mrs Sterne-Lewis's relationship to the dead man."

"Lord, I'm sorry, Mr Bowe," Newman appeared mortified. "We're still in the habit of keeping that a secret. She was his daughter. Born out of wedlock, which her husband never knew about."

Maddy, evidently ready to chip in again, said, "See, they'd had a sympathetic, or easily bribed, registrar back when she was born. He'd listed her mother as a widow and invented a husband who'd died at sea."

Toby cut off the whistle of surprise he was about to make. His mother would probably say he was being impolite. "A forged birth certificate?"

"You could call it stretching the truth. I daresay a lot of it went on it the past. And even if a man's listed as the father of a bairn, it doesn't mean he is." Maddy smiled. "Mrs Sterne-Lewis used to like me to read to her. You won't be surprised to hear she loved a murder mystery, and I can remember one set in an advertising agency where a character says, 'Not every puppy appears in the kennel book' or something like that."

"*Murder Must Advertise*," Alasdair said.

"Yes, that's it. When I got to the kennel book bit, Mrs Sterne-Lewis asked me to stop reading, because she wanted to tell me a secret, one she'd kept quiet about for too long. She said somebody else had to know. That's when it all came out about her being born out of wedlock and how such a thing was scandalous in the spring of 1852 although I doubt it was uncommon. I'll just get us a top up." Maddy rose, to fetch the teapot. "She'd never told her husband, partly because she hadn't known the truth when she married him. Went to the altar believing her father had been buried at sea."

Toby found the story entirely believable. Exactly the sort of subterfuge studio publicity departments employed so well.

Alasdair held out his cup for a refill. "Thank you. When did Mrs Sterne-Lewis discover the truth?"

"When her uncle James was coming to the end of his life. He and his wife had brought her up, almost as his own, because the birth had been traumatic and left her mother very ill. She died when my mistress was barely weaned. Anyway, after Mrs Sterne-Lewis's uncle told her the truth, she carried that knowledge all by herself right up until 1929, when her husband died. That's the point at which she started to track down Drayton."

"I've got some questions about that. Forgive me if we need to clarify everything." Toby flashed his hosts an apologetic smile. "We're honestly not that dumb. It's simply that we're obliged to report back to Messrs Stewart and Coppersmith on everything we learn and if we're not in a position to answer their questions, we'll get the equivalent of fifty lines."

"Maddy was tickled pink when Mr Ludlum told her you were in cahoots with those two," Newman said.

"Mrs Sterne-Lewis would have appreciated it, as well. She didn't just like her mysteries between the pages of a book. The adventures of real-life detectives, too." Maddy offered round the biscuits once more. "What did you want to clarify?"

"For a start, what her uncle told her had happened to Peter Drayton." There was perhaps a more pressing question but Toby was holding that in abeyance as he was beginning to dread the answer.

"He told her that he didn't know. That the man was supposed to have gone to work abroad—there was a letter sent along those lines—and then everything went silent. The mother had clung to the hope that he'd reappear, right up until her death, because they'd been very deeply in love. When that didn't happen, she persuaded herself he'd died abroad. She couldn't live with the idea he'd abandoned her and perhaps that contributed to her death. Made her less able to recover from her illness."

"As it turned out he didn't abandon her, Mrs Dacres. Did he?" Alasdair stirred his tea, evidently gathering his thoughts because he didn't take sugar so there was nothing to be stirred.

"I can imagine you making a film of the story," Maddy said, "with Miss Marsden playing the abandoned woman."

"Too near the knuckle for Landseer, I fear. Now, the thing my colleague *hasn't* asked is perhaps the most important." Alasdair flicked his eyebrow in Toby's direction. "What was the mother's name? Was it Proudfoot?"

Maddy looked blankly at her husband. "Proudfoot? I've never come across that. Have you, Jim?"

"No. Mrs Sterne-Lewis was born Elizabeth Geraghty."

If Toby's hands hadn't been occupied with cup and saucer he'd have clapped them. "Mr Newman, you've made my day. If this were Sherlock Holmes territory, you could call it *The Plethora of Proudfoots*. We've had members of that family trying to break into the vault at the Old Manor, writing papers about ancient languages—that is relevant, I promise—and being the grandmother of the coroner who led Drayton's inquest."

"It's just like the plot of one of the books I used to read to Mrs Sterne-Lewis," Maddy said. "Will you have time today to explain what all those points mean?"

"I think we owe that to you." Alasdair took a long draught of tea. "For the moment, we'll say that Drayton had another sweetheart, one whom his father believed he wanted to disentangle himself from. Which would make sense if he'd got Miss Geraghty with child. Whether Mr Drayton senior knew about that but didn't mention it to the police when the family spoke to them, we clearly can't say. This other sweetheart was Mary Proudfoot and we believe she was the coroner's grandmother."

"Mrs Sterne-Lewis didn't mention her but she probably didn't know about her. Perhaps her mother didn't, either." Maddy shrugged. "I can see why you made the link. I'm sorry we couldn't confirm it."

"No need to apologise. There was a Geraghty connected to the inquest, as well. The chief constable." Toby glanced at Alasdair. "I hope you're going to be jotting all this down."

"I will as soon as I've drained my cup. Too good a brew to be wasted."

"While he does that, can I ask about the Geraghty family? You mentioned a cousin, called Rose. Was she on the maternal or paternal side?" Toby asked.

"She was the daughter of Miss Geraghty's brother, which was why she and my mistress were so close, almost like sisters. James had been very supportive all through what must have been an awful situation. Rose came to visit one day, didn't she?" Maddy looked to her husband to continue the tale.

"Yes. That was before you came on the staff and not long after I was employed. I collected her from the station and she was a lovely woman. No airs and graces."

"I never had the chance to meet her," Maddy said, "although I believe she'd visited regularly in the past. Mrs Sterne-Lewis was devastated when she died, it coming so hard on the heels of her losing her husband. I think those two shocks were the start of her memory going."

"All noted, thank you." Alasdair tipped up his notepad to show the evidence. "You don't by any wondrous chance know if they had a relative who ended up being a chief constable?"

"Hmm. I doubt Rose herself had any connection to your chief constable because the surname would have gone down the male line, via James's son Henry. The Geraghtys did have lots of important connections, though, which was why everything about the baby was hushed up and covered over, both when it happened and subsequently." Maddy put her hand to her chin, face crinkled in thought. "There was something my mistress said towards the end, when she was rambling a bit, about how her family would do anything to protect their reputation. I thought she just meant inventing a husband who'd never existed but she could have meant something different."

"She could indeed," Toby said. "She didn't mention anything else that could be relevant?"

"I don't think so. Mrs Sterne-Lewis wouldn't talk to me directly about what she thought had happened to her real father, just that she had her doubts." Maddy looked at her husband, who shook his head.

"Did she ever speak of anyone called Gray or Southerton, or indeed Williams?" Alasdair asked. "They knew Drayton from working at the Great Exhibition."

209

"The first two names don't mean anything, although Williams rings a bell."

"Maddy has a good memory for names, better than I have," Newman cut in. "I never forget a face, which is worse in the long run because you say hello to someone and you've no idea who they are."

"Context is everything for me," Toby said. "If I met my dentist in the street, I'd be aware that I know him but wouldn't tell from where."

"Williams was the godfather," Maddy exclaimed. "I never saw Mrs Sterne-Lewis's birth certificate but she did show me the record of her baptism. Wanted to prove that she'd been welcomed into God's family even if she wasn't regarded as legitimate in law. I think one of the godparents was called Williams and I know she'd lost touch with him and then run across him again during the great war, when they were both involved in a charity event raising money to support our lads. That's all I can tell you, I'm afraid."

"That's enough to be going on with." Births, marriages, baptisms, they all left official records which could be accessed. And even if those records didn't always state the truth—as in the case of Mrs Sterne-Lewis's birth certificate—they had a chance of confirming what had been mere speculation. "I have one final question, before we tell you what we've discovered so far. Rose. Was she married and to whom?"

"That I couldn't tell you. My mistress only ever called her Rose Geraghty. I did wonder whether she'd forgotten her cousin's married name but I suppose she might have had another reason to keep it quiet. Jim?"

"I'd have been told it but you know me, in one ear and out the other." It appeared to be a truthful answer.

Once he'd noted Mrs Sterne-Lewis's date and place of birth, and the parish where she'd been baptised, Alasdair had no further questions for their hosts. That allowed the actors to launch, as promised, into an account of everything related to Drayton, including a spirited impression from Toby of Cutting's "How to get a man into a crate" theory. But avoiding, however, any mention of just how close Williams might have been to the dead man. At the end of it, while the Newmans were better informed and all present agreed that Drayton's death was highly unlikely to have been accidental, no new conclusions could be drawn. Apart from the fact that if Williams had been the murderer, he must have been an extremely cold fish to be able to stand godfather to the dead man's child.

***

"You're going to be unbearably smug about this, aren't you?" Alasdair said, as he drove back towards London.

"I shall be a model of restraint. No shouting 'I told you so!' despite the great temptation." Toby sighed happily, watching the countryside pass by. "Am I allowed to say that I think today, to use another sporting analogy, has left the Landseer lads a solid two nil up against Cambridge?"

"You'll be laughing on the other side of face if it turns out rose Geraghty married Gerald Proudfoot or another of the clan."

"I'll be bloody mortified."

"But you can't deny the family Proudfoot are linked to the case in more than one way." They'd hit a good stretch of road, so Alasdair—as excellent a driver as he'd been a pilot—put his foot down.

"I don't. I simply think we've misunderstood their role. Mr Stewart didn't. He suggested the coroner and chief constable were in cahoots and he speculated that a discussion had taken place between them to control the

211

inquest's verdict." Toby tapped the dashboard. "They're all involved. The whole boiling. With the exception perhaps of Gray and Southerton, who may be innocent bystanders."

"Until it turns out that Rose was bigamously married to one of that pair, hence all the secrecy," Alasdair said mischievously. "That was a joke, by the way. People must be spinning in their graves as we cast aspersions upon them."

"At least one of them deserves to be rotating like a propellor. A hundred years they've got away with it and it's time we established the truth."

"Will we name names, though? Think of the stink it could cause if we accuse people who still have relatives alive now, especially if they're as influential as Geraghty and Armitage were. What proof would we have that we're telling the truth?"

Toby considered the point. The culprit and any collaborators would be long dead, beyond the reach of any justice apart from whatever reckoning came at the pearly gates. So, was this merely a matter of satisfying his own curiosity, alongside that of Alasdair and the two Cambridge dons, in which case the truth needn't go any further? "We don't need to disseminate our conclusions very far, although there are people who should be informed. The staff at the Old Manor for example, as well as the Newmans and the O'Neills. Granger, too, so he can put a postscript on the police records."

"I agree with all those proposals. Keeping our conclusions entirely to ourselves would feel at the least self-indulgent." By which Alasdair probably meant less than satisfying; he did quite enjoy having the fruits of his mental labours recognised.

"Maybe this will become a Woodville Ward case, with the only hard evidence turning up when we're long gone.

Some fantastic scientific discovery will mean that the amateur detective of 2022 who is fascinated by our work will be able to say, 'Aha! That's the link we needed.'"

"True. Although I don't think we're anywhere near having a conclusion, yet. I wonder what Mrs Sterne-Lewis's doubts revolved around and why she couldn't mention them to her trusted nurse. That her godfather had killed Drayton?"

"I was thinking the same. Perhaps he let something slip when they met again. Or felt he wanted to make some great confession as the prospect of facing his maker drew nearer."

"That meeting couldn't have been that long before he visited the grave for himself. Assuming it's Hugh Williams in both instances and not Mr Red Herring Williams. Too common a surname. As bad as the vicars Smith and Jones." Alasdair slowed as the road began to wind. "We should ring Forsythia Cottage when we get home. Add some more things to their man Howe's list for checking. Toby?"

"Sorry, I was just reflecting on you saying, 'get home' and our home situation not being quite the same as Jonty and Orlando's. Do you think we'll ever be able to have our version of the Cambridge set-up? A house we can live in together as though we were married or is that only available within a male dominated society like the university?"

"Not solely. Other men through the years have managed to set up a household together. We met one in our last case."

That had been a clever deception, with ostensibly a man, his wife and their two personal secretaries in the kind of set-up nobody would blink an eyelid at, unless they understood exactly how the romantic pairings stood. "I couldn't pretend to be your assistant or gamekeeper or whatever, though, could I? I hardly think you're proposing we both enter sham marriages and then move into two secretly interlinked houses, either."

"Heaven forbid. Still, there has to be a way. Perhaps we should get Sir Ian's considerable brains on the case. As long as we're making plain that it's a longer term solution we're looking for, rather than something to apply next week or else he'll have kittens."

"Kittens? Sabre-tooth tiger cubs, the sort that might have chased that poor mammoth whose tusk is causing such consternation. That's reminder enough for you to make sure you give Fiona your most longing looks in this new film. And perhaps we should suggest to the scriptwriters that they have our two characters living in St Bride's, occupying separate sets of rooms, rather than out of college and in one house together. Every little piece of camouflage helps."

Which was a devastatingly sad fact.

Chapter Thirteen

"Geraghty." Jonty shook his head after ending the telephone call from Alasdair, which had updated them on the actors' visit to Nurse Dacres the previous day. "You could knock me down with a feather."

"Nobody has ever been able to knock you down with anything less than a battering ram, I'd say," Orlando retorted. "You've always been built like a small wall."

Jonty grunted. "Ha ha. Howe's going to be delighted, though."

The librarian had taken to his investigative role as to the manner born and was already bearing fruit in terms of moving the investigation on. He'd turned up, via the Ascension College archive, various bits of material related to the Great Exhibition. Among them were papers relating to when an item belonging to Ascension—not, alas, a mammoth tusk—had gone missing and been found the other end of the country. While neither Gray and Southerton were mentioned among any of those papers, both Peter Drayton and Hugh Williams were listed and had made statements about the errant artefact, which was a cloak from a New Zealand chief.

The possible, if tenuous, connection to Gerald Proudfoot and the family with the items from New Zealand had been noted, although Jonty had felt it was a simple coincidence because the name Proudfoot hadn't occurred in any of the papers. Howe had promised he'd been diligent in keeping an eye out for any of the surnames of interest and they had no reason to doubt his efficiency. Orlando had reserved his judgement on whether the cloak had any bearing. What might be relevant was the supposed existence of a list from the dismantling of the exhibition, detailing who had supervised sending what to where or having it collected. They'd naturally reported all of this to Toby and Alasdair.

"I hope Howe can get his paws on that list. We need something to outdo our actor pals. We'll also have to set him onto the business of connecting the two men called Williams, if he can, with a side order of anything Geraghty related." Jonty ushered Orlando into their sitting room, where a pot of coffee awaited. "Although we surely can assume that there were no Geraghtys mentioned in the papers he fished out at Ascension or he'd have pointed out the fact."

"I've never known him to be less than thorough." Orlando glanced over to the window, to see Adam going past, clearly manoeuvring his bicycle. "Where's he off to? I thought he had a walk with his sweetheart lined up."

"He does, but he's doing a little job for me, first." Jonty sipped his coffee. "While you were at your bridge orgy last night, I was in hall, relating our findings so far to Dr Panesar. He appeared particularly interested in the iron slag and said he'd like to see it, so I've despatched Adam off to his laboratory with the stuff. I doubt it'll come to anything, although it might keep Dr P from blowing up anything for an hour or two."

"He didn't want to inspect the other things?"

"No. Said if the O'Neills had given them the once over he'd have nothing more to add." Jonty tipped his head in thought. "On reflection, he was being more than his usually mysterious self. I don't know what bee he had in his bonnet and whether it'll turn out to be a maker of honey or simply a misidentified wasp."

"One of your better analogies. Did you tell him about the Ogham message?"

"Yes. And that's what appeared to pique his interest. I— oh, hell's teeth and damnation." Jonty laid down his cup.

"We're losing our touch, old man. So bound up in linking surnames we've missed something more obvious. At least I can console myself that our two younger colleagues were equally remiss."

"As usual, I have no idea what you're referring to."

"I'm referring to Proudfoot searching for the tusk and what the message might mean to him. *The place where the ash tree was burned and purified.* Proudfoot the metal expert." Jonty leaned forward, counting off points on his fingers. "You have to purify metal from its ore to make it usable for manufacturing artefacts, which involves heating it—burning, if you like."

"I believe you also have to burn charcoal to generate enough heat to make the process work." Orlando nodded. "And the ash could simply be a play on words. Rather than a species of tree, it refers to the ash a fire produces."

"I hadn't thought of that but yes, it could. I had it more in mind that the ash tree provided fuel for the refiner's fire—do they use that wood to make charcoal?"

"I wouldn't know. As a general theory, it does make better sense of the cryptic Ogham phrase, though. Even the reference to a place, which would be the smithy or workshop where they did the metalwork. Perhaps Proudfoot had his own laboratory where he tried to replicate ancient techniques." Orlando tapped the arm of his chair. "I wonder if either O'Neill or Howe can find out if Proudfoot was involved with something similar for the Great Exhibition?"

"I think it would top everything off if Proudfoot was actually an expert on copper smelting. I know they had lots of examples of copper ore and the like at the exhibition, although our slag appears to be the wrong colour. Apropos of which, do you remember Mama trying to make a quip on your name not long after you first met?"

217

"I do indeed." It had tickled Orlando greatly to find Mrs Stewart regaling him with tales of her own mother visiting the Crystal Palace and being tempted to steal some of the cuprous objects. "If we've hit on the truth, we've also hit on a different motive for Proudfoot to go hunting in various vaults. He wanted his tusk back because, contrary to what Alasdair suggested, he knew about Drayton and he didn't want anything of his found in association with the man's dead body. Not within the timescale that somebody might remember Armitage making it specifically for him."

Jonty nodded. "I wonder if the iron slag was his, as well. Do you know, one of those lumps would make a jolly useful weapon. If it had been used to clonk Drayton one, either by Proudfoot or whoever he was in cahoots with, he might have wanted to get rid of that connection, too."

"He might. Although why didn't he remove the slag and the tusk from the chest when he—as you put it so poetically—clonked Drayton one?"

"Because he was interrupted? Heard people coming, so slammed down the lid of the chest, meaning to return later. He never got the chance and so became increasingly frantic that his victim would be discovered, with the incriminating evidence right beside him."

"To the point he felt he had to get rid of it once and for all? That would also suggest he had a motive to kill Drayton which enough people would know about. We now know that motive can't have been that he got Mary Proudfoot pregnant. Although getting another woman with child might be enough to raise the hackles of a brother who didn't want to see his sister abandoned. Enough to start a violent argument, one that ended up going too far." Orlando drained his cup. "I hope Dr Panesar doesn't wash those specimens you loaned him. I suppose there might still be blood traces after all this time?"

"As you've just said, I wouldn't know. Still, Dr P wouldn't do anything amiss. He said he'd treat those specimens like gold." Jonty picked up his cup once more. "I'll ring down to the library and heap more questions onto Dr Howe's broad shoulders. Perhaps a joint meeting with him and Dr Panesar in a few days would be fruitful."

"Agreed." One that would hopefully bring them a few steps closer to a solution.

***

Dr Howe had been delighted to arrange a report on his progress. He'd suggested that Jonty, Orlando and Panesar meet him in his little office, where he'd have the relevant papers to hand. All involved had readily agreed: it was a place which had seen fruitful investigational meetings on previous occasions and while Orlando wouldn't say such a location would bring them luck, it had good associations.

The tea and little cakes they found waiting for them on arrival were most welcome, it having been a busy day so far. Howe made them as all as comfortable as he could within the cramped confines, then began to lay out what he'd found.

In what Orlando thought an exceptional piece of work, the kind of thing which would have benefited many a past investigation, Howe had used his many sources of information to tick off much of his list of questions. Firstly, he'd confirmed both the dates and the wording on Mrs Sterne-Lewis's birth certificate, that the fictitious father's name had been given as Peter Geraghty and that her mother, Louise, must have been a good four or five months pregnant when Drayton died. Secondly he'd been told by someone at the parish where Mrs Sterne-Lewis had been baptised, that her godfather was indeed Hugh Williams. Thirdly, and most importantly, he'd located a copy of Geraghty the chief constable's autobiography, which was in the university library, him being an alumni of the college next door to St Bride's.

"That doesn't surprise me at all," Jonty said. "No wonder my father didn't like him. A good St Bride's man, was Richard Stewart, and he'd not have been impressed by anyone associated with our rivals."

"I've come across Mr Stewart's name in our archives," Howe said, "and been told about him by those fortunate enough to have met him."

"He was a good judge of character," Orlando averred.

"So I believe. And while I clearly never met Geraghty and won't judge him on his choice of college, I think your father's estimate of the man seems correct, given what I've read so far." Howe handed over the autobiography for Jonty to flick through. "I can confirm that he *was* related to Mrs Sterne-Lewis via her paternal uncle. Her husband was a man of great wealth and influence and Geraghty was determined that all his readers should be aware of the fact they were connected. I say *all* his readers but I doubt the book had much of a circulation. A self-supported effort, albeit that being no bad thing in itself."

"Like Peter Rabbit." Panesar's eyes danced. He'd been sitting unusually quietly, taking everything in and clearly poised to make some revelation. "One of my favourite books. So very naughty, all Miss Potter's characters."

"Kindred spirits to yours, then." Orlando chuckled. He doubted that choice of reading was the only surprise Panesar would reveal.

Jonty passed the book to Orlando. "Dr Howe, from my brief inspection, you've gone above and beyond the call of duty reading this tome. I bet it's nowhere near as entertaining as *The Tale of Two Bad Mice*. Did anything else turn up in it relating to our case?"

"Only an oblique reference to amateurs needing to keep their noses out of official business. It's in the chapter dealing with the start of the war, so it may be a reference to Mr Stewart or indeed to you two." Howe grinned.

Orlando, handing the volume to Panesar after no more than a cursory glance at the text, bridled at the thought of being besmirched, however obliquely. "He's a fine one to talk, given how he appears to have prevented justice being done."

"There's evidence in the text to support that. He was great friends with Armitage the coroner, who gets a glowing reference in there." Howe pointed at the autobiography, which Panesar was holding as though it were one of his explosive devices which had got into an unstable condition. "He relates another case they worked on together, around the time King Edward died, where he as good as boasts they ensured a convenient outcome was delivered, despite the best efforts of what he described as an ignorant jury."

"That's what my nephew George Broad—His Honour Judge Broad, QC, although forever Georgie to us—would call 'having previous'." Jonty, who was squashed fairly close to Howe, patted the librarian's arm. "Well done, sir. Another stitch in the net we're drawing around these people."

Howe inclined his head, chiselled features awash with pleasure at being able to help. "I'll keep working at it. What I've learned so far comes merely from a skim through the text, looking for names and relevant dates. I'll go back and read it all with more care, because I may have missed something."

"Was there any mention of the man who identified the iron slag as such for the benefit of the inquest?" Panesar asked. "What was his name, Professor?"

"I have it in my notes." Orlando, with a quiver of excitement, flicked back to the jottings he'd made when they'd been at the Old Manor. This surely was the build-up to a fresh revelation as he was damn well sure Panesar knew the answer to the question already. "Dr Parker. Why?"

"Because I think he got his facts wrong. Not with the Neolithic items, which were his specialised field. I checked up on him, you see, after you loaned the supposed iron slag to me. Which isn't iron slag at all." Panesar produced the lumps from a bag, laying them on the desk before sitting back triumphantly.

Jonty whistled. "I didn't realise that was another arrow in your quiver, Dr P. Metal working expert as well as everything else."

Panesar raised a hand in self-deprecation. "I'm not. We have plenty of people at the university who've been studying metallurgy for years. It's a relatively new department but a highly competent one, so I've been picking their brains. Any of us might have mis-identified these, although a person worth their salt shouldn't have done, despite the fact they do contain some ferrous material. According to those I consulted, they're meteorites."

"Meteorites?" Jonty shot Orlando a glance. "Someone's mentioned meteorites. When and in what context?"

Orlando didn't need to consult his notes to give the answer. "The context of Gerald Proudfoot. O'Neill said he wrote a paper about them, which we ignored because of the man's interest in metalworking. Could he have been looking for the meteorites when he went into the vaults? They'd be rarer than iron slag and might have been worth retrieving."

Jonty picked up one of the items concerned. "My grandfather apparently made a remark, which we thought applied to Proudfoot, about antiquarians and votive offerings. Gentlemen, this is not our sphere—do you know if meteorites could be used as an offering or have a connection to something similar?"

"Quite possibly." Panesar nodded. "Meteorites do get worshipped in some parts of the world, because they're items which fall from the heavens and burn bright, like Lucifer. As we already have the vague New Zealand connection, it might be worth mentioning that such objects play a significant part in the Māori culture."

"Which is why Gerald Proudfoot may have chosen the particular vault he tried to access before he attempted the Old Manor," Orlando pointed out, miffed that *he'd* dismissed the New Zealand elements so quickly. "Dr Howe, did anyone display meteorites at the Great Exhibition?"

The librarian picked up another volume, from which several bookmarks peeped out. "According to this catalogue which I've borrowed from the archive at Ascension, I suspect you could have seen just about anything there. Strangely enough, I seem to remember..." He opened the volume at the first marked page, shook his head, then went to the second. "Look at this."

The catalogue had been annotated in ink, possibly at the time of the exhibition as the marks were starting to fade, although they were still legible enough. A reference to meteor steel was circled.

"There are some half a dozen items ringed in such a manner. A hotch-potch of things that don't make any sense to me but must have done to whoever made the annotations and might to you." He read each entry aloud, although nothing rang the sort of bell that meteors had done. Much that had been marked, such as the Koh-I-Noor diamond, seemed standard fare for visitors although the industrial items seemed to be of more specialised interest.

"I do hope we haven't stumbled across some fiendish plot to substitute the Koh-I-Noor for a clever replica, so realistic that the switch hasn't ever been discovered. And that Drayton wasn't killed because he stumbled upon the truth." Jonty was clearly jesting, although it would be supremely ironic—given the use the Old Manor's vaults had been put to—if the real crown jewels came into the case.

"I can assure you no such switch took place." Panesar spoke with the sort of finality that none of those present would dare argue with or enquire about.

"I've scrutinised the names listed at the front of the catalogue, superintendents of classes and the like, but none of our pals appear there. They might be listed elsewhere, given that it's a huge work." Howe frowned. "Is it worth going through all the text?"

"Only if you suffer insomnia." Orlando gave the librarian an encouraging smile. "To bring the matter from royalty back to the base common and popular, as it were, we continue to link Proudfoot closely to the inanimate objects in the chest."

Panesar raised his hand. "If I may be so bold, I think you also have another possible explanation for what was inscribed on the tusk. If the meteorite struck an ash tree and caused it to burn that might be referenced in the message."

Jonty groaned. "Dr P, I think the world of you and respect every one of your theorems, but I feel I now have as much a surfeit of Ogham meanings as I do of Proudfoots and Geraghtys. I'm desperate for a solid fact or two. Dr Howe, is there any chance you can rescue we three men in the investigational boat? Give us something that takes us closer to knowing who killed Drayton."

"I wish I could." Howe spread his hands helplessly.

The gloom which descended on the gathering couldn't even be overcome by the excellence of the cake on offer. Orlando was about to suggest they call it a day when a knock came on the office door and what appeared to be a porter's face peered round it. "Beg pardon, sirs. I've something from Ascension for Dr Howe."

"Thank you. If you could hand it to one of my colleagues…it's a bit of a scrum in here."

The porter gave the envelope to Orlando, who relayed it across. Once the man had gone, he asked the question that was no doubt on Jonty's lips as well. "Is this the list from the dismantling of the exhibition?"

"It is. Let's hope it's the answer to Dr Stewart's prayer." Howe cleared his desk, with the help of Orlando, who gathered up all the refreshments and took them outside. By the time he returned, several sheets of foolscap were on display, with more waiting.

"There appears to be no system to how things are listed, so let's all take some and work through them," Jonty suggested. "We're primarily looking for the Old Manor but any names that are relevant should be pointed out. Even if they happen to be Proudfoot."

Southerton turned up among the first names Jonty read, along with Drayton himself. "Anyone else finding our old pals?"

Orlando nodded. "Gray's the first entry on my list and H Williams is the second. I don't see anything in terms of where or what they're in charge of which links to the case, though."

It was Panesar who found the relevant reference, on the second sheet he'd been given. "Here we are." He laid his piece of paper down for them all to see. "Three chests, to the Old Manor. Under the control of Mr M Heathfield."

"Heathfield?" Jonty groaned again. "I think I'd rather it was another blooming Proudfoot."

"That name means something?" Howe asked, glancing up sharply.

"Only in so much as it's the same surname as another person who tried to access the vaults. A right silly ass pal of my brother Clarence's." Jonty, shrugging, looked at Orlando, seemingly for guidance.

"Let's work through all of these before we discuss him further. More revelations might appear." They acted on Orlando's suggestion, finding numerous mentions of all five men although none leaped out as being related to the case. All, Heathfield included, appeared to have been properly employed in the proper return of borrowed items.

"I didn't find Drayton in any of mine," Howe said. "I've got the later numbered sheets, if that's significant.

"It might be, if they're in chronological order of when things were dispatched or collected. I have sheet one and Drayton's right at the top of it." Jonty scrutinised his papers again, as did the others. The conclusion was that he'd disappeared by sheet four, while the Old Manor reference—which was the first to feature Heathfield—appeared towards the top of page five. They started to make notes of this, before Panesar suggested he should get his camera and photograph the relevant sheets.

"An excellent idea," Howe said. "Could you do that as soon as possible, though, as I'd like to return all these things to Ascension, before my office becomes an annex of their archive."

Panesar nodded. "As soon as we've concluded this meeting."

Howe moved the papers to one side, the notable ones at the top of the pile. "I'm pleased this list arrived while you were here. Not simply so you could see it. I'm intrigued by the significance of Heathfield."

"Why?" Jonty asked.

"Look at this." Howe picked up the catalogue, turning to the last page, one he hadn't bookmarked. "You can just make out a name here. Presumably the person to whom this belonged."

Orlando leaned forward—even viewing it upside down, the writing was fairly clear. *Michael Heathfield*. There followed a list of item numbers which wasn't as easy to read.

"I checked back through the catalogue and these are all exhibits which are attributed to a Mr M Heathfield," Howe said. "One assumes this is his personal reference copy."

"Dr Stewart, did you ever establish whether Freddie Heathfield is still alive?" Orlando asked.

"I did and he isn't." Jonty rubbed his chin. "They could be related."

"Would you like me to see what I can find out?" Howe offered.

"Perhaps but hold fire on it. I think this is a job for Toby Bowe—didn't he have a chap of that name in his squadron, Professor?"

"I believe so. He speculated on whether his Heathfield could be related to ours."

"That's just what I'm hoping. Let's get our actor pals on the trail." Jonty leaned forward to take the last piece of cake from his plate. "We've been comparing this investigation to completing a jigsaw puzzle but I'm beginning to think it's more like one of those things you used to like when they first appeared, Dr Panesar. Where you join the dots."

"Ah yes." Panesar nodded. "Although in this case it's names we're connecting to see what image emerges."

Jonty hastily swallowed a piece of cake, almost choking in the process and needing Howe to slap his back. "Sorry about that. Getting too excited about this new lead. I'm thinking that perhaps the people we've already linked aren't the main part of the picture but merely outlying areas. If Heathfield was involved in getting that crate back to the Old Manor, he might have known about its contents. Or wondered about them afterwards."

Orlando would agree with all that. He'd not admit it, but Heathfield *felt* right, in the way that they'd all thought Proudfoot, for some reason, didn't. "We've imposed on your time quite a lot, Dr Howe, although if you could scrutinise that autobiography, we'd be very grateful."

Howe, who'd looked slightly crestfallen at not being asked to follow up on Heathfield, smiled at the suggestion. "It would be my pleasure. I'll add Heathfield to the list of names I'm keeping an eye out for."

"Is there anything I can do?" Panesar asked.

"You could ask your metal-mad pals if the name Heathfield means anything to them," Jonty suggested. "You could also let us host you two for dinner one evening soon. As a small recompense for the progress you've helped us make."

"Hear hear. We'll consult our diaries in a moment." Orlando picked up one of the meteorites, turning it over in his hands, possibly as an adjunct to thought. "Gentlemen, I fear we've sorely neglected the classic trio in all of our excitement at identifying clues. Means, motive and opportunity. While we are narrowing down opportunity, at least so far as establishing who was working with Drayton at the time of his disappearance, the other two are no clearer."

"You don't favour either of these as the object that was used to strike Drayton down?" Panesar picked up the other meteorite, miming with it the act of hitting someone. "I

228

believe blood residue is very difficult to dispose of and I may know someone who could check them for us. I doubt we'd be in a position to match it to Drayton—nobody is, I assume, proposing an exhumation?—but it could be identified as human, one hopes."

"That would be splendid," Jonty said. "Especially if anything else turned up in the evaluation, like a part knocked off or some tiny fragments of hair stuck down a crevice. Would you be interested to do the same with one of the hand axes? It was said to have blood on it."

"Of course. Send me anything you want tested and I'll see what I can do."

"I'll get young Adam to nip down. He enjoys being a Madingley Road Irregular." Jonty chuckled, probably because the Holmes allusion always wound up Orlando. "A shame that we don't have some modern scientific test for analysing motive, though."

"We do have the distaff line to continue exploring," Orlando pointed out. "A supposedly jilted sweetheart and another woman with child. Dr Howe, when you go through that autobiography, can you make a note of anything that might concern a discarded lover or a hint of illegitimacy? If Geraghty went so far as to intimate that he and Armitage affected the outcome of an inquest, he might have been bold enough to sneak in an obscure reference to the other time he made sure that justice wasn't served. As Dr Stewart put it, he's got previous, because he made an allusion to Proudfoot."

"That wasn't him, it was Armitage the coroner." Jonty motioned with his finger, as though putting a mark on a scoreboard. "One up to the English department. That was during the inquest, by the way. A quote from the sonnets, perhaps referring to the family Proudfoot, Mary of that ilk being his grandmother."

"I see." Panesar thought for a moment. "Why would he mention his own family connection? A little private joke, trying to show what he could get away with?"

"Perhaps. Dr Howe might find something in that autobiography that gives a further clue to his character." Orlando gingerly laid the meteorite back on the table. "We'll reconvene at Forsythia Cottage, then. By which time we might have even more information to digest."

Jonty reached into his pocket for his diary. "So long as said information is more in the digestive nature of fillet steak than ancient mutton, I'll be happy."

"It might turn out to be mammoth, Dr Stewart," Panesar said gleefully.

"Tough and impenetrable? That'll be about right for most of the clues in this case." Orlando chuckled, but what he'd said was too close to the truth to be completely amusing.

Chapter Fourteen

The last time Toby had seen Charlie Heathfield was at a squadron reunion in 1949. It had been a less than sober affair, partly because—perhaps to have been expected—those present found that the ties that had once bound them so closely no longer exerted such a pull. Toby had tried to be sociable, chatting to all and sundry and making sure he did more asking than talking, which usually oiled the conversational wheels, but he'd found that he had little in common now with most of his one-time comrades. Only two he'd found notes of connection with, but those were men he'd kept in touch with anyway, because one knew his family and another was in the film industry. Heathfield had been among those people whom Toby had found it less than easy to converse with, although the man himself had appeared as blithely untouched by any social awkwardness as he'd remained untouched by German bullets.

He'd equally not seemed to be at all surprised when Toby got back in touch with him in order to arrange meeting for a drink. The latter had made it plain from the start that he wanted to pick his old comrade's brains about an old case he'd got himself embroiled in solving. While this eliminated any element of surprise, it gave an explanation as to why Alasdair would also be coming along. Heathfield had said he'd be more than happy to help, although he couldn't think offhand of any mysteries that had come his way. "Apart from the fact my belt seems to be getting shorter," he'd quipped, "although I suppose there's no real mystery in that."

When Heathfield strode into the bar where they'd arranged to meet, he certainly seemed to have put on a few pounds in the previous few years. Perhaps his ability to eat and drink as much as he wanted, yet remain whippet thin, had finally deserted him. Still, the awkwardness of their last meeting didn't reappear, probably because there was a clear purpose to *this* meeting which meant that the making small talk and catching up was less painful. Actually, Heathfield had a lot to say, having taken up a job in the airline industry, got himself married and being the proud father of a bouncing boy. Once he'd shown off pictures of the child and listened to news of Toby's career—some of which he already knew about because his wife was an avid fan—something of the old camaraderie had been rekindled.

"We've a new project coming up. Murder mystery, set at the time of the Great War, although not Holmes and Watson," Toby said. "We've met up with the two real life amateur detectives we'll be playing and via them got involved with solving an actual case from around the same time. Which may sound odd, but we've done a bit of amateur detecting before."

Heathfield nodded, as though this were nothing peculiar. "Sounds intriguing. How do I come into it?"

"Not you personally so much as people who might be your relatives." Alasdair's eyebrow emphasised the importance they placed on their guest's potential input. "Two Heathfields have cropped up and Toby wondered if you might be able to enlighten us about them. A long shot, we know."

"Long shots can hit the target, and the Heathfields are a pretty tight-knit bunch so it wouldn't surprise me if I know of your two chaps. Assuming they *are* chaps. I'm not aware of any murderers in the family, though, or murderees." Heathfield chuckled. "Victims, I mean. We're a boring lot."

Toby doubted that. "The victim was called Peter Drayton, he was involved with the Great Exhibition and he seems to have died around the time it came to an end in 1851. It's not easy to get our hands on much in the way of facts, hence us calling on anyone who might have a connection. We have two Heathfields we're interested in, the first being Freddie. He would have been born around twenty years or so after Drayton's death."

"Well, I'm blowed." Heathfield was so surprised he put down the glass which hadn't so far left his hand. "That could be the pater. They say I'm a chip off the old block if that helps to confirm it."

"It might." Toby didn't elaborate. "Did he have a Welsh connection? Something to do with rugby?"

"Yes. Selected for the national team but couldn't play because of injury. He was never picked again. What skeleton does the old man have in his closet? Oh, have I put my foot in it?"

Alasdair waved his hand. "It's simply that Drayton was found dead in a sealed chest, some sixty years after he must have been put there."

"The Mistletoe Bough." Heathfield had turned pale, paler than he'd ever appeared in the face of the enemy.

Toby shared a glance with his lover, who was evidently also at a loss. "Sorry, I don't follow."

"We had an Irish nanny for a while. She got the sack when mater discovered that she was scaring me and my sisters with her ghost stories and the like. They still give me the creeps." Heathfield took a fortifying drink. "One was about a bride who wanted to surprise her husband, so she hid in a chest, intending to pop out. Only the lid closed on her and she was trapped. Found years later, all wasted away. A mere shrivelled corpse in her wedding finery. Pater went mad when he heard the nurse had been telling us that tale and not just because it was hardly suitable for young ears. He said that it wasn't simply an old legend. That such things really did happen."

233

"Well, well. Did he give any indication about what he was referring to?" Alasdair asked.

"No. He always refused to talk about it. Why?"

"Because if he's the Freddie Heathfield who tried one dark night to get into the vaults at the Old Manor—the Stewarts' country home—then he might have been referring to Drayton's body." This new information needed to be fed back to Cambridge as soon as convenient.

"Was that Clarence Stewart's place? I've heard all about the antics he and the pater got into. My grandfather didn't approve of the friendship because he didn't particularly like *Clarence's* grandfather. I'm afraid that's all I can tell you on the subject, because the name Drayton doesn't ring a bell. You'll perhaps remember, Toby, that I may not be over blessed with brains but I do have a good memory for names." Heathfield drained his glass, then motioned for the waiter to have it refilled.

Alasdair, glass still half full, took a sip. "Is Michael Heathfield a name you remember? He'd have been alive in the 1850's."

"That could be my grandfather, the one I just mentioned. I think the dates would work out, because we do tend to be later than usual on the begetting front and he'd have been quite old when he had Pater." Heathfield began to do his sums, mouthing figures and counting on his fingers before shrugging. "Yes, I think that could be him. I never met the man, obviously, but I can tell you that he's where the Welsh connection comes in. Married to a girl called Williams. Which is clearly another name that means something, given the way Alasdair's eyebrow just jerked."

"We know about a Hugh Williams, friend and colleague of Drayton, who came to mourn him when he finally found where the man had been buried." Was it too much to hope that Heathfield would pull him out of the recesses of memory?

"Her brother was called Hugh. I know because he was Pater's godfather. He'd also be some species of great uncle to me."

"If it's the same chap as our Hugh, he appears to have been a bit of a serial occupant of the standing at the font role," Alasdair said. "We have him as godfather to the dead man's illegitimate daughter."

Heathfield whistled. "It's very labyrinthine—if that's the right word—this investigation lark. Does it strike you as a bit of a coincidence that all these folk appear to have a hand in things?"

That element of coincidence had started to worry Toby, but he ploughed on regardless. "Michael Heathfield was involved in having stuff sent back to its rightful owners when the Great Exhibition ended. Including the chest in which Drayton's body was found."

"Lummy. You don't think the old man bumped off this Drayton cove?"

"We have no idea who did, Charlie," Alasdair said. "We've lots of names and plenty of speculation about who might have done what and why, but we're perilously short on hard facts. Any you could give us would be very welcome, especially if they helped to clear your family from suspicion."

"Yes, it hardly looks good for us, does it? My ancestor works with Drayton, sends off a crate with his dead body in it and then Pater apparently tries to get his paws on the thing." Heathfield rubbed his brow. "Any other shocks you want to give me?"

Toby shook his head. "I hope not. It was never my intention to cast aspersions on any Heathfield, living or dead. Unless any of the aforementioned had collections of meteorites or were given cricket bats inscribed with secret messages in old languages."

Heathfield gave Toby the sort of look he might give someone he suspected of losing their marbles. "Not that I know of. Pater collected stamps and Hugh Williams—" He stopped, mouth clamping shut.

"Please go on." Alasdair lowered his voice. "Whatever you say will be treated in the strictest confidence."

"I was about to say he collected young men but that's unfair because it's based on nothing more than family gossip."

Evidently nothing further was forthcoming on the matter of Williams's interests, so Toby said, "I've one more thing to discuss and it's not a direct Heathfield reference. Unless people called Proudfoot, Geraghty, Armitage or Sterne-Lewis are impenetrably woven into your family history, particularly any women with those names."

"Not forgetting Gray and Southerton, whom we keep overlooking. Shall I jot down that list, Charlie?" Alasdair offered.

"Yes please, or else one name might get lost and sod's law says it'll be the important one." Heathfield waited for Alasdair to write the list, then studied it. "Most of those mean absolutely nothing, I'm pleased to say. Geraghty might."

"Geraghty?" The dark horse that kept coming up on the rails.

"Yes. Although I'm blessed if I can think why." Heathfield picked up his drink as though to finish it then clearly thought better of doing so. "I'll go and see if there's somewhere here to call Mater. She's even better with names than I am. I'll subtly ask her about the other stuff while I'm at it. I can be subtle, you know."

236

Once Heathfield had headed off in search of a phone, Toby said, "I bet he can, where his mother's concerned. Be subtle, I mean."

"I guess that's a skill we all acquire. Sounds like Williams would have had to learn discretion, too."

Toby snorted. "Not discreet enough, if he acquired that reputation. It would potentially explain why he didn't get on with the Draytons, though."

Alasdair took another sip from his glass. "Heathfield seems a reliable witness, more so than I expected. Aware of his own limitations, which is a good thing."

"He always was. Perhaps that's why he got home safely after every sortie. Right," Toby rose, "I'm taking this opportunity of visiting the little boys' room. Don't let Charlie reveal any information in my absence. That would be a low blow."

Toby returned to their table barely a minute before Heathfield did. The man looked more chipper than prior to the telephone call, so whatever he'd discussed with his mother had lifted his spirits. He almost drained his glass, then said, "Glad to say that Mater can confirm what I've told you about Hugh Williams and the like. Not sure if I should be glad about the fact she says our Michael Heathfield was definitely involved with the exhibition at Hyde Park, but if that's the truth, so be it. She said Pater once got a few too many of these inside him—" he indicated his drink, "which was totally out of character, so as a result, he told her about something which was worrying him concerning his father. How he might have been involved with a crime being covered up although Pater had never been able to get many details out of the old man. Perhaps that's why he went into those vaults, if he was trying to find out more. He rather fancied himself as a Sherlock Holmes type and he might have spent ages coming to the conclusion he was on the right trail in going there."

"I said we were being blinded by Proudfoots." Toby couldn't resist making the point. "Although I now fear I'm awash with too many other surnames and connections to see my way straight. What did your mother have to say about the list of names?"

"She mostly drew a blank, apart from Geraghty. We've one of those lurking about in the old family archives and not at all where I thought she'd be." Heathfield raised almost as eloquent an eyebrow as Alasdair's uninsured one. "Hugh Williams, he who was latterly said always to have a young man in tow, married a girl called Rose Geraghty, who was considerably his junior. Is she the Geraghty you're looking for?"

"She's among them, yes. Assuming, as we keep having to do, that it's not a case of two different people with the same name. Was your mother as surprised at him having taken a wife as you seem to be?" Toby asked.

"She wasn't alive at the time, but she was shocked when the story emerged, because by that point she knew him quite well. Not the marrying type, according to her, although I guess it takes all sorts to make a world." Heathfield waggled his glass at the waiter. "Would you chaps like another? I seem to be ahead on the game."

"Just a small one for me," Alasdair said, with Toby echoing the response. "We understand that Rose may have reverted to using her maiden name. Was that after her husband died?"

"It may have been earlier, because the marriage only lasted a couple of years before they separated, which is why it was all a bit hush-hush. Risk of family scandal. I asked the Mater if either remarried and she thought not." Heathfield pursed his lips between thumb and forefinger, as Toby had

238

seen him do when waiting for the call to scramble. "There's a lot here to take home with me and tell Molly about. Which reminds me that I promised her I'd ask about your next film."

"We'll have to swear you both to secrecy before we can answer that." The drinks arrived and the rest of the conversation with their guest revolved around matters Landseer.

Once they'd reached the point where Heathfield said he had to depart or he'd for the domestic high jump, Alasdair waited until the man was well out of earshot before saying, "Miss Dacres—as was—said there was something a bit iffy about Rose's marriage, didn't she?"

"Yes. Identity of husband kept under wraps. As might apply if she discovered he wasn't the sort of man she thought he was." Toby wouldn't be more explicit, given that the bar was getting busier and the consequent risk of being overheard: Alasdair would know what he meant. "We need to get this information up to Cambridge as soon as possible. Too late to make a phone call?"

"Not if we ring from here rather than wait to get home. I hope we don't have to haul them out of bed. I can't face a grumpy Professor of Applied Mathematics."

As it turned out, both men were not only awake, they were in the midst of entertaining Drs Panesar and Howe, having apparently just reached the port stage. The evening was obviously proceeding well, given the loud and merry voices in the background which could be heard when Jonty answered the call and had to explain why it sounded like he was in the midst of the crowd at Twickenham.

"I can barely hear you. Let me tell the rabble to pipe down," Jonty said.

"You might want to let them listen in on the extension, as we've juicy stuff to relate. Alasdair is here and sends his regards, but we're on a public phone so I'll have to relay whatever he wants to say." Toby grinned at his lover's frustration with such a situation.

"Send him *our* regards. I'll go and organise this mob."

Once Panesar and Howe were said to be ensconced by the instrument in Jonty's study and he and Orlando were apparently trying to share the one in the hall, Toby started his tale.

"For a start, Charlie Heathfield—he of my squadron—is the son of Freddie, of the vault escapade." He related the tale of the nanny, *The Mistletoe Bough* and Freddie's reaction to it.

"We should have been able to hazard a guess at that," Jonty said when the story concluded. "It seems a classic case of Mama getting the wrong end of the stick. She said Freddie was rambling about Guinevere, but what if he said Ginevra?"

A person who must have been Panesar could be heard whispering, "Ginevra?" to which another voice, surely Howe, replied at a normal volume, "Ginevra was featured in a story based on that legend of the hidden bride. It would have been published fifteen or twenty years before Freddie attempted to break into the vault. He might have been referring to it."

"Agreed." Jonty sighed loudly. "Once more you have staggered me, Toby. I had so many of Clarence's vapid pals inflicted on me over the years that, to be frank, I'd have sworn none of them possessed a single brain cell, let alone the capability of carrying out a reconnaissance operation."

"Don't be so hard on your judgement," Orlando said, having evidently borrowed the mouthpiece. "As it proved, he *didn't* have the capability, at least not of taking the task through to a successful conclusion. The body remained unfound. Here's Jonty again. He's bursting."

"The cover up also explains the false address given for the company who handled moving the crates," Jonty stated. "Although how did Freddie—or whoever he was working for—establish Drayton might have been foisted on us in particular? Apart from the ancestor having sent a chest to the Old Manor?"

"We don't know for certain, but we think he'd been acting off his own bat and doing some sleuthing. Charlie described him as a bit of a Sherlock Holmes type. I heard your snort there, Orlando. Anyway, he'd got wind that his father—Michael, of the Great Exhibition—may have been involved in covering up a crime and was trying to find out more. Alas, the details died with Freddie. There's more, though. Hugh Williams was Freddie's godfather and his sister was Michael's wife." Toby paused for breath. "Still with me?"

"Absolutely," Jonty and Panesar said almost simultaneously.

"Hugh was also married, for a brief time, to Rose Geraghty. Mrs Sterne-Lewis's cousin," Toby added mainly for the benefit of Jonty and Orlando's guests. If the pair reacted badly to the next part, their hosts would have to cope with the fallout. "This despite the fact that he appeared to have a preference for his own sex. The marriage was not a success."

"We were discussing my friend Dr Crick earlier," Panesar said, in a bizarre change of conversational direction. "He and his colleagues are trying to work out the structure of the DNA molecule. I think they have an easier task than ours, trying to work out which are the key connections and which are merely coincidental."

"To be perfectly honest, it's the coincidences which bother me," Toby confessed, still trying to catch up with the DNA reference. "If it were a film plot, Sir Ian would be having stern words with the scriptwriters. All these interconnections between families and the same people cropping up hither and yon. It feels unreal."

"Professor Coppersmith is waving madly here as he evidently has an answer to your concerns. I'll pass you across."

Jonty's voice was replaced with Orlando's. "I've been pondering this also and have some thoughts. Everything only appears coincidental because we're looking at events years after they happened. As someone might in the year 2152 if they were considering the case of Dr Stewart's highly suspicious demise and kept being confronted by various Stewarts, Grangers, O'Neills, my Italian relations and descendants of Sir Ian. All of whom can be connected now, one way or another, and all of whom might still have connections a hundred years hence. Imagine that people were acting in concert over the murder, for a variety of reasons. Landseer to cover up the fact that they'd tired of our suggestions for script changes and done him in, thereby also doing a public service by ridding the country of a notorious pest. Ow! That was my bad shoulder."

"Serves you right," Jonty could be heard muttering, followed by something like, "notorious pest, my arse."

"Carry on," Panesar said, with more than a hint of amusement in his voice. "I'm enjoying your reasoning."

"Thank you." Orlando sniffed meaningfully. "To our future detectives all these names continually cropping up might seem coincident and far-fetched, especially as they'd be unlikely to have concrete evidence of, say, Toby and Alasdair's meetings with Sergeant Granger. As we have no evidence of who was talking to whom a hundred years ago. Here's the pest again."

"Orlando's right," Jonty said, "despite how rude he's being to me. It's a cross I have to bear, gentlemen. Anyway,

242

I can imagine those folk a hundred years hence finding clues as flimsy as the ones we've found. A line of descent through a sibling or a close friend, followed by what might be termed an irregular family connection in the Artigiano del Rame branch of the Coppersmiths, then the fact a film was made by Landseer about us. The people looking at those might think it too far-fetched to connect us up or assume we worked together but we know how all of us link up at present and it makes complete sense.

"I think I follow," Toby said, starting to feel more reassured. If these men, with both their academic and investigational history, could swallow the internecine complications then perhaps he should too. "If all these people knew each other in the past, it wouldn't be unreasonable to assume that they had every opportunity to talk, argue, collaborate or whatever. I'm also beginning to see that there's no reason their descendants couldn't still be in cahoots. I know, based on what my parents have said, that the families Firestone and Bowe have a long-standing friendship. I suspect they've known each other since some Neanderthal Firestone went around apprehending folk who'd stolen their neighbour's mammoth steaks and an equally ancient Bowe earned his nuts and berries by acting out scenes of derring-do to amuse his peers on the long summer nights. No doubt one of Alasdair's ancestors was similar involved in the entertainment, depicting his wooing of one of Fiona's great, great and all the rest grandmothers. Maybe following a thrilling chase in pursuit of a sabre-tooth tiger who'd been terrorising her."

Alasdair leaned close to the mouthpiece. "Do excuse him. At this rate our imaginary scenario will become a real one and it'll be Toby being done in for the sake of the country's sanity."

"Are they always like this?" Howe could be heard whispering to Panesar, who replied that he couldn't speak for the actors but that their hosts were often worse.

"Speaking from my experience of researching sources," Howe said at a normal volume, "nothing in this case raises an alarm. We have people who knew each other through work or romantic relationships, through academic collaboration and family connections. Nobody comes without what you could call a provenance."

"You've convinced me. Once again truth is stranger than fiction." Truth had the advantage of not having to be subject to an editor or a censor, either. "Back to Charlie Heathfield. I think we've related all we need to."

"We have to tell you what Dr P has turned up," Jonty said. "Maurice?"

"There is evidence of human blood on one of the meteorites from the chest although not on the hand axe. The latter does have blood on it but apparently from an animal. One might speculate it's from the last meal the tool was used to prepare before it was lost or discarded." Panesar cleared his throat. "As a result of which I do have a theory I'd like to share, if it's convenient."

Fortunately, given than Toby was hoping for an early night with his light of love, Jonty leaped in to forestall any theorising. "I'm sure we'd all love to hear it, but I'm afraid I'm feeling too tired to do any theory justice. I'd like to come to the thing with a clear head, so might I suggest that we meet again at a convenient time? If we're all available next Sunday, I could arrange a private lunch at St Bride's. For all six of us, which I know will throw the four suits thing into a cocked hat—I'll explain that after this call, Drs P and H—but method is more important than metaphor in this instance."

"That's an excellent idea," Toby said. "It'll also give us a few more days to gather our thoughts and assess anything else that comes to light. Would it be too much like a clichéd scene from a book that we each come with a theory and take turns to outline what we think?"

"Not clichéd at all." Panesar sounded delighted at the proposal. "Such a meeting of minds may well have a synergistic effect, hastening our arrival at the truth."

Orlando could be heard harrumphing and muttering about what sounded like a poisoned box of chocolates.

"Pay no attention to my colleague," Jonty said. "He's not referring to how he's proposing to kill me but to a book he read back in the year dot which has a similar set up, with people saying how they thought a murder was done."

Orlando harrumphed once more, before taking over the telephone again. "I don't think it played fair. Talking of which, should we share anything that emerges before we meet or do we hoard it and spring it at the last minute, a la he-whose-name-we-shan't-mention?"

"If I may interject as an almost-neutral," Howe said, "while the spirit of sport might argue for openness, it could prove impractical to do that in an even-handed way."

"Agreed." Toby could see how the St Bride's men could share a key piece of information very easily via pigeonholes, while the actors would be hours if not a whole day behind as they waited for the post. "What if we only report on something huge? Like if we discover that Mary Proudfoot was in hospital for the whole second half of 1851 so couldn't have struck the blow."

"I approve of that approach," Orlando said. "With the stipulation that, at the lunch itself, everyone prefaces their theory with anything less sensational that they've turned up. I appreciate that gives an advantage to the person going last as they'll have all the additional information at hand to weave into their theory."

"Or disprove it entirely!" Jonty said in the background.

"Then that's a plan, subject to consultation of diaries." Toby brought the call to an end and manoeuvred himself and Alasdair out of what wasn't the biggest of booths. "I'm relying on our Cambridge colleagues to be men of honour and not suddenly produce a vital clue over the clear soup."

"How do you know I won't do the same? I might have paid Granger a douceur to scour the 1851 archives for a definitive sign that my theory is correct."

"You wouldn't dare pull such a dirty piece of work." Toby lowered his voice as they headed for the door. "All privileges would be withdrawn. And then I'd propose to that soup millionaire's daughter on your behalf."

Alasdair had turned slightly pale at the first threat but laughed at the second. "That's threat enough to keep me on the straight and narrow."

"What is your theory, by the way? In the Great Drayton Handicap, which horse is your money on?"

"You'll have to wait until Saturday to find out." Alasdair raised his arm at a passing taxi. "In the matter of the Great Hamilton Bed Hurdle, however, you can find out what I'm proposing within the hour."

"That knocks all matters investigational into a cocked hat."

Chapter Fifteen

Saturday late morning, Alasdair and Toby were back in Cambridge, where the chase had begun. Morgan had driven them up, the manservant having a sister who lived locally and valuing the opportunity of dropping in to see her for a few hours. When they arrived at St Bride's, they made a point of asking for Archer, the porter with the crush on Fiona. He turned a fetching shade of red when presented with a photograph that was not only signed but bore a private message, one which he refused to let his colleagues see. Despite this unfair play, Archer was allowed to take the visitors up to the room Jonty had booked, which the porter did wearing a broad smile quite out of keeping with the supposedly serious nature of his job.

The private room was in the oldest part of the college and bore all the hallmarks of its age, with what appeared to be the original panelling still in place. Thankfully there was also the evidence of modern improvements, with a radiator pouring out plenty of heat on a day which had turned wintry, rather than simply autumnal. Their hosts were waiting by an elegantly laid table, one which was soon to be heaped with delights: Jonty had promised that the catering at St Bride's was generally top notch. So long as it was palatable, Alasdair didn't mind, as he'd been nurturing the feeling that today would be the pivotal moment in the case. They didn't have all the facts they might wish to have but to obtain many more could be an unrealistic expectation. Surely, with what they had, six such notable brains could between them come up with the solution to Drayton's death?

Hard on the heels of the actors' arrival, two other dons came through the door. Even if Alasdair hadn't been expecting Dr Panesar, he might have guessed the man's identity from the description he'd been given, while Joshua

Howe was more strikingly handsome than anticipated. Proper introductions and pleasantries were made over sherry although everyone present would know time was of the essence if they were to do justice to six theories—and to the food. Jonty proposed that they tackle two between the soup and the meat, two between meat and pudding and another two over coffee. He'd arranged with the kitchens that a suitable gap be left between courses so that their offerings could be properly appreciated and not spoiled with talk of dead bodies.

As they cradled their aperitifs, Jonty said, "Professor Coppersmith has an unusual proposal to suit the unusual occasion."

Orlando nodded. "I know that we hardly ever use our first names in college but as it would be a touch awkward for our visitors, I propose that we do so over lunch."

All present gave their agreement, while Alasdair noted with approval how Orlando had used the word "first" rather than "Christian" in what must have been a nice touch of deference to Panesar. The arrival of the opening course hastened them to the table, where conversation turned to the upcoming film until the last spoonful of excellent clear soup had been scooped up. At which point Jonty asked, "Would you like to open the investigational batting, Maurice? As your mention of a theory to air prompted this meeting taking place."

"It would be my pleasure." Panesar inclined his head, pushed forward his soup bowl and rested his hands on the table. "At the risk of sounding like one of my students playing the game that seems to be all the rage with them, I believe it was Gerald Proudfoot, with the meteorite, in one of the storage rooms."

Alasdair recognised the reference; he'd played that particular board game, although he hadn't enjoyed it as much as he'd expected to. It was nothing compared to being involved in a real case. There was one thing he wanted to clarify, though, so raised a finger preparatory to asking the question. Orlando had evidently spotted his intention, because he forestalled the move.

"I'm sure we'll all have questions or points we wish to have elucidated but might I propose that we make a note and keep them until all the theories have been shared? That will ensure everyone gets to air their thoughts without prejudice, as it were."

"I'm sorry," Alasdair said. "You are quite right."

Once the others had given their agreement, Panesar carried on. "I'll refer you to the detective's three main points of reference. Means, the meteorite, which was Proudfoot's to start with, along with the tusk. Opportunity we can take as established, as far as it can be at this remove, given that he was involved with the items in that chest. Motive, the man having slighted Mary Proudfoot, his sister. Not motive enough, I'd concede, to deliberately plan a man's violent death but sufficient to spark a disagreement, especially if Proudfoot had seen the letter Drayton has written about travelling abroad." He paused, finger wagging. "I can see you getting agitated, Jonty, and I'm guessing you want to ask if I'm saying that Drayton wrote that first letter?"

"I am," Jonty said, with a quick glance at Orlando. "Me replying to a direct question is playing by the rules, surely?"

Orlando inclined his head. "In these specific circumstances, it's allowable. Maurice, pray continue. This is fascinating."

Panesar drew his finger along the tablecloth, as though writing. "Drayton had written that first letter because he was intending to run away with Elizabeth's mother and didn't want to expose her to any embarrassment. He'd have reappeared after a while with a wife and child—a six-month

249

baby, as one might say. Proudfoot sees the letter and confronts Drayton, who happens to be in the chest—perhaps retrieving the meteorite or the tusk, which Proudfoot has come to collect. In the heat of the dispute, Drayton gets struck and falls in a heap. Proudfoot, rightly or wrongly, thinks he's killed the man and panics because there's circumstantial evidence making it look like a deliberate act on his part. His meteorite, his tusk, his sister. So, instead of stating the truth to the police and facing a manslaughter charge, he decides to cover up his crime. He seals the lid to the chest—after removing Drayton's keys from his pocket or otherwise obtaining them—takes the letter and not-so-calmly walks away. Afterwards, he's remorseful and confesses to his sister but she persuades him not to do anything that risks blackening the family name. He doesn't know what has happened to body, because the chest has already been despatched, he knows not where. So, he sends the letter to Drayton's parents, after he's prepared another one copying the man's style, just in case that's needed. He also accesses Drayton's rooms to make it look as though he's packed and gone. Each step in covering up the death, and every passing month where he says nothing, takes Proudfoot further from the point where he can simply go and confess what actually happened. As time goes by, Drayton plays on his mind, to the point he becomes obsessed with finding the chest. He narrows down the possible places it may have gone and gradually works round them, but without success. This all has to be done secretly because by now Mary is an Armitage so there's another reputation to protect. The inheritance he and his sister leave their descendants is that if Drayton turns up, every effort must be made to hide the truth."

Did everyone else at the table feel as disconcerted as Alasdair? He'd his own theory, beautifully worked out, which didn't have Gerald Proudfoot as the murderer, but Panesar's elegant display of reasoning had taken all the elements and woven them into a cohesive whole. Even the question he'd been about to ask when Orlando stopped him—about what Proudfoot would have been doing at the exhibition—had been answered.

Will I be having doubts about my own thinking after each theory is expounded?

Alasdair was evidently not the only one having such disconcerting thoughts.

"Very nice, Maurice," Orlando said. "While that doesn't accord with my theory, I don't see any enormous holes in what you've said."

Howe quietly cleared his throat. "As a mere beginner at this game, I find my colleague's exposition rather alarming. It appears to hang together much more cogently than my effort. Is it always like this?"

"Not in terms of the particular set up, but in essence, yes," Toby assured him. "You bat about ideas, put together stories that fit what you know and see how convincing those stories are. With due deference to Maurice, who's played a blinder of an opening innings, we may have the same thoughts when we've heard your theory. Or indeed all six of them. Who goes next, Jonty?"

"I'd propose that you do. Simply because you're sitting to the left of Dr P and the honour can go that way round the table, like a decanter of port. Rather than widdershins." Jonty chuckled.

Toby took a leather-bound notepad from his inside pocket. "I have jotted down a few aides-memoire but I hope I have my speech pretty well off by heart. I'll have to extemporise the first bit, though, because it's an apology to our esteemed friend." He patted Panesar's arm. "Means and opportunity are all very well in normal circumstances but

251

Drayton's case is far from normal. If the means of death are a blow with a meteorite, combined with a clever ruse to get Drayton into the chest, then anybody could have done that, even the smallest of women or indeed the three months pregnant Louise Geraghty."

"I don't disagree," Panesar remarked, immediately putting his hand to his mouth. "My apologies to you. I forgot the rules of the game."

"I suspect we'll all break them at some point." Toby flashed his neighbour the most charming grin. "I did check with my mother, by the way, to see if she could have clobbered anyone in such a manner when she was expecting me. The answer was a hearty 'yes'. Going back to my argument, the same latitude would apply in terms of opportunity. We can't really eliminate anyone from being present at the scene, as Maurice has already demonstrated by giving Proudfoot a valid reason to be there. So, it comes down to motive and the other old friend of detectives, *cui bono*. If we assume that this wasn't simply an argument that got out of hand, but was to some extent or other planned, who would benefit by Drayton's death? On first appearances, nobody leaps out as profiting materially unless Drayton left a small fortune to somebody. In which case, surely that would have been mentioned at the time he disappeared. I have a confession to make at this point. Something I got Granger to look into."

"I call cheat!" Alasdair slapped the table. "He tries to do this when you play draughts against him, too."

Toby ignored the jibe. "It's within the parameters we set about what should and shouldn't be revealed in advance. Granger merely confirmed firstly that nobody had tried to get Drayton declared dead once the appropriate time was up and secondly that he hadn't made a will. I hope that doesn't upset anybody's theories?" He glanced round the table. "So, only two folk had anything to gain. Mary Proudfoot, either if she wanted shot of Drayton or desired to take revenge for his dalliance with Miss Geraghty. Horatio Armitage, so he could clear the field of his supposed rival or for revenge on the man for his treatment of Mary. At this point I'm going to steal an idea from Maurice, because it's better than mine."

"Feel free. Academics do it all the time," Panesar said with a chuckle.

"I was going to have Armitage arranging to see Drayton supposedly to plead Mary's case. 'She sends these roses, picked by her own fair hand.'" Toby gestured dramatically. "But instead, I prefer that he goes to the exhibition ostensibly to retrieve his brother's piece of handiwork—the tusk with the message on. In either case, he's really there in order to confront Drayton in a place away from family and friends. What prompts that course of action? Mary Proudfoot having received a letter saying Drayton's heading off to pursue his new career. Armitage, who met Mary through Gerald, is totally besotted with her and is furious at the offhand way she's been treated. One mustn't dismiss the possibility that Drayton seduced Mary and the subsequent risk to her reputation because of that. I can imagine Fiona, in character, confessing something similar to Alasdair. The Landseer scriptwriters employing their clever language that gets past the censors but not the audience."

"I can imagine it, too," Jonty said. "The thick is plottening nicely."

"Anyway, Armitage is waiting for Drayton in the room with the chest—all labelled for the Old Manor—and his brain starts to whirr, him being a man who likes to shoot game and knows exactly how that kind of crate is used for specimens. Nobody knows he's meeting Drayton so he can simply do the man in, tip him into the chest, seal it and mark it ready for dispatch, leaving it for Heathfield to send off all

253

unknowing. In this case the identity of the delivery men and who utilised them is merely a red herring." Toby paused to take a sip of water. "Horatio and Mary forge the letters as part of the cover up, because they have the perfect template in the one Drayton sent to her. Remember that his parents thought it authentic, so the writer must have had good knowledge of Drayton's hand and style. Maybe they even used the original, changing it somehow. And, as Maurice said, they passed down to their descendants the need to cover up the crime. I have one final thing to add and it will hopefully stop Alasdair having an apoplectic fit which he appears to be on the verge of, if his eyebrow's anything to go by."

If they'd been alone, Alasdair would have made an extremely rude retort, but he satisfied himself with a mere, "You leave my eyebrow out of this and get on with your tale."

"I was going to say that the Heathfield bit is also a red herring. Michael didn't know he'd been involved in disposing of a body until Hugh Williams told him. Hugh having had his doubts about Drayton's disappearance and doing much the same as we've done. Worked out what had happened to the body but had no proof of who did it." Toby returned the notepad—which he hadn't needed—to his pocket and picked up his glass.

Alasdair hadn't been concerned about Heathfield's involvement when he'd shown his agitation earlier. His thoughts had been going down quite a different line, but he'd keep that until it was his turn. Still, Toby had produced another decent piece of reasoning, especially with his emphasis on motive.

"May I add something to what Toby said?" Howe asked. "It may support both his and Maurice's hypotheses."

Jonty nodded. "I think that's allowed."

"Thank you. It's simply a reference in Geraghty's autobiography in which he speaks about Armitage being an excellent coroner, one who knew where his duty really lay and that some obligations weighed heavier than what the man in the street might think important. The chief constable didn't seem to think much of the man in the street." Howe's expression registered his disapproval. His was a ruggedly handsome face, one that suggested trustworthiness, although Alasdair knew he shouldn't judge on appearances. One of the men in his squadron, who'd been possessed of a visage of child-like innocence, had turned out to be a serial bigamist. "Geraghty's only criticism of Armitage refers obliquely to a case which may be Drayton's, where some remark from the coroner's chair nearly let the cat out of the bag."

"The sonnet quip that could refer to Proudfoot?" Jonty said.

The librarian shrugged. "Possibly. He bookends the remark with some stuff about blood being thicker than water and the importance of family loyalties. Circumstantial but all of one piece with the two theories we've heard."

A knock on the door heralded the arrival of the main course. By previous agreement, all discussion of the case was put on hold, Alasdair nudging the conversation in the direction of St Bride's rivalry with the college next door, the history of which he wanted to hear. That discussion hadn't run out of steam when the last pieces of roast potato and soupcons of gravy had been disposed of.

"Clearly there's enough in this tale to last an entire meal in itself," Toby said. "Perhaps we should organise a reunion to do justice to the subject. You need to see the proposed script, anyway, so perhaps Sir Ian might delegate that duty to us and we could kill the proverbial two birds?"

"Splendid idea. The professor and I need to tell you all about the time we had to defend somebody from the ghastly place." Jonty pulled a disgusted face. "A case of establishing the truth having to take precedent over college honour. Now, if we carry on round, it will be Orlando's turn to outline his theory. One of which I have no prior knowledge because he's been playing his cards close to his chest as usual. Would you like to proceed or wait for the table to be cleared?"

Orlando's answer never got aired, a knock on the door announcing the arrival of the St Bride's waiting staff. When they'd taken the dishes away and tidied the cloth, he said, "I've always wondered if it's a case of them being telepathic or if it's simply many years of experience which helps them know when to appear."

"A mystery which not even we could solve," Panesar observed with a chuckle. "Professor, your theory?"

Orlando smoothed the cloth in front of him. "I'm pleased to be following Toby, as my thoughts have followed the same broad track as his. *Cui bono*? However, I found dwelling on that question less than profitable, there being to my mind—as Toby noted—no clear candidate. Therefore, I took the approach of starting with the end and working backwards. We have the incontrovertible fact of Drayton's body in a chest in a vault and rather than ask myself who benefitted from his death, I've concentrated on who benefitted from his body not being found."

"Ah. Very clever," Jonty murmured, with evident pride at his partner's mental acuity.

Orlando nodded his thanks. "If you wanted to gain financially from another man's death, then you'd need the body to be discovered or at least the fact of death being made plain. You wouldn't have sent those letters, for one thing. I'm glad that Toby confirms nobody appeared to have gone about claiming a large inheritance. So why might a murderer need their victim's body to remain undiscovered? At least two reasons. Because making it look like Drayton had run off would put the victim in a bad light, and to cover up the killer's involvement by casting doubt on the time or location of death. I would argue that the covering up was planned from the start rather than as a temporary measure, with the killer clearing Drayton's things from his lodgings and employing the falsified second letter after the first. That first being a genuine one from Drayton to his family, intended as part of covering up his elopement with Louise Geraghty. Ah, thank you."

Jonty had opened a second bottle of claret, to follow the one that had accompanied the roast pork. He topped up everyone's glasses as Orlando continued his account.

"I believe we have two men working in concert and we don't have to look far to find the first. Who sent that chest back to the Old Manor? Michael Heathfield. The same man who was rumoured to have been involved in covering up a crime and whose family were said—by no less reliable a source than Richard Stewart—to have a penchant for mischief. Freddie trying to find Drayton's body could be said to verify that. Yes, Toby?"

"I know I shouldn't interrupt but, like Joshua, I have some relevant information to support your theory. Alasdair, do you recall Charlie Heathfield saying that his grandfather Michael hated the Stewarts?"

Alasdair wagged his finger in admonishment. "To be specific, he said the old man didn't particularly like Jonty's grandfather. It could explain why he sent the body down to Sussex."

"It could indeed." Orlando appeared delighted at the news. "Give the Stewarts the problem. That accords even more with the 'mischief' remark and its postscript. If you

257

recall, Richard Stewart's comment was followed by something about the Heathfields making other people think they were to blame. We probably all know men, or women, who are very good at persuading other people to do what they want and, in the process, making them think it was all *their* idea. Perhaps that's what happened here, with the actual killer believing he'd been the one to suggest using the Stewarts, although that's mere speculation."

Panesar wagged his head. "All of us are ultimately indulging in mere speculation. Unless someone is hiding a piece of definitive proof with which to accompany their theorising, in which case we must all cry 'foul!'"

"I promise I'm not." Orlando took some wine. "In this instance, I'm assuming some knowledge by Heathfield of Jonty's grandfather's slapdash ways with the contents of his vault. He'd know there was a chance that crate wouldn't get opened and if it was, and the body found, Heathfield could have said he'd found the crate sealed and simply despatched it with the other things, never suspecting Drayton might be in there. They had no fingerprinting or the like in those days, so they'd have been as short of evidence as we are to link him, or the killer, to the crime. Now, before Jonty says that my argument begins to contradict itself, let me explain the apparent dichotomy. Heathfield's name wasn't among those who gave statements to the police so he couldn't have had an obvious connection to the dead man. I propose that's because his involvement with despatching items didn't overlap with Drayton's, therefore it never appeared that they worked together. That's supported by where their names are on the list of who sent what where. He may even have specifically taken over Drayton's role when the latter apparently disappeared. He had a friend working in the same department, after all, who could have engineered his involvement."

258

"Hugh Williams," Jonty said, then apologised profusely. "I'm afraid that nearly fifty years of batting ideas back and forward is a habit hard to break. I'm trying my best to behave, honestly."

"It's no doubt proving a sore trial for all of us," Toby assured him. "I think we've all done remarkably well, considering. Orlando, are you proposing Hugh Williams as the murderer?"

"I am. He makes the connection between the families Geraghty and Heathfield and he's a man I feel we may have misread. I believe Drayton's death was premeditated, with Williams as the instigator. I see him not as a suitor for Drayton but for Louise Geraghty." Orlando paused, clearly to let his words sink in. "Williams was his rival in love and was horrified when he discovered that Louise was pregnant and that she and Drayton were intending to elope. If I may divert for a moment to the two known accounts we have of him, I'd say that Williams's interview with the police was intended as a blind. The old chestnut of, 'How can I possibly have killed this man when I'm so concerned over him?' With a side order of wanting to be kept informed, if he could, about how the investigation was progressing. His visit to the grave in 1919 was simply driven by remorse at what he'd done all those years previously, perhaps the season of Lent stirring repentance in him of his sins as it stirs Jonty to penitence at stealing my peppermints."

"May I point out that the offence is usually quite the contrary?" Jonty gave a dramatic roll of the eyes.

Orlando snorted. "Williams desired Louise Geraghty and thought that if he could get Drayton out of the way, with the added pretence that the man had deserted her in her hour of need, then she might cleave to *him*. She wouldn't and so he married Rose Geraghty in an effort to maintain closeness to the woman he really loved. Not unnaturally, the marriage

259

failed because Rose could never live up to his ideal and she got fed up with playing second fiddle. Incidentally, the cover up at the inquest was simply to protect the reputation of the Sterne-Lewises. Too much probing into Drayton might have risked revealing him as Louise's father and *her* illegitimacy."

"I know we're not allowed to butt in," Howe said, taking his opportunity while Orlando took a drink of water, "but I'll burst if I don't say how fascinating today is proving. Every theory aired appears to have a ring of truth to it."

Toby nodded. "I'm newly persuaded by each one and keep wanting to revise my theory to include other folk's ideas. How do you think the actual murder was committed, Orlando?"

"By Williams, who knew about the special crate and ostensibly planned its use, previous comment about Heathfield pertaining. Williams arranges to meet Drayton strictly on the quiet, saying he has a confidential message from Louise, who is supposedly worried about the wording of the letter to his parents. During this fateful meeting Williams can't believe his luck on seeing the meteorite and decides to use *that* rather than whatever he's brought with him to do the deed. He clonks Drayton, purloins the letter, then tips his body in the chest along with the weapon and some other stuff. He quickly seals it and goes back to his own work, with nobody having taken any notice of him and with the intention of posting the letter immediately. If he's seen leaving the room he can act the innocent, saying he was looking for Drayton and couldn't find him. As events turned out, he and Heathfield benefit from some good planning and a lot of luck. As does Louise Drayton, whose family rally round to support her when it appears she's been abandoned." Orlando sat back, hands folded.

"I suppose it's my turn now and I'm not sure how to follow that," Howe shook his head. "I'd counted myself fortunate, having come in relatively late to this business, when most of what we know had already been established. As though I was reading a cricket match report that had been written at tea on the final day. I'm not so sure now, especially as my account seems rather thin compared to those already outlined. If I may have a minute to flick through my notes?"

"Of course," Jonty said. "We all have the advantage of experience in finding a theory that explains as many of the clues as possible. Some things may never be explainable, of course. Take your time, because there's another bottle of claret on the sideboard which is calling out to be opened and allowed to breathe a bit. If Toby would oblige, as he's already had his turn?"

"My pleasure." Toby left the table and set to work, employing the corkscrew in a manner similar to an effective piece of business he'd used in the last Holmes film. Alasdair doubted anyone else at the table would recognise it but he appreciated the touch. He also appreciated the studious expression on the librarian's face, which rendered him even more attractive. Alasdair could see Howe as a fourth billed actor, playing a wing commander or a first lieutenant. Quite possibly Fiona's brother, in which case he'd likely be killed about half-way through the film. He suddenly felt guilty at imagining such a fate, despite it only being a cinematic death in action, although he didn't feel any remorse for fancying the bloke. Any man could look at the cakes in the baker's window, even if he had no intention of buying them.

"You're miles away, Alasdair," Toby said, as he placed the bottle on the table and took his seat.

"Guilty as charged. Thinking about film business, when I should be concentrating on murder." Which was correct, if not the entire truth.

"Well, I'm as ready as I'll ever be." Howe took a final look at his notes. "From the start I've thought the culprit was one particular person and I've had to force myself not to go looking for evidence to support that assertion rather than assess everything objectively. Appalling practice, I know and exactly the sort of thing one might deride the college next door about."

"The late, lamented Ariadne Sheridan would also have said it was what she'd expect from historians," Orlando said. "If there's room in your film for a secondary character of high intelligence, the kind of role perfect for a character actress, then Ariadne would be ideal. Sorry, Joshua, for intruding on your exposition."

"Intrude all you like. It's probably better than what I have to say." Howe grinned. "It has always struck me that Mary Proudfoot was the wronged woman in all this and that she likely took up with Armitage on the rebound. I propose that much of the 'how it was done' is as Maurice described, for example the reason for her meeting Drayton being supposedly the return of the meteorites and tusk. The main difference is, of course, that Mary did the deed and not her brother. Now, I fear that Maurice will shout 'foul play' and send me from the field because I have run across one piece of circumstantial evidence that strengthens my argument. Mary gets a mention in that autobiography because Geraghty was keen on cricket and he'd met her at some club function. The main point of the story was to illustrate what a good player he thought himself but it's mentioned that Mary also played and was a jolly useful bowler. Very fast for a woman. That would suggest she had enough strength to commit the deed."

Toby gave Howe a fairly flirtatious smile. "Maybe we should all have a read of that book and see what else we can turn up to support our own theories."

"I refuse to do so on family principle." Jonty snorted. "Go on, Joshua. It's interesting to have our first woman in the dock, as it were."

"It's her being a woman which links to the aspect Orlando focussed on. The body being hidden. I can imagine the men she knew rallying around to protect her, she being a woman greatly provoked. Or, at least, making herself out to be." The librarian's toss of the head spoke volumes. "Those men being primarily her brother and Horatio Armitage. I did consider whether Drayton senior was involved, given the nature of his comments at the time his son disappeared—did he know his son had seduced another woman and got her with child?—but I decided he'd have had to be a very hard man indeed to connive in his son's death, even if only after the event. The three key elements in the death being successfully covered up are the letters, the inquest and the crate. Mary would surely have received letters or notes from Drayton so would be able to imitate his style. The inquest was led by her descendant, who was no doubt aware of the great family secret that might rear its head and be quietly dismissed. As for the chest, we come back to our old pal, by which I mean Hugh Williams, rather than Michael Heathfield."

Howe paused to take a sip of wine, which allowed Alasdair to chip in. "As someone who's been merely a spectator so far, I have to declare that you're all too good at this. Toby tells us that Heathfield is a mere dupe and I believe him. Then Orlando says Heathfield is directly involved and I believe that, too. I feel like a pendulum, swinging hither and yon, and there's still Jonty to give his reasoning, although I suppose I'm next."

"You are," Jonty confirmed. "I'm the unlucky man who goes last. Joshua, back to the chest."

"Hugh Williams struck me—by mere instinct—as a man of honour. I suppose I was influenced by the tears and the visit to the grave, but now I see those as remorseful. I have been speculating whether he knew Proudfoot or Armitage, or both, via the exhibiting of their objects. I can imagine him walking in on Mary when she'd just killed Drayton and taking charge, getting her away and getting the body—and Gerald's tusk—sealed up. His motive would be less sympathy for her, than anger at Drayton for having seduced his friend Louise." Howe spread his hands. "That's the best I can do."

Panesar gave him a round of applause. "You have by no means disgraced yourself. I find it intriguing that we have all taken the same set of facts and arrived at such a range of conclusions. How we'll be able to decide between them is a hurdle yet to be jumped, though."

"Do we need to choose between them?" Howe asked. "Which is part of the bigger question of what happens if we do all come to a consensus of opinion. We know that whoever the culprit is, they're long gone. Unless something definitive turns up at the eleventh hour, I don't think we're in a Woodville Ward situation, where the solution seems beyond reasonable doubt."

"Quite right," Toby said. "Our proposal, if it's acceptable to the company, would be to make a proper record of our conclusions, which could be stored in both the library here and at the Old Manor. We would share it with everyone who'd helped us in the case, with the proviso that the outcome is based on the balance of probability, rather than conclusive proof."

"I vote for that proposal." Jonty raised a hand, at which everyone else did the same. "Motion carried. Which is opportune, because I believe I can hear footsteps on the stairs to signal the imminent arrival of something which will ideally be suet based and awash with custard."

The pudding—jam roly poly—must surely have been ordered to please Toby but it went down well with all present, especially as the custard couldn't be faulted. Alasdair was pleased he'd get to explain his theory as soon as the plates were empty and before the stodge affected whichever part of his brain promoted sleep. Luckily a pot of strong coffee was delivered hard on the heels of the highly efficient St Bride's staff arriving to clear the table. With an empty, if admittedly less than spotless, cloth in front of him and a cup to hand, Alasdair could commence with the penultimate theory of the day.

"It's now my turn and before I come to my idea, I have to say I've found this case frustrating. Too much of everything." Alasdair enumerated on his fingers. "Two visitors to Drayton's grave, two people who could have influenced the inquest, two midnight visitors to the vaults, two women in Drayton's life, let alone all the families and their connections. Then we come to all the instances of what I'll call Smart-Alec-ery. Messages in Ogham, allusions at inquests, forged letters and cryptic hints in journals. I decided that what I had to do was sit back and take stock. When I'm preparing for a new role I try to get to the key points of both the character and the storyline."

A derisive snort came from Toby's direction. "I've always thought the only key point for you is to be heroic and successfully woo Fiona while I hang around suffering attractively. With as many buttons of my shirt undone as Landseer can get away with."

Alasdair grunted. "Shall we make him stand outside?"

"He'd only make the staircase untidy," Jonty said. "What did your stocktaking produce, Alasdair?"

265

"That the key point wasn't how Drayton was killed or even why he was put in that chest but why two separate people tried to break into the Old Manor vaults. What on earth did they have to gain?" Alasdair paused for effect, appreciating the expressions on the other men's faces, especially the slightly baffled one on Toby's. "Heathfield we can easily explain away, because we have enough evidence to suggest he'd been trying to figure out the family secret of the covered-up death and was attempting to confirm his theory that the dead man had been sent to the Stewarts. Proudfoot's motive is more of a puzzle; why would a man go to all that trouble for a tusk, for example? His friend Armitage could easily have made him another engraved item. And if Proudfoot killed Drayton, or was involved in hiding his death, why start potentially stirring up trouble when he'd got away with it for years? Surely no guilty person would seek to disturb the dead."

As Alasdair paused to drink some coffee, Panesar said, "I have heard people here, both fellows and students, condemning the cinema as providing the lowest form of entertainment, barely more tolerable than bullbaiting. I won't repeat what I've heard them say about those who act in films. I only wish they could have been here today to witness our guests' reasoning. It would put several of my students to shame."

Alasdair's insured eyebrow made an attempt to show both gratitude and a high degree of intellect. "Praise indeed. I hope the rest of what I have to say doesn't make you change your opinion. When I considered Proudfoot, my thoughts perversely kept going back to the things I'd found so frustrating, such as there being two vault intruders. What if they'd both had broadly the same motive, getting to the bottom of a crime a family member had been involved in covering up? In this case, Gerald's sister Mary, who'd killed

Drayton when she discovered he was involved with another woman. And what if the message on the tusk was more like the one on the cricket bat, a reference to his character? The ash tree has all sorts of significance in mythology—healing, tree of the gods, etc. What if Gerald was as keen on establishing the truth as we are? A purifier of stories, if you like." He raised his hand. "I know, it's all highly speculative, for which I apologise, but Mary Proudfoot in the role of murderer is something both Joshua and I have no issue with. Armitage helps her to cover up the deed, earning himself her hand in the process. When Gerald discovers what went on, well after Drayton died and probably from Maximillian Armitage, he's appalled and determined to get to the bottom of things. I've nothing else to add that hasn't already been said about why and how reputations continued to be protected."

Alasdair gave Howe a nod, recognising their independently arriving at the same conclusion. Whether it was the correct one, he couldn't say, and the confidence he'd had coming into the meeting had ebbed somewhat.

Jonty cleared his throat then folded his hands in front of him, almost as if in prayer. Perhaps they could all do with some divine inspiration. "Now it comes to me and I'm not sure if I'm fortunate to be last. What I do know is that I've revised my original theory. When I came here, I'd had Hugh Williams firmly in line for the dock, dating from the time we heard about his visit to the church. Then when we discovered he married Rose Geraghty I had to have him as the primary suspect. In my eyes, Williams as both godfather and relative by marriage showed him wanting to have some oversight of Drayton's child, given that he'd been in love with the man. Whether that was requited or unrequited I don't know, although I favour the former. The reason Williams's marriage broke up and he became persona non grata within the family was Rose discovering his true nature and romantic history. The family reputation that he collected young men shouldn't be ignored, although I accept that doesn't mean he couldn't have found women attractive as well."

"Quite right." Orlando inclined his head, no doubt appreciating the nod towards his theory.

"Like Maurice, I saw Williams as having means, motive and opportunity and had favoured the manslaughter line. I also agreed with Joshua, envisaging Williams's resentment when he discovered Drayton had got his good—platonic—friend, Louise Geraghty, with child and perhaps didn't intend to do the right thing by her. I'll come back to that, as it's even more relevant to the new theory I've hatched. Excuse me." Jonty took a drink of water. "Williams felt betrayed on all counts, got into a row with Drayton and the rest is as Maurice outlined. Or I should say *was*, in my original theory. I've had a light on the road to Damascus—or at least to the Old Manor vaults—moment over luncheon. I'm proposing that rather than detail it, I'll end my monologue after I've laid out the key points which have led me to switch horses. It'll then be time to open the floor to discussion."

"That has my support," Orlando said sombrely. "I have the feeling I've seen a similar light."

Toby shook his head. "I'm still waiting for it to shine on me but perhaps it will when Jonty lists his clues."

"Then I'll begin. We have Alasdair to thank for nudging us in what I hope is the right direction. He's right that we've been too tied up with secret messages and the like. I'd say we've underplayed one very obviously falsified document, which is Elizabeth Geraghty's birth certificate. We've also speculated that Louise Geraghty was Drayton's real love and that perhaps the couple were intending to elope. But the

268

date of Elizabeth's birth would suggest they'd had plenty of time to have got married normally, let alone by special licence, before Drayton died. So why didn't they? We've also focussed on what people might have wanted kept quiet but have we asked ourselves whether other things could have brought even more stigma to a family than illegitimacy?" Jonty crossed his arms, awaiting a response.

Toby was first to pitch in. "Are we saying that Mary Proudfoot really was the love of Drayton's life? That perhaps he merely had a dalliance with Louise Geraghty, instantly regretted, one with unforeseen consequences—which is why his father believed he wanted to get away from women but assumed, like us, he meant Mary."

"I'd say so. Perhaps we read too much into that little remark about the policeman sympathising with wanting to get away from her." Jonty spread his hands.

"I'll share my thoughts," Panesar said. "Louise influenced control over what went on the birth certificate. Ultimately, only a woman would be able to say for certain who the father of her child was. Or wasn't. For all we know, and this is more wild speculation, Drayton actually never had relations with Louise. She could easily have pretended he'd got her pregnant, to trap him into marriage, knowing that she'd be the one most likely to be believed if it became a case of her word against his."

"But—as Jonty pointed out—they *hadn't* married, Maurice." Howe cradled his cup. "Her family would have had plenty of time to force Drayton to the altar."

"Unless they didn't know she was expecting, because she kept it hidden," Alasdair said. "My cousin Alice was only a month or so short of her due date before she began to show. Louise may have been too embarrassed to tell her family, hoping that she could force Drayton to propose before it was too late. That might have been motive enough

269

to kill him if he didn't. With him gone there'd have been nobody to argue against her assertion of who was the father. I can't, however, think of an answer to the question about what was more of a disgrace than a bastard child."

"Insanity." Orlando's voice, quiet and solemn, bore some note of deeply personal pain. "A stigma that taints by familial association and which might provoke a more robust protective response from family and friends than a mere chivalrous instinct. Dr Howe—Joshua—could you work the oracle and access the details on Louise Geraghty's death certificate?"

"I could, although insanity may not be given as…oh, I see." The light had clearly struck the librarian, too. "It's the date and location of death we want, isn't it? To establish if Louise didn't pass on when her daughter was a baby and was perhaps put into an institution."

"That might also accord with Mrs Sterne-Lewis becoming rather confused and easily upset towards the end of her life," Jonty said. "We've naturally assumed that was due to dementia but what if it was an inherited trait? Think of her attacking the vicar with her umbrella. It might seem humorous seen in one light but not in another."

"The flowers with the body. They remind me of Ophelia in Hamlet." Toby shivered. "Can we explain all the rest of the story in line with Louise being the killer?"

"I believe so," Panesar said. "Much of what followed would have been as one or other of us has already surmised."

The atmosphere in the room had subtly changed, as though the six men each had the feeling that they were approaching the centre of the maze as opposed to taking tentative steps down what might be a dead end. Even the St Bride's birds outside the window had hushed their tones.

Panesar continued. "The men around her would have rallied round. As Orlando spoke, I could see in my mind's eye a scene being played out like a Landseer film. Louise had come to confront Drayton accompanied by one of her champions. Most likely her brother James because of the Hugh Williams connection. They don't attend the interview, Louise insisting she does this alone, but they become worried and burst into the room to find Drayton dead or dying in the chest and her throwing in on top of him anything to hand. Williams insists James gets her away quietly while he goes to work sealing the chest and putting into train the rest of it. To use yet another Shakespearean reference, perhaps snapping up the unconsidered trifle of a half-written letter."

"Yes, that has some logic," Alasdair said. "It's a neat way to explain why those items were in the chest when they shouldn't have been, if Drayton had them laid out ready to go into another packing crate and she simply grabbed them. It also gives another reason for the break in relations between Williams and the Geraghtys. Sharing a great secret doesn't always bind people together; it can put strain on a friendship. Maybe he also felt sorrow about that when he visited Drayton's grave."

"But the visitors to the vaults?" Toby ruffled his previously immaculate hair, as he was occasionally wont to do when he couldn't see the outworking of something. "Heathfield yes, especially if he'd discovered his father had unwittingly been part of such a conspiracy to deny a man justice, because this is what it all comes down to. Proudfoot, though? Are we suggesting his foray was simply in search of that wretched tusk?"

"No," Jonty said. "Sorry to say, Toby, but I think Alasdair got that eighty percent correct. I bet Gerald was looking for a body although on behalf of his sister, who

271

wanted to know where her lover had gone. The time lag before he went poking around was due to him having taken years to discover what might have happened."

Toby, with a slight but attractive pout, nodded. "You could be right. And what about the Armitage connection? Why should a family want to cover up a murder that they didn't commit and that caused one of them sorrow?"

"Because the coroner and the chief constable were great friends, a loyalty which might override a familial one?" Howe didn't seem that convinced by his own argument.

"I'd combine that with a degree of coercion," Orlando said. "Geraghty had two potential holds over Armitage. They'd previously contrived together the outcome of an inquest, something Armitage wouldn't want revealed. Geraghty clearly knew about the Proudfoot connection so he might have been in a position to know about the complaint levelled at Gerald. The mention of his great-uncle being a housebreaker could have been enough to bring Armitage into line, possibly on both occasions an inquest was influenced."

Jonty tapped the table. "I like that. It could also be the best explanation so far for the baffling sonnet quote he made. A little hint that he knew more than he was allowed to say. I wish he'd had the guts to mention all this to my father, even if he swore him to secrecy. We could have—no. I was about to say that we could have looked into it while some of the main players were still alive but obviously we couldn't."

"With apologies for sounding trite, it's better late than never," Panesar said. "Might I propose that we all take a few days to consider the solution we've reached. Too easy to simply fall in with something in the heat of the moment."

"I'm all for sober reflection." Alasdair ignored the snort from Toby. "Who do we report any qualms or second thoughts back to? And who gets the task of writing up our conclusions? Not Toby, as his grammar is appalling," he added in riposte to his lover's grunt.

"I can do that," Orlando said. "Once I'm certain no objections will be lodged, I'll get it drafted and copies circulated to all of us. There are bound to be pieces of evidence supporting aspects of the case that I inadvertently omit."

Alasdair doubted that but held his tongue. Lengthening the process by which the report was produced would allow extra time to include anything new and also be a guard against them making fools of themselves. If Howe's investigation showed that Louise Geraghty had died while Drayton was still alive and that the date on her daughter's birth certificate had been falsified as well as the details of the parents, they'd risk egg on their faces by prematurely declaring her the murderer.

Toby had evidently had similar thoughts. "There's no great urgency, is there? Drayton has waited a hundred years for justice so a few more weeks won't make much difference. Better to wait for all the horses to be weighed in before prematurely declaring the winner."

"You think we might have it wrong?" Jonty asked.

"Actually, I don't. I just wish I had a solid piece of proof in my hands." In saying which, Toby probably spoke for all those present.

"Then I suggest that any of us who find ourselves in church, chapel or anywhere else we'll be saying our prayers, might put in a word tomorrow with the Almighty," Jonty said. "I'm never sure if it's fair, asking for a clue—rather like asking to win a rugby match—but it can't do any harm."

Epilogue

St Luke's little summer had come and gone, leaving November to make its entrance with heavy rain and a wind that seemed to have blown non-stop from the steppes of Siberia. University life was in full swing and the various events of the last few months were working to their conclusion.

The script for the Landseer film had been scrutinised by Jonty and Orlando, amendments suggested, the reworking scrutinised again and finally given the seal of approval, young Adam being thrilled skinny—as he put it—that his idea for the poison had been used. A tentative date for the premier had been noted in various diaries in Cambridge and Sussex, including Thomas Stewart's. It wasn't simply as a thank-you for his agreeing to filming at the Old Manor: according to Jonty's niece Alexandra, the family member with whom Thomas was particularly close, his friendship with Fiona Marsden was blossoming. Possibly because the man who was due to walk the actress down the aisle had been discovered with his pants down—literally—in the company of a barmaid from Balham, so the wedding was off. Sir Ian had made sure that the Landseer publicity machine had gone into battle mode to protect his star, as far as it could, which had prompted Jonty to say it would have been interesting if Louise Geraghty had been lucky enough to have had a man like that in her life. As he observed, "If Sir Ian had been in charge, they'd never have found the body."

To which Orlando had replied that the studio head must surely be hoping Thomas would pop the question. After a decent interval but preferably before the film came out because the publicity would be fantastic.

As for Louise herself, Howe had found the relevant death information. The woman had died of heart failure, at a private institution for the mentally ill, in 1899, presumably never having seen her daughter since she was a babe in arms. Various other minor points, such as who'd married whom and when, had also been verified, although none of them provided definitive proof. No objections to the Louise as murderer theory having been lodged, however, Orlando had taken a lead on writing up the case and circulated his first draft to all who'd been present at the lunch. A few changes were suggested to him, which he incorporated, but the thing remained in his possession rather than in any library, unshared with the wider group of people who'd helped solve the case. *If* it was solved. As the six amateur detectives all confessed whenever they shared their snippets of news, that elusive piece of proper proof wouldn't come amiss.

They'd all had the chance to read Geraghty's autobiography and a less inspiring tome it would be hard to imagine, except the diaries of Dr Owens, their rival from the college next door. Nobody had turned up anything from it that Dr Howe had somehow missed.

The last of the Guy Fawkes fireworks were merely a memory when a letter appeared in Jonty's pigeonhole. He didn't recognise the writing, although the postmark suggested it had been sent from the environs of the Old Manor. He was about to open it when a pang of conscience struck. If this was related to the case then he really should read it in the presence of Orlando at very least. Gathering the others together might be premature if it was simply from the vicar informing him that they were having a whip-round for the church roof and asking if he would like to contribute.

It was late morning before he was able to run Orlando to ground in his college room, by which time Jonty was having second thoughts about the letter's importance. "It may be nothing," he said, waggling the envelope, "but given that it comes from Sussex, it might just be the answer to our prayers. Even those sent up by an old sinner like you."

"Stop talking twaddle and open it."

The address at the top of the first sheet rang a bell. "It's one of the estate lodges."

Dear Dr Stewart

I hope you don't mind me writing but we thought you might want to hear this. I also must apologise if your ears have been burning. That would have been us. Mrs Hammersley and I belong to the same knitting circle and ever since you came asking about Mr Drayton it's been a topic of conversation among us all. Especially because Mr Bowe and Mr Hamilton are involved. I've been rather an object of envy among some of the other ladies having met one of them. I haven't dared to mention the offer of dinner which he made.

"It has to be from Bessy Cutting, surely?" Orlando said. "Can we sneak a look at the signature?"

Jonty carefully folded the sheets of paper so nothing else would be revealed. "Quite right. I have high hopes, which I'm trying to restrain."

Anyway, we've been racking our brains for anything that could help and asking anybody else who might know something. We call ourselves the Old Manor Irregulars.

"There seems to be a positive craze for amateur detection. I'm not complaining, though," Orlando added.

"Neither am I. Unless it turns out this is a mare's nest."

I won't bore you with a long tale of everything that people said. Folk do talk a load of nonsense at times. The important bit, as far as Bob and I are concerned, is this. One day, after the knitting circle had broken up for the afternoon and everyone was going home, Miss Topley

276

nabbed me and Mrs Hammersley and asked if we wanted to go round for a cup of tea the next day. She tends to keep herself to herself, Miss Topley, so we knew something was up.

"I suppose one should be grateful she isn't a Miss Proudfoot," Jonty said, "wanting to tell Mrs Cutting that her ancestor Mary did the deed."

"Don't tempt fate."

When we went to Miss Topley's, she was keen to tell us that her father was on the jury for Drayton's inquest and she went to watch the proceedings. She was a young woman at the time and interested in the law. She's a solicitor now, very well thought of, so I'd say that if she had something to tell, it would be worth listening to. She and her father always believed there was something dishonest about the proceedings. Like Mr Stewart, Mr Topley was convinced the chief constable was behind it all. He wore a smug, self-satisfied look all through the proceedings and kept sending the coroner notes.

Orlando nodded. "Nothing new in that but glad to have it confirmed."

They lodged a complaint about how the inquest had been handled but nothing came of it, of course. Probably buried away somewhere. That didn't stop her father trying to find out more. She wishes he'd spoken to Mr Stewart about it, two heads being better than one but Mr Topley thought he and his daughter were the only people who smelled a rat. Then the war got worse and Miss Topley volunteered to do nursing. When she returned, Mr Topley had caught the flu and not long after it took him, like it did your parents. One poor dead soul from sixty years previously didn't seem to matter so much.

"It's almost as though the universe collaborated in not having Drayton's death looked at. I don't subscribe to the

277

view that God takes a hand in human affairs to the extent he'd contrive a war and an epidemic just to foil us, by the way." Jonty smiled ruefully.

"Perhaps it's taken your mother thirty odd earthly years of nagging the angels into action to get things resolved." Orlando tapped the paper. "I have high hopes."

Jonty sighed. "Yes, well, as a long-term watcher of sport, I have to say that when it comes to the teams I support, it's the hope that kills you."

Clearly us talking about the death being investigated now got Miss Topley thinking. She knew that her father had tried to find out more about Drayton, putting appeals in the personal columns of the newspaper for any information about him. She went and fished out her father's stuff from back then, to see if he'd had any replies although she wasn't hopeful because he hadn't mentioned getting any further. There was a letter, one that came in the August of 1918, which was long after he'd given up on getting any response because the adverts had been placed in early 1915. Mr Topley had pinned a note on it saying he needed to reply but Miss Topley doubted he'd done so because he'd been taken ill a few days after the date on the letter. She showed us it, although she didn't want to part with the thing, because of a particular, rather odd, connection with her dad. She says if any of you want to see the original, she'd be happy for you to do so.

"See? I told you this would be good." Orlando gave Jonty a quick, reassuring hug across the shoulders.

We didn't copy it word for word, as that seemed rude, and I won't go into all the bits about why the reply was so late but it was something about the man who sent it being very ill all through the autumn and winter of 1914. He recovered, although he didn't come across the story of the inquest until a few years later, having been unable to read the newspapers at the vital time. Once he'd heard about Drayton's body being found, he started scouring the papers for any further news.

"Williams," Jonty said, voice shaking. "It has to be." He turned onto the next page.

This man was called Hugh Williams, if that means anything. He said he knew the truth about Drayton's death and he was sorry, but he'd vowed not to reveal it, despite the woman who'd done it now being dead nearly twenty years. He said the only clue he'd give was sonnet one hundred and forty. Miss Topley had gone to look it up and it made no sense to her, although one part of it was rather troubling. At that point she didn't want to say any more, not even why she'd been upset.

Because I know you're a bit of a dab hand with Shakespeare, you might be able to shed some light.

The letter concluded with general best wishes and a note that she was looking forward to seeing the new film.

"I don't suppose you have a copy of the sonnets to hand?" Jonty asked.

"I confess I do."

Jonty should have guessed that, given how fond his lover was of the early ones. The book was soon located and the sonnet found. "Well, here's what must have upset Miss Topley. *As testy sick men, when their deaths be near, No news but health from their physicians know.* That would almost read like Williams had predicted her father's death."

"Here's the hint, though. *For if I should despair, I should grow mad, And in my madness might speak ill of thee.*" Orlando raised almost an eloquent an eyebrow as Alasdair could. "Is there Evensong in the chapel tonight?"

"Said, not sung. Why?"

279

Orlando laid the letter from Bessy Cutting inside the book of sonnets, marking the page. "I think even an old heathen like me should go and offer thanks. For these."

Jonty gave his lover a quick peck on the cheek. "Your gratitude will mean more than that of any number of righteous men. Oi! That hurt. Men of my age shouldn't be subjected to pinching."

"Then men of your age shouldn't resort to insults."

Jonty sighed happily. A solved case and clever verbal slights. Life was very good.

THE END

Printed in Great Britain
by Amazon

37118895R00169